black chain

black chain

a novel

DOMINIC MARTELL

db

Published by Dunn Books. First edition October 2021

This title is also available as a Dunn Books ebook.

Library of Congress cataloging-in-publication data is on file with the U.S. Copyright Office.

HARDCOVER: ISBN 978-1-951938-09-3
PAPERBACK: ISBN 978-1-951938-10-9
EBOOK: ISBN 978-1-951938-11-6

Designed by archiefergusondesign.com
Maps by Joe LeMonnier

Manufactured in the United States of America

Tatoi Airport

To Istanbul: 1080 km by auto **E75**

Peristeri

E75

U.A.E. Embassy

CITY CENTER

Railway Station

UNHCR EXARCHEIA

Syntagma Square St George Lycabettus

Acropolis

PIRAEUS

Venizelos Airport

4.0

km

Saronic Gulf

athens

Istanbul Airport

Black Sea

Rumelifeneri

Bosporus

Ferry Terminal

Golden Horn

YENIKAPI Topkapi Palace

Hagia KADIKÖY

Sofia

0   10

km

Sea of Marmara

black chain

1

The Yank shows up in the doorway just after the *soupe au pistou* lands on the table, and Pascual knows instantly that the one is going to spoil his enjoyment of the other.

Being half Yank himself, Pascual can spot them a mile away; even as fashions on either side of the Atlantic have converged, something about the gait, the tentative air, the cut of the jib gives it away. As the Yank pauses on the threshold, scanning the cheerful tumult of a bar in the tumbledown quarter of Noailles in the heart of Marseille at *l'heure du déjeuner*, there is an outside chance he could be just another tourist looking for a cheap lunch, but that hope vanishes when he locks eyes with Pascual and smiles.

Pascual refuses to acknowledge him, concentrating on his soup, until the Yank heaves to at his table and says, "Pascual Rose, I believe? Or would it be Pascual March today?"

Pascual gives him his haughtiest look, watching the phony smile fade to a bland neutrality, and says, just for form's sake, "*Vous vous trompez, monsieur. Vous me prenez pour quelqu'un d'autre.*"

"*Je ne crois pas,*" the Yank says with a creditable accent and pulls out the chair opposite Pascual. "Nice try, but we've got you on video. You're my guy." He sits, and his eyes go to Pascual's left hand on the table. "The two missing fingers kind of seal the deal. That's what the files call a distinguishing mark."

The Yank is somewhere in his forties, gray at the temples and with the hairline starting to retreat, just a bit jowly, a little slope-shouldered, not a military man from the look of him. Most likely a spook, then. A journalist might know both his names, but Pascual doesn't like the sound of that video. "And who the hell are you?" he says.

The smile comes back for an instant, triumphant, and then goes away again. "Ed Melville, pleased to meet you. Mind if I join you for lunch?"

Pascual returns to his soup. "What if I said I did?"

The man who is calling himself Melville today shrugs. "That would only postpone the conversation we're going to have."

Pascual swallows and says, "You can pick up the tab, then."

"I can do that." Melville manages to flag down the sullen waiter in his soiled apron and with a minimum of awkwardness succeeds in ordering the *plat du jour*, a fairly plebeian *steak frites* Pascual has learned to avoid. "You've got quite a range of dining choices in this neighborhood," says Melville, looking out the window. "There's the kebab joint across the way there, and I passed some kind of African place on the way here. Amazing smells. And the market stalls just around the corner here. Very colorful. You've chosen a great place to go to earth."

Through the window Pascual can see two African cigarette peddlers arguing in front of a mobile phone shop, watched with suspicion by the Corsican baker sucking on his hourly cigarette in the adjacent doorway. "It's a slum," says Pascual. "Even more than it was before the pandemic kicked the hell out of it. But I like it." He finishes the soup and shoves the bowl away. "How did you find me?"

Melville flashes the smile again. "We followed the money, of course."

"What money?"

"Ha. Very good. You're living on a shoestring budget, that's for sure. I'd guess you have some local income, probably in cash. Your ATM withdrawals can't possibly be feeding you and paying rent. But they've been just enough to give away your location."

Pascual stuffs a piece of bread in his mouth. "You must have leaned on CaixaBank. I should have anticipated that."

"We didn't need to lean on anybody. Least of all your wife and son, if that's what concerns you. Didn't go near them. We looked at their phone data, but if you're talking to them, it's not on the phones registered to them."

"I'm not an idiot."

"No, nobody would accuse you of that. Anyway, all we needed was a little cooperation from some colleagues in Madrid to start with. The bank was happy to help them track down a known money launderer and possible terrorist. And then, once we saw the withdrawals here in Marseille, the DCRI was very helpful. They're the ones with access to the video from the ATMs. And the facial recognition software, of course. They were kind enough to put a couple of men on the task of spotting you and tracking you down. I have to say, you've done a pretty good job of going off the grid. How much are you paying to live in that dump?"

Pascual washes down the bread with a gulp of rich red Provençal plonk and sets the glass down a trifle more emphatically than he intended. "It's a squat. It's one of the places that was declared unsafe when those two buildings collapsed a few years ago and killed eight people, just up the street here. The *mairie* got suddenly very concerned about the wellbeing of its poorer constituents and evicted them all until the buildings could be shored up. This one's been declared safe, but the landlord doesn't want to put any money into it. He lives in Paris, and I think he's hoping for another disaster so he can get the insurance money. A fellow I know put in new locks, invited a couple of pals to join him there. We're quiet and we keep the place up. We're doing the landlord a favor."

Melville sits shaking his head. "You had a fairly comfortable life there in your little Catalan town, by all accounts. Why would you give that up to come here and hide?"

Pascual gives him a withering look. "You have to ask?"

"All right, I get it. You've made some enemies."

"It's my so-called friends that worry me."

Melville acknowledges that with a nod. "The offer still stands. The agency will be more than happy to set you and your family up with good cover, good amenities, anywhere you want. All you have to do is say yes."

"I don't want to work for the agency."

There is a brief stare-down and Melville says, "You don't have much choice, sad to say. You owe us."

Pascual shrugs. He has known this day would come eventually; he has staved it off for nearly two years, and he decides he will have to be content with that. "So what the hell do you want?"

The steak and fries arrive, and Melville picks up a knife and fork. The steak gives him a battle but some vigorous sawing manages to detach some pieces he can fit in his mouth. When he tires of chewing he says, "Does the name al-Azma mean anything to you?"

Something roils the soup in Pascual's belly, part excitement and part dread. In truth the monastic life has begun to wear on him and the prospect of a more eventful way of living is not unwelcome. The dread comes because he knows the nature of the events that any contact with the Central Intelligence Agency is likely to generate. "It sounds like an Arabic name. Can I have some context?"

"How about in a Syrian context? Does that help?"

It takes Pascual a few seconds. "Seems to me there was a Yusuf al-Azma who put up a fight against the French during their mandate in Syria. He got himself killed leading a bunch of irregulars against the French army. In about 1920, I think. Considered a martyr of modern Syrian nationalism."

"Oh, very good. I think you may have nailed it. You're not aware of something called the al-Azma Cell?"

"Never heard of it."

"Well, neither had anybody else until two weeks ago. We suspect it's a new incarnation of the Syrian Electronic Army."

"Which was a bunch of Syrian hackers, if I'm not mistaken."

"Or possibly Iranian. The cyberwar arm of the Assad regime, anyway, such as it was. They cropped up at the beginning of the war and raised a little Cain, launching DoS attacks, defacing websites and so forth, mostly nuisance value stuff. And then once Assad had driven out or killed all his dissatisfied citizens, they sort of went away. Some of them got caught, some of them got killed. Now some of them apparently are back."

"And they've finally done something serious."

Melville smiles and wipes his mouth with a flimsy paper napkin from the dispenser on the table. "Now why would you assume that?"

"Because you wouldn't go to the trouble of finding me if you weren't desperate."

"Desperate's a little strong. Let's say they've managed to make a major nuisance of themselves."

"And you think there's something I can do about it."

"Well, if there are Syrians involved, that's right up your alley, isn't it? You spent a few years in Damascus."

Pascual shrugs. "A long time ago. How do you know they're who they say they are?"

"Well, good question. On the internet, nobody knows you're a dog, and all that. The tech guys say it checks out. There are digital fingerprints and signatures and such that are hard to hide. Whoever they are, they're in that camp or they're being paid by that camp."

"OK. Now, what the hell is all this to me?"

"It might mean a payday for you. It looks to me like you could use one."

"What would I have to do?"

"You'd have to be an honest broker."

Pascual works on that for a moment. "Who wants what from whom?"

"We want our data back."

"Ah." Pascual watches Melville jab at his plate. "What, somebody at Langley clicked on a special offer for Viagra?"

"We're a little better than that. Everybody's got good hackers nowadays. Suffice it to say they found a way in. And now our data's locked up tighter than a drum and our best guys can't crack it."

"And so you're going to have to pay."

Melville nods, working on a mouthful of fries. "We're going to have to pay, and we're going to have to make sure we don't get cheated. That's where you come in."

"Why me? I'm not much good with the technical stuff."

"You don't have to be. You just have to be able to follow instructions."

"Again, why me?"

"Because you have a reputation in the right circles as a disinterested party. We proposed you and they accepted you. And the financial plumbing that will make it work is in your name."

Pascual sighs. "Just send them the Bitcoin, or whatever it is they want. Isn't that how these things are done?"

"Normally. That's not how this is being done. One, they don't want cryptocurrency. Two, they don't want to be traced. They've got some special setup in mind for transferring the ransom. They want to keep everything offline, which is interesting for a bunch of hackers. But that's what they're demanding. And that's why we need a bagman. It's a low-tech solution."

"I see. How much money are we talking about?"

Melville saws at a piece of gristle, frowning. "They want ten million dollars."

Pascual watches him chew. "And you're going to give it to them."

Melville looks up from his plate, and there is no humor in his look now. "We will explore ways of getting it back. But right now we really need our data."

"What do they have against cryptocurrency?"

"Who knows? It seems to work for most crooks. But crypto is, of course, at least in principle, traceable. They want to avoid that. I'm not sure how they hope to do that, but I'm sure you will keep us informed."

Pascual swirls the last of his wine in the glass and then quaffs it. "So what's this data you let them put the clamps on?"

Melville just looks at him for a moment, completely expressionless. "You don't need to know that, do you? All you need to know is where to go and what to say."

Pascual smiles. "And one more thing."

"What's that?'

"What's in it for me?"

Melville spears a forkful of fries and raises it toward his mouth. He pauses and says, "How about a million bucks?" He jams the fries into his mouth and chews, watching Pascual.

Pascual waits for him to swallow. "A million dollars?"

"Or the euro equivalent, if you prefer. In a nice anonymous account in some tax haven, under whatever identity you wish, all completely kosher."

Even Pascual can do that math. "A million is ten percent. Is that the going rate for a bagman?"

"Are you trying to tell me a million isn't enough for you?"

"I'm just trying to see how much leverage I have."

Melville shrugs. "How much do you want?"

Pascual gives him a long, contemplative look. Being offered a million dollars over lunch in a down-at-the-heels Marseille bistro is no more surreal than any number of other things that have happened to him; it is all too believable. The problem is the baggage that will come with it. "I'll settle for the million and a promise I won't be bothered again. I can make a million last a while. If you'll let me."

Melville nods a few times, dabs at his lips with the napkin and tosses it away. "I'll have to clear that with the higher-ups. But I don't see that it should be a problem."

Pascual's gaze drifts out the window into the rue d'Aubagne. The Africans have moved on and the baker has gone inside; a pretty Muslim girl in a hijab looks up from her phone and happens to make eye contact with Pascual, fleetingly, before hurrying away up the street. Pascual watches her go, wistfully, and thinks about how much promises from the agency are worth. He decides that the million dollars will probably be real enough and that they will assist in handling whatever comes after that.

Pascual sighs and says, "Where do I sign?"

Pascual meanders after lunch, idling through the market past piles of fruit and heaps of cheap plastic goods, fielding smiles and gripes and philosophical reflections from acquaintances in three languages. He realizes it is beginning to feel like a farewell tour. For a moment he wonders idly about the mechanics of administering a small fortune in a remote tax haven, but where money is concerned Pascual learned long ago to believe it when he sees it.

He turns up a narrow lane and makes for a doorway with a cheap tin plaque bolted onto the wall beside it announcing the *Hôtel Pharaon*. A hand-lettered sign on the door says *OUVERT SONNEZ MERCI*. Pascual does as instructed, pressing the button set into the wall before he pushes through the door and mounts the stairs.

At the top of the flight is a cramped lobby with a counter, the classic pigeonholes behind it and a fluorescent tube above it providing a cruel light. A man is standing at the foot of the next flight up and shouting, "*Quoi?*" Two or three floors above them a woman screeches something that is inaudible because of the echo in the stairwell. The man makes a dismissive gesture and turns to scowl at Pascual. "What are you doing here?"

"I've come to use the phone." Pascual fetches up at the desk and leans on it. "If I may."

The man is roughly Pascual's age, some way past fifty, but in much worse shape, with less hair, more belly and a correspondingly embittered expression on his face. He shuffles around the end of the counter, hands jammed into his trouser pockets. "Ah. So, only to exploit your position once again."

Pascual grins at him. "That was part of our arrangement. I work cheap and off the books, at times when nobody else will work, and in return I get to use the phone. What's your beef? You even dock my pay for it."

The man grunts and brings an antediluvian analog telephone up from below the counter. He sets it in front of Pascual. "Why don't you buy yourself a phone? Ten-year-old *petits voyous* straight from the Congo have phones. You can get one for twenty euros from that *bougnoule* in the rue Rouvière."

Pascual puts the receiver to his ear. "If I had a phone my wife would give me no peace."

"*Ah, ça alors.*" Conceding, the man wanders away into a back room and Pascual punches a number into the phone.

He expects the call to go to voice mail, but after three rings a woman's voice says, in Spanish, "You're at work early."

"I just stopped in to use the phone. I'm surprised you answered."

"I've been keeping the secure phone near me. I knew you'd be calling."

"How's that?"

"There have been signs. Whispers at the bank, my mobile acting oddly. I knew someone was looking for you."

"Well, they've found me."

"Nobody too dangerous, I hope."

"Just the usual crowd."

"The *yanquis* or the Germans?"

"The *yanquis*. They want to give me money."

"And what do they want you to do for it?"

Pascual smiles; any other woman would have asked how much, but Sara goes straight to the heart of the matter. "Nothing too strenuous. I'm to deliver a ransom payment."

"Who's been kidnapped?"

"I'm told it's a matter of access to data. Somebody in Washington got hacked."

"*Dios mío.* With all their experts?"

"Everybody's got experts. Anyway, the point is, they're offering me a lot of money to do this, and I'm inclined to accept it."

There is a brief silence at the other end of the line. "It's your conscience."

"Enough to make things easier for us. Enough to buy some privacy, maybe. So we could have a home again. Somewhere."

The silence goes on for a while this time. At last Sara says, "I trust your judgment."

Pascual has to laugh. "That's more than I can say. What do you hear from our son?"

"He's well. Settling to work, I hope. Exams coming up, he should have the degree next spring."

"That's more than his father ever accomplished. I'll give him a call."

"Do that. He misses you. How is life in Marseille?"

"Much as it was when you were here."

"I am distressed to hear it. When do you leave?"

"Soon, I have been given to understand."

"And after that? Will we be seeing you?"

Pascual draws a deep breath. "As soon as I can manage it, *vida mía.*"

"I'm waiting for you, then. *Cuídate, cariño.*"

"As always. I'll keep you posted. *Ciao.*"

Pascual stands for a moment with his hand on the phone after hanging up, beginning to make calculations. The hotelier emerges from the back room and gives him a questioning look.

"I'm giving notice," Pascual says. "As of next week. You're going to need a new night clerk."

The man blinks at him. "You can't just walk out like that."

"I can, actually," says Pascual, turning away. "It's what I do best."

"Monaco," says Pascual. "I might have passed through it on a train once or twice. I don't think I could ever afford to get off."

"It's a high-rent district," says Melville. "But you'll be able to afford it now."

Pascual stands at a window, looking out at a slice of Marseille's Eighth Arrondissement, a high-rent district if there ever was one. Below him a sloping street plunges toward a distant boulevard, lined with trees and stretches of high stone wall concealing the gardens of the wealthy. "What do you see out there?" says Melville.

"Secrets," Pascual says, turning from the window. "My wife knew this district quite well when she lived in Marseille, years ago."

"Really? What did she do?"

"She was a high-priced call girl."

Whatever Melville expected to hear, it wasn't this; he blinks stupidly at Pascual.

Pascual wanders to the table. "Her best clients lived around here. Business titans, political heavyweights, a bishop or two. Pillars of the community. She killed one of them one night when he tried to stick a bottle up her." Pascual pulls out a chair and sits. "She was acquitted at trial on grounds of self-defense. A rare victory for justice."

When Melville recovers he says, "I bet she doesn't have much trouble keeping you in line."

Pascual smiles. "I treat her with the utmost respect. Why Monaco, do you think?"

Melville reaches for a manila envelope. "It's a financial center. Lots of banks. They seem determined to do everything the old-fashioned way, with a minimum of electronic communication. So they need physical proximity to financial service providers. That's my guess. You're going to be investing in a hedge fund. That's the way they want to do it."

"A hedge fund. I have a vague notion of what that is."

"It's a kind of investment fund, where you give a fellow a chunk of your money and hope he can make it grow. He pools the money he gets from you and other suckers and goes off to speculate in the markets. It's less regulated than other kinds of mutual funds, and so there's a greater chance of making a killing. Or losing your shirt. Most of them are for big investors only, with stiff minimum investments. Even in the new regulatory environment they're still a good option for money laundering because the assumption tends to be that all the Know Your Customer procedures have been done before the money gets to the hedge fund. You can just sink a load of cash into a hedge fund and then wait till it's safe to make a withdrawal and have it wired to your cousin in Colombia. Or in our case, kiss it goodbye."

"Ouch."

"Your investment is the ransom payment. When they get the money, we get our data back."

"You hope."

Melville smiles. "That's where you come in. You're the go-between, the honest broker. Your function is, in essence, to hold the money in escrow until we notify you that we've recovered the data. You'll go through all the procedures for making a subscription to the fund, show proof that you have the money and can transfer it at any time, and then say OK, now make with the goods. When we get the code and confirm that everything works, you wire them the money."

Pascual nods slowly. "Ten million dollars. That must be some really important data."

"It is." Melville hesitates. "I know ten million sounds like a lot, but it's not what it used to be. Not where hedge funds are concerned. You'll just be a midrange client. Enough for them to be polite but not enough to fawn."

Pascual suppresses a laugh. "And what's the hedge fund?"

"This one's called Zenobia Capital."

"Aha. The Syrian connection." When Melville looks blank Pascual says, "Zenobia was the queen of Palmyra, back when Palmyra was a thriving city instead of a pile of sunbaked ruins in the Syrian desert."

"Your grasp of history is impressive. The fund's been in operation since 1999. Ownership is a little opaque. We're still working through all the shell companies and foundations and such."

"So, what am I going to do, hand them a check? Ten million dollars in cash would more than fill a suitcase, I imagine."

"You'd need an old-fashioned steamer trunk. No, you will pay them, whoever they are, out of the UBS account for Regenta Holdings Ltd."

"Good God, that still exists?"

"Of course. All those accounts Pascual Rose set up as part of his last business venture are still active." He pulls a passport out of the envelope and slides it across to Pascual. "As is Pascual Rose. Given the size of the assets listed when you applied for citizenship, the Maltese government was happy to replace the passport you reported stolen two years ago."

"That was very responsible of me. I'd forgotten all about it." Pascual sighs as he opens the passport issued in his real name more than thirty years after he abandoned it. "This won't set off alarms whenever I try to cross a border?"

"It might pique some interest among a certain type of intelligence officer if they happen to notice it. But nobody will stop you. You're not on any watch lists, not anymore. We went around and had a quiet word with the relevant agencies. Pascual Rose was never prosecuted for anything and he's a demonstrably real person. He also happens to own a number of shell companies incorporated in various places, none of them under any kind of sanction. He's too valuable to let lapse."

Pascual tosses the passport aside. "I see. What's he living on these days?"

Melville reaches into the envelope again. "That's a little murky, but all you need to know is that he doesn't have any trouble paying off his credit card bills every month." Melville produces a platinum premium card issued by a major bank and hands it to Pascual. "Like I say, you'll be able to afford a room at the Hermitage."

"I tend to lower the tone in a place like the Hermitage."

"That's where we were told to book you in. Use the card to go buy yourself a wardrobe upgrade this afternoon. That's all they care about in a place like that."

"And who am I talking to once I get there?"

"Once you get there, you just wait. They'll contact you."

"How?"

"Probably by paging you at the desk. We offered to give them a phone number but they declined. You'll need this anyway." Melville tips the envelope and a mobile phone slides out. "It's pretty well encrypted and should be hackproof, as far as anything can be. The password's on that sticker on the back. Don't download anything, don't use it for anything that's not related to the job." He pushes the phone toward Pascual with his fingertips. "Also on the sticker you'll find my personal number. Don't hesitate to call if you need guidance. Memorize it and destroy the sticker."

Pascual glances at the sticker and sets the phone down. "I'll need account numbers and passwords and so forth for the bank."

Melville reaches into the envelope again. Without a word he shoves a single sheet of paper across. "It's all there. Again, memorize and destroy."

"I didn't realize there'd be homework. How have you been talking with these people so far?"

"By e-mail, just like with any other hacker. The addresses go nowhere, of course, and they keep changing. Whoever contacts you in Monaco will be the first confirmed sighting of a human being."

"Do I demand credentials? Or do I just hand ten million dollars to the first guy that buys me lunch?"

"I think their credentials will be what they know. When in doubt, check with me. But in any case, the main part of your job is to show them the money. At that point, we see if we get our data back. If we do, you give the word to your banker to wire the funds and your job is over. It's up to us then to see if we can track them down and get our money back, maybe eventually haul somebody in front of a judge. Of course, any information you might be able to contribute from your face-to-face contact with them would be appreciated."

Pascual smiles. "So. I'm not supposed to be all that honest a broker."

Melville raises his hands in a gesture of concession. "Don't do anything to jeopardize the deal, or your personal safety. But you will be debriefed."

Pascual sits nodding slowly, trying to think of questions he should ask, guarantees he should demand. "And when is all this happening?"

Melville shrugs. "When can you leave?"

Pascual scoops passport, cards and phone toward him. "Does now work?"

3

After a pleasant morning's run along the coast from Marseille, the sea sparkling beneath an azure sky, arrival in Monaco is a bit of a disappointment, as the train slips into a tunnel and eases to a stop at a long, curving platform in what looks like a particularly well-appointed subway station. Pascual has to negotiate multiple levels and passages before he emerges into sunshine with a view of yachts moored in a harbor below and nary a taxi in sight.

A brief consultation of his new phone convinces Pascual that nothing can be very far away in Monaco and it will be a pleasant downhill stroll to the Hermitage Hotel. After Marseille, Monaco looks like a theme park, all pastel colors and lush gardens, spotless. He arrives at the Hermitage in a light sweat and with tender spots where his newly purchased wing tips have set to work on his feet.

Pascual has stayed in his share of top-shelf hotels, always at someone else's expense, and has never been able to take them seriously; no human being could possibly require the degree of pampering and obsequiousness they offer. One thing he has never suffered from is feelings of intimidation or inferiority; he has witnessed enough squalid behavior among the wealthy to feel quite at home. As he approaches reception in a soothing environment of cream-colored, flower-bedecked opulence, his principal concern is how soon he will be able to take off his shoes. His passport and credit card arouse no apparent suspicion, and he fends off a marauding bellhop with designs on his overnight bag and manages to find his own way to the elevators.

Whoever booked the room has done him proud; his lavender-themed suite has French doors onto a balcony with a view of the sea. Only a few hours removed from a crumbling squat in Marseille, Pascual stands wiggling his toes in the thick carpet, looking past waving palms at the shimmering Mediterranean and wondering how long he will have to wait before the curtain goes up.

Not long, as it happens. Pascual has just flung himself on the bed after an obscenely expensive luncheon at the agency's expense on the hotel's outdoor terrace, watching sailboats disport offshore, when the hotel phone at his bedside purrs. He lets it ring a couple of times, wondering idly what will happen if he simply refuses to answer, before rolling slowly to pick up the receiver.

"Monsieur Rose?" The male voice is deep and, to judge by the *r* in Rose, possibly not that of a native French speaker.

"*À votre service.*" Pascual manages to get his feet to the floor. "With whom am I speaking?"

"Your car is here, *monsieur*. We await you at reception."

Pascual identifies an Arab, with fluent French but learned as an adult. "Very good. Where are we going?"

"*Chez Zenobia, monsieur*. If that is convenient for you."

"Perfectly." Pascual rubs his face, wishing he had had the moral fiber to forgo the wine with lunch. "Give me five minutes."

"*D'accord, monsieur.*"

Pascual runs a comb through his hair and eases his feet into the unforgiving shoes. He struggles with his tie, puts on his jacket and slips passport and phone into the thin leather portfolio that contains the documentation he will need to establish his relationship with Zenobia Capital. He has been thoroughly rehearsed on the particulars of Pascual Rose's resuscitated financial empire and can produce a bank statement for Regenta Holdings that shows ten million dollars and change, ready to be disbursed.

There is no mistaking the two men who are waiting for him when he steps out of the elevator. Pascual has seen men who look like this before, bodyguarding regime heavyweights in Damascus and shaking down lorry drivers at desert border crossings. These two are in suits, unmistakably Arab and unmistakably *baltajis*, hard cases, one bearded with the swollen look of a weightlifter, straining the suit, and the other a tall, lantern-jawed specimen with thick black eyebrows and mustache that contrast with his scouring-pad gray hair. The gorillas size him up as he comes across the lobby, their faces utterly blank. Bluto and Silverback, Pascual thinks, extending his hand. "I'm Pascual Rose. Are we going far?"

Silverback says, "Not at all, *monsieur*. Five minutes away." He gestures toward the exit. The car is a black Mercedes S600, waiting in front of the hotel with a casual scattering of Lamborghinis and Jaguars. Bluto drives, taking them out of the hotel forecourt onto a road that descends in a graceful curve to sweep around the harbor. From the shotgun seat Silverback says, "First time in Monaco?" He does not sound especially interested in the answer.

"I was here once before," Pascual says, improvising for no reason other than to dent that leaden mask. "Many years ago. I lost a hundred thousand francs at the casino one night."

The man vents a grunt that could be sympathy or disapproval. "You had very bad luck or perhaps very bad judgment."

Irked in spite of himself, Pascual says, "I won a quarter of a million the next night."

Silverback shoots him a skeptical look and says, "I hope you spent it on a woman. They don't put it in the brochures, but they have very fine prostitutes in Monaco."

Pascual gives it a moment and says, "Some of us don't have to pay for it."

That kills the conversation until they arrive at their destination in the flat, low-lying district to the west of the harbor. Halfway along a quiet street stands a modest-sized but elegant Italianate house squeezed between taller neighbors, pale yellow with quoins at the corners and elaborately carved window hoods, set back from the street beyond a small front garden shaded by two tall palms and guarded by a wrought-iron fence. The overall effect is quiet money and lots of it. A plaque on the gatepost reads *Zenobia Capital S.A.M.*

Silverback leads Pascual up the front steps and rings the doorbell while the Mercedes oozes away. A buzzer goes off and he pushes inside into a hall with a high ceiling, a parquet floor and a marble staircase. He leads Pascual up the stairs into a hallway running the length of the house, turns toward the front and after a single rap on a door ushers him into an office. Here a dark-eyed honey blonde, dressed to kill in a figure-hugging forest-green dress, sits behind a desk. From the look she bestows on the gorilla, Pascual surmises that she knows him and is not a fan. She nods at them and goes to tap gently on an inner door. She opens it and leans in to murmur something inaudible, then stands aside and motions them in.

They enter a sleekly modern office, with multiple flat-screen computer monitors and laptops on an oval desk that looks like an overgrown surfboard, an array of chairs and a sofa. Behind the desk is a small, dark man in a suit. Unlike the two gorillas, he looks as if he belongs in it. He is nicely groomed, his hairline retreating in good order on either side of a central tuft, and he sports stylish square-framed glasses and a dapper little mustache. He rises as they come in. "Ah. You must be Monsieur Rose."

After the handshake, Pascual is offered a chair in front of the desk; Silverback slouches on the sofa. The man sinks back onto his chair. "I am Didier Sabbagh, head of compliance. Welcome to Monaco." His French is impeccable. "Is the hotel to your satisfaction?"

"Very much. Just what one expects in a place like Monaco."

"You have flown in from Dubai?"

Pascual is unsure how good his cover story has to be for this little charade; presumably all that matters is whether the wire transfer goes through. On general principle he chooses not to tell a lie that can be easily checked. "I came on the train from Marseille this morning. I've been in France for the past few weeks."

"You have interests there, no doubt."

Pascual waves a hand, airily. "A little all over."

Sabbagh sits nodding for a moment, his smile fading. "You have an interesting history. As far as it can be discerned, that is. The public record contains some gaps."

This is alarming; Pascual has been led to believe that things have been stitched up in advance and all he has to do is follow instructions. "I will be happy to provide any documentation that may be required."

He brandishes the portfolio.

Sabbagh nods. "I'm sure there will be no problem." He hesitates for a moment, looking faintly troubled. His eyes flick to the gorilla on the couch and back and he says, "Certain elements of the onboarding process have been waived, at the request of the partners. I have been assured that your credentials are impeccable and that the terms of your investment have been thoroughly discussed with you and are acceptable."

"Perfectly." Pascual nods with a gracious smile, relieved to hear confirmation of the stitch-up and starting to get a clearer picture of Monsieur Sabbagh's position.

Sabbagh's expression eases a little. "Very well. I assume then that you come prepared to transfer ten million dollars to the management account of Zenobia Capital, for the purpose of a subscription to the fund. There will be certain formalities to be attended to first, of course. There will be a certain amount of *paperasse*."

"There always is." Pascual flashes a nonchalant smile.

"Indeed." Sabbagh returns the smile and then pulls a thin stack of paper forms toward him. "I have prepared the necessary forms for the application. We will require some basic documentation, of course."

"I trust I can provide everything you need."

"Excellent. There remains the matter of the money."

"I can arrange a wire transfer from a corporate account at UBS in very short order." Pascual raises a finger. "But there is a condition to be fulfilled first."

"Yes." Sabbagh carefully squares the edges of the stack of forms. "So I am informed. I have been instructed to complete the registration process, confirm that the money is available and then notify certain parties and wait for instructions." Again his eyes go briefly to the man lounging on the sofa.

Pascual says, "Presumably they will not be long in coming. For my part, I will proceed to wire the money when I receive confirmation from my advisers that all conditions have been satisfied."

He knows it's crooked, Pascual thinks as he watches Sabbagh trying to work all this out. He knows this is no ordinary investment and there is a ten-million-dollar quid pro quo involved. He's trying to run a legitimate hedge fund, and he's got crooks telling him what to do. Looking like a man who has swallowed something rotten, Sabbagh says, "Well, then. Let us have a look at this *paperasse*. There is a good deal of it to get through."

"Normally it takes a few days for the paperwork to clear," says Pascual quietly into his phone. "But I've been assured that I won't have to wait around. Once the wire transfer goes through, I'm free to go." He is standing at a window at the rear of the house, looking down into an enclosed yard where a Vespa scooter sits beneath an orange tree and Bluto stands smoking a cigarette, tie loosened to ease the pressure on his massive neck. "The transfer's set up online through the USB account. Once you give me the word, all I have to do is log in and click on Kiss It Goodbye."

"Well, don't do that just yet." In Pascual's ear, Melville's voice conveys just a hint of strain. "I'm sitting here watching our tech guy trying to find our data, and he doesn't look happy. Where are you? Are you still at their office?"

"Yeah. They've put me in what looks like the staff lounge. There's coffee, and they've offered me booze. I'm tempted, because it's getting on toward cocktail hour here. But I'm going to try to keep my wits about me."

"Do that, by all means. Hang on a second." There is a silence that lasts for half a minute and Melville is back. "Look, are you sure they sent the code? My guy here says he hasn't gotten a thing. The data's still locked up tight."

Pascual comes away from the window, suppressing a surge of anxiety. "I couldn't tell you what the hackers have or haven't done. The only guy I've dealt with is Zenobia's compliance officer. Once he had verified with USB that I am who I say I am and the account is good, he watched me set up the transaction on my phone. When it was ready to go, he made a phone call, saying I'd checked all the boxes and was ready to wire the money. Then he put me back here and told his secretary to make sure I had everything I needed. That's when I texted you."

"Christ. That was an hour ago. How hard can it be? Are they contacting the hackers by camel?"

"Maybe they're asleep. Hackers aren't known for keeping regular hours."

"Levity is not really helpful right now. Look, whatever you do, don't put that transaction through until I confirm we've got the data. Don't let your phone out of your hands. Don't let them pressure you, don't let them hoodwink you. You wait for confirmation from me, personally."

"Understood. How long do I give it?"

"Good question. Shit, see if you can stir things up a little. Go find out what's going on."

Pascual sighs. "All right." He ends the call and slips the phone into his pocket. He opens the door and steps out into the hall to be confronted with the sight of Silverback rising from a chair. "Monsieur requires something?" The stance he assumes says clearly that he is there to keep Pascual from going any farther.

"Monsieur would like to know how long he is going to have to wait."

"Ah, I could not say. Would you like something to drink? Something to eat? I will have the girl bring you something."

"Let's let the girl attend to her business, shall we? What I would like is to speak to Monsieur Sabbagh." Pascual tries to step around him, but he moves to block the way.

"Don't trouble yourself, *monsieur*. Make yourself comfortable in the salon and I will see if Monsieur Sabbagh can attend you." The expression on the lantern-jawed face is blank, the touch on Pascual's arm casual. The message is unmistakable, and Pascual decides he is not prepared to contest the issue.

"Very well." He returns to the lounge and goes to the window. He has a brief vision of an escape by Vespa, but Bluto is still there, and Pascual decides that the drop is too far in any event. Ten minutes later he hears footsteps approaching in the hall and then a rap on the door. It opens and a man Pascual has never seen comes in. He is short and compact, shaven-headed and jowly, a bulldog with a face made to show ill temper. Instead of a suit, this one wears jeans and a black motorcycle jacket. He closes the door behind him and makes a visible effort to soften his expression. "Monsieur Rose."

Pascual nods. "And who are you?"

The look hardens a little, reverting to form. "I represent your counterparty. I'm here to assure that this transaction goes through as expected." His French is good, with a barely detectable accent that may be Arabic or may be something else.

Pascual assumes an innocent look. "The transaction can proceed at any time. I only require confirmation that you have complied with your part of it."

The black brows clamp down. "The key has been sent. You can access your data at any time."

"You'll forgive me if I wait for confirmation from my principal."

"He has sent confirmation, *monsieur*. By return e-mail. I can show you." He turns, reaching for the door handle.

Pascual almost goes for it; he takes two steps toward the open door before he remembers Melville's last instruction and stops in his tracks. "One moment. Allow me to contact him by phone."

The way the man stiffens tells Pascual all he needs to know. "That won't be necessary. I can show you the e-mail."

"Indulge me," says Pascual, reaching for his phone. Melville answers instantly when the call goes through. "What's going on?"

"Did you get your data? They're telling me here they sent it and you confirmed receipt by e-mail."

There is a brief silence. "They're fucking with you. We got nothing, I sent nothing. I think this thing's going belly up. Get out of there if you can."

"I'll see what I can do." Pascual rings off. The bulldog is glaring at him. "You're a bad liar," says Pascual.

The man shrugs, not in the least embarrassed. "There seems to be some confusion. I suggest you wait patiently while we sort things out."

"And I suggest you get serious about executing your end of the bargain. I'll be at the Hermitage." Pascual starts to move past him and is stopped by a hand on his chest.

"Please. Allow us to accompany you to your hotel."

During the short stare-down that follows, Pascual makes some rapid assessments and decides that his chances of shaking free of Syrian thugs are virtually nil at the moment and will rise once he is delivered to the Hermitage and has some breathing room. He nods. "Thank you. That's very kind."

How many men will they need to keep him from leaving the hotel? Pascual stands at the open French doors of his hotel room and considers, watching the horizon go orange and the sea a deep shimmering aquamarine as evening descends. Not that many, he decides. A man in the lobby to watch the elevators, two or three others in the street, including Bluto, who has been lounging in the little plaza across the road all afternoon, to keep an eye on whatever side doors there may be.

He comes back into the room, swirling his minibar Scotch in the glass. A more vexing question is how long they intend to keep him here, and why. His estimation of the quality of the opposition crashed with the clumsy attempt to deceive him. To go to the trouble of conscripting a hedge fund to arrange a ten-million-dollar ransom and then to resort to the basest subterfuge to avoid handing over the goods does not speak to a high standard of criminal competency. He wonders what will be next.

His phone vibrates in his pocket. Pascual extracts it and swipes. In his ear Melville says, "Time to bail. The whole thing's off."

Pascual's stomach goes cold. "What happened?"

"They got hacked."

"What? Who got hacked?"

"Our hackers. Your Syrian pals. Somebody hacked them. That's why they couldn't deliver."

Astonishment gradually cedes to mirth and Pascual has to stifle a laugh. "You're kidding."

"I wish I was. Are they still watching you?"

"Still there. What are they up to?"

"They're probably going crazy trying to get their data back. They won't want to let you get away as long as there's a chance they can deliver. They try any more funny stuff? They lean on you at all, to make the transfer?"

"No. But if they do, I'm giving it up. My commitment to the agency doesn't extend to gritting my teeth while my fingernails get torn out."

"It won't come to that. We've already gone into the account and canceled the transaction, and we're changing the passwords. But I'd bail if I were you. It's just possible they may try to use you as a hostage."

"That's reassuring. What if they try something? Can I scream for help, call the police?"

Melville takes his time before answering. "Be advised, if any law enforcement agencies come asking us about you, we never heard of you. We'll buy you back from the Syrians if we have to, but we're not going to try to explain you to Interpol."

"Your concern for my well-being is touching. How did you find out about the hack?"

"Simple. The new hacker contacted us. Now we have a new set of demands to deal with."

This time the laugh escapes Pascual. "You're having an exciting day, aren't you?"

Pascual can tell Melville is not amused. "It could get exciting for you if the Syrians are frustrated enough. I'd move if I were you."

Easier said than done, Pascual thinks, putting away the phone. There is a three-story drop from the balcony of his room and no doubt a Levantine arm-breaker or two waiting for him in the lobby. He closes the French doors and turns to give a wistful look at the obscene luxury in which he will now not be spending the night. For a moment he is tempted to postpone all decisions until the morning and take advantage of this unique opportunity, but the word "hostage" is resounding faintly at the back of his mind.

Alerting the watchers by attempting to check out of the hotel is out of the question. The Hermitage has no doubt had guests bolt before and will take an unannounced departure in its stride. They have his credit card number. Pascual takes stock and decides that very little of what he brought with him is essential. He has long since ditched the new wing tips for his well-worn loafers; as for the rest of his new wardrobe, easy come, easy go. With his phone, passport and wallet in the pockets of his sport jacket, Pascual is ready to make a run for it.

Or rather a casual stroll, he thinks. A man in search of a congenial place to drink might wander at his leisure through the public areas of the hotel, incidentally noting exits and strategically stationed vagrants. He might then be able to form a plan.

Pascual is making for the door when the housephone rings. Them again, he thinks. Ignore it? He stands frozen while it rings again. Best to know what they have to say, he decides, and goes to answer it.

"Monsieur Pascual Rose?" If this is another Arab, her French is even better than the rest, and she has a silky voice to purr it with. Pascual identifies himself and she says, "Céline Crovetto here, of the Seek Fun."

This cannot possibly be what she said, and Pascual is at a loss for a moment. "Seek Fun?"

She spells it out. "The SICCFIN, *monsieur*. Service d'Information et de Contrôle sur les Circuits Financiers. I am here with my colleague Loïc Meyrueis, and we would very much like to have a brief word with you."

Pascual is speechless for a moment. It may not be Interpol, but the Service for Information and Monitoring of Financial Networks sounds as if it is fully capable of ruining his evening. He says, "What, you're here at the hotel?"

"At reception, yes. Can we have a few moments of your time?"

Pascual can almost hear Melville screaming at him. Best practice from the agency's point of view would no doubt be to politely assent and then make for the back stairs at speed, but Pascual makes quick assessments and decides that whatever Melville may prefer, he would much rather spend the evening explaining himself to regulators than risk being clubbed into submission by Syrian thugs. "Certainly," he says. "I'll be right down."

When Pascual comes out of the elevator he spots two parties in quick succession: Silverback ducking behind a spray of flowers and his visitors coming away from the reception desk toward him. Whatever image her voice may have conjured, in person Céline Crovetto is on the formidable side, stout and matronly with a severe pageboy haircut that does not become her. Her colleague is perhaps ten years older, somewhere in his fifties, hawk-nosed and gimlet-eyed, with the unmistakable look of the retired copper. The handshakes are perfunctory.

"And to what do I owe the pleasure of this visit?" Pascual is scrambling to anticipate, evaluate, fabricate, masking it with his most ingratiating smile.

Crovetto responds with a slight raise of a squarish chin. "We would like to discuss the reason for your presence in Monaco."

Pascual's smile widens. He has spotted a gap in the fence. "If I could make a suggestion," he says, "this discussion might best be held somewhere outside the hotel. Your office perhaps? I am perfectly happy to accompany you there."

"There is no need, *monsieur*. I'm sure the hotel can provide a secluded space for a consultation."

"I would prefer that it take place elsewhere," says Pascual, stiffening a little. "There are people in the hotel who know me, and I have a reputation to uphold."

They stare at him for a moment and then trade a look. When Crovetto looks back at Pascual, she is almost smiling, but not in amusement. "Very well," she says. "Come with us."

"The deal's off," says Pascual. "Canceled. It fell through." He waits to see what impression this will make on his inquisitors. They are in a windowless room in a police station on a quiet street a short drive downhill from the Hermitage. In Monaco even the sweatboxes are well-appointed; this one has padded chairs and a table free of coffee stains and scratched graffiti. The fact that a couple of regulatory officials are on casual visiting terms with the local cops has raised them in Pascual's estimation.

Crovetto is frowning faintly; Meyrueis is giving Pascual a look of deep professional skepticism. "Why?" he says.

Pascual shrugs. "I got cold feet. I received information at the last moment that Zenobia Capital was not sound. Not to be trusted with my money. There are unsavory rumors."

The investigators trade another of their looks, the telepathy of old partners operating at full strength. Crovetto says, "There are unsavory rumors about you, *monsieur*. More than rumors. It would be more accurate to say that the factual, documented record of your doings for the past thirty years is wholly unsavory."

Pascual would be the last to argue with that, but he has a role to play. He looks down his nose at her and says, "I have never been charged with a crime. I am unsure even why you took the trouble to come and find me this evening."

Meyrueis leans in. "Because we were alerted to your intention to invest in Zenobia Capital, and upon examination your name set off every alarm bell in our system."

"I congratulate you on the responsiveness of your system. But I don't see why it should have."

"Because of your proven links to terrorism and money laundering." Meyrueis enunciates with the pedantry of a man explaining something to a particularly thick child.

Pascual issues an exasperated sigh. "The terrorism allegations have never been proven. The only criminal charges ever brought against me were dropped in Germany, last year. As for the money laundering, I was deceived. There was an attempt to manipulate me by criminal elements. I reported it, cooperated fully with the authorities in Spain, Germany and the United States, and was cleared of all charges."

"Yes," says Crovetto. "It made a bit of a splash, especially when it became evident that certain influential parties were working hard to smother the story. What seems to be indisputable is that the financier Pascual Rose is largely a fabrication."

"It is my real name. You have the proof in front of you." Pascual pokes his chin at his passport on the tabletop. "That issue was also settled when the criminal charges were dropped."

Meyrueis stirs and says, "That is not in dispute. What is in dispute is why you should be using it now instead of the name you have lived under for the past twenty-five years."

"Because I have chosen to do business under my real name. Pascual March is merely a convenient pseudonym to avert publicity. Look, if you can find any law I've broken, charge me. If what you're concerned about is my relations with Zenobia Capital, then you can easily verify that I've pulled out of the deal. Talk to Monsieur Didier Sabbagh at Zenobia. I'm guessing he's the one who alerted you, right?" Pascual waits for a response but gets nothing. "Very well. To be frank, he himself didn't seem entirely at ease. And I suspect it was for the same reason I wasn't. I think there is pressure on Zenobia from external parties. He seemed to be intimidated by certain . . . elements who were present during our interview."

The look that passes between Crovetto and Meyrueis this time tells Pascual he has struck close enough to home that he might yet deflect attention from his own position. He can still hear Melville saying, "We never heard of you," and if pressed he is ready to give up Melville, the agency and a million dollars, but he is hoping that SICCFIN will be more interested in keeping Levantine gangsters out of Monaco than in probing the dodgy finances of a disreputable Spanish speculator.

Meyrueis promptly alarms him by saying, "What is the origin of the capital you intended to invest with them? How did you come by ten million dollars?"

"I liquidated a number of assets. I can refer you to my accountant for details."

This is pure bluff, but Meyrueis apparently has no comeback. Crovetto says, "Who warned you about Zenobia?"

Pascual settles back on his chair, folding his arms. "Advisers."

There is a brief silence. Pascual senses that nobody believes the load of codswallop he has just shoveled, but that the collapse of the Zenobia deal has at least for the moment resolved the main concern of the Service d'Information et de Contrôle sur les Circuits Financiers. He is hoping that Crovetto and Meyrueis will perceive that Pascual Rose is an instrument of the influential parties Crovetto mentioned and conclude that it is not worth their while to delve deeper. The two officers hold another silent parley and then shove back their chairs and stand. "Wait here," Crovetto says, and they leave the room.

"You're leaving Monaco tomorrow, then?" says Crovetto, twisting to look at Pascual in the back seat as Meyrueis starts the car.

"As quickly as possible," Pascual says, meaning it. "I certainly have no further business to conduct here. I regret that my trip to your pleasant little country seems to have been wasted."

"Save it," growls Meyrueis. "Do us all a favor and don't even think about investing in Monaco in the future."

None of it was my idea, Pascual wants to say, but holds his tongue, grateful that whatever consultations his inquisitors undertook in the twenty minutes they were out of the room seem to have persuaded them that seeing him out of the country without further ado is the best course of action. He watches the harbor go by, lights shimmering on the water, a party in full swing on a brightly lit, rakish three-decker motor yacht at anchor, and feels a pang at the thought of the soft bed in the Hermitage on which he was privileged to lie for a brief moment today.

Crovetto turns to face Pascual again and says, "These advisers of yours."

"Yes?"

"I don't know who they are, but I think I know what they are. Tell them it would be appreciated if they would consult us the next time they want to run an operation in Monaco."

"I'll make sure they get the message," says Pascual.

"And one other thing."

"What's that?"

"A word of advice to you. You would do well to remember that the people behind a well-planned operation always have somebody they can throw to the wolves when things go wrong. Ask yourself who that might be in this case."

Pascual has already come to much the same conclusion, but he nods, gravely. "I thank you."

Somebody's phone makes a warbling noise. Crovetto digs in her handbag and comes out with her mobile. She answers, listens, and says, "*C'est pas vrai. Merde.*" Meyrueis gives her a sharp look and she returns it. "Where?" she says to the phone. She listens, signs off and says to Meyrueis, "Boulevard de Belgique."

"What is it?" says Meyrueis, already braking and looking for his turn.

Crovetto shakes her head a few times, slowly before answering. "Sabbagh." She gives Pascual another look over her shoulder, this one almost accusing. "The police are there." Meyrueis nods, squeals around a corner and steps on the gas.

Nothing in Monaco is very far away, but the Boulevard de Belgique is several terraces farther up the side of the mountain, and it takes a few hairpin turns and a tense ten minutes or so to get there. The police are indeed there, their flashing lights coming into view as Meyrueis sweeps around a curve and slows. High apartment buildings line the uphill side of the street, and the commotion appears to be at the foot of one of them, perhaps fifteen stories high. Meyrueis slows and pulls to the curb as a policeman waves them to a stop. Two patrol cars, white with red stripes, block the way beyond him. Clusters of people have gathered on the pavements on both sides of the street, standing mute and motionless, attention fixed on the spectacle in front of the building.

"Stay here," snaps Crovetto as she opens her door. Pascual watches her and Meyrueis approach the copper who stopped them, confer briefly, flash credentials and then walk on past the patrol cars. Pascual gives it a few seconds and gets out of the car.

Hands in his pockets, he strolls to the edge of the crowd on his side of the street and stands on his tiptoes for a better view. "*C'est affreux*," mutters an old woman, turning away and shoving through the crowd with a look of disgust.

Affreux indeed, Pascual thinks, horrific in any language, looking at the sprawled remains of Didier Sabbagh on the hitherto clean Monaco pavement. He appears to have bounced off a parked car, but what he did to the windshield and hood is nothing compared to what the car did to him. Pascual recognizes the tuft of hair on the top of his head and his stylish glasses, lying a few feet away.

"A suicide, *sans doute*," mutters one of his neighbors in the crowd.

"If it was, he changed his mind halfway down," says another. "I heard him scream. I will never forget that sound."

39

Yes, a suicide, Pascual thinks, turning away. *Sans doute.*

"I heard him *hit*," says someone behind him. "That, my friend, I will never forget."

"At least it was clear I couldn't have killed him. I'd been at the police station for the past hour." Phone to his ear, Pascual stands looking down into the rue d'Aubagne through a cracked windowpane, watching a retail drug transaction take place in a doorway. "But the cops kept me up all night anyway."

Melville takes a moment to reply; he sounded a little groggy when answering, and it occurs to Pascual that on the other side of the Atlantic the time is approximately six o'clock in the morning. "And what are they thinking?"

"For some reason they did not choose to share their thoughts with me. I was able to gather that Sabbagh lived in the building, in the penthouse suite. The consensus on the street seemed to be suicide, which is no doubt what it was intended to look like."

"You think it was assisted."

"I'd be very surprised if he wasn't ushered over the rail by a couple of Syrian thugs. And I told the cops that."

"What did you tell them about your part of it?"

"I told them it was an investment and I'd backed out because of information received. I tried to get them worked up about the criminal infiltration of the hedge fund. I was expecting the SICCFIN people to have more to say about that, but I guess seeing the guy splattered in the street like that got them focused on the Syrians, too. They knew there was something fishy about my end of the deal, but they didn't have any grounds for detaining me."

"Of course not. It was a legitimate investment. All the documentation would have stood up to examination. They might have delayed it a while, but they would have approved it eventually. Even so, you don't want to be too available for further investigation. Will they be able to find you again?"

"I told them I was flying out of Marseille back to Dubai. They seemed to buy it."

"Good. Sounds like you handled it."

"So. No million bucks? I didn't even get to spend the night at the Hermitage."

"You got a new wardrobe out of it."

"I had to ditch the clothes. I did get a nice day trip to Monaco out of it, I'll give you that. Tell you what, put a thousand euros in my wife's bank account and we'll call it quits."

"Not so fast. You're not finished."

"I'm finished trying to stare down Syrian gangsters, I can tell you that."

"You're done with them. I told you, we have a new set of demands to deal with."

"We?"

"We. You and us. We're going to need your services to deal with this new hacker. And you'll get paid, don't worry."

Pascual heaves a sigh. He is tempted to tell Melville where he can put it and take to his heels, but the phrase "get paid" has a certain resonance. "Who's this one and what does he want?"

"I'm not going to talk about it over the phone. Things are in flux. There are negotiations going on. Just sit tight and wait for me to contact you."

"For how long?"

"If it goes beyond a day or two, the whole thing's probably gone up in smoke."

"I can't say I'd be too sorry."

"Your million bucks included."

"Damn you," says Pascual, turning away from the window. "They better be there when this is all over."

Melville's call wakes Pascual in the middle of the night. "How soon can you get to Athens?"

Pascual sits on the edge of his cot, phone to his ear, rubbing his face with his free hand. "What, Athens, Greece?"

"No, Athens, Georgia, what the hell do you think? Of course Athens, Greece. Where the Acropolis is, for Christ's sake."

"I know it. I've been there."

"Excellent. I'm flying there tomorrow. Get yourself to Athens, ASAP. When you get there, book yourself into the St. George Hotel and call me."

"Just what is Pascual Rose going to be doing in Athens?"

"That's still a little up in the air. I told you things were in flux? Well, they've stabilized enough that we know the action's going to be in Athens. And we still need you. The terms are the same. Do the work, you'll get your million."

"Will I need another new wardrobe?"

An exasperated sigh makes its way across the Atlantic and into Pascual's ear. "I'm not sure how this one's going to play out. We're still trying to figure out who we're dealing with and what the logistics are going to be. But there will be a role for you. Business casual ought to do it."

Pascual starts to laugh. "Nothing about your business is casual, in my experience."

"Get your ass to Athens," growls Melville, and cuts off the call.

6

For Pascual, Athens was where it ended. In Athens in 1989 he finally realized that what he had dedicated his life to was not a cause but a homicidal extortion racket. In Athens on a hot summer day much like this one he delivered himself to the enemy, the security agencies of the United States and Israel, against whom he had been plotting murderous attacks for the best part of his youth. He betrayed nearly every organization and individual who had ever trusted him and became the greatest snitch, grass, stool pigeon and turncoat of all time. He has never regretted it.

Athens was a shambolic place in the late eighties, and that was before it was ravaged by twenty-first-century economic, political and biological crises. From the window of the slightly battered Nissan taxi bringing Pascual into the city more than thirty years after he last set foot here, Athens looks like a city that has given up. Pascual has experience of such things; New York in the seventies had the same look.

New York still had its pockets of quiet, fiercely guarded money, of course, and Pascual is hoping that the St. George Lycabettus Hotel might provide some relief from the pitted, graffiti-splattered cityscape he has ridden through to get here. The grizzled taxi driver, gray, ungroomed and splenetic, is nearly as devoid of English as Pascual is of Greek, but he is able to communicate to Pascual that their route will be roundabout due to disturbances in the city center. "Much problems. *Anarchikoi*." Pascual sees no anarchists but gets an eyeful of urban decay as the taxi pushes through sluggish and ill-tempered traffic. It finally grinds uphill into an amply leafy and shaded quarter with narrow streets and little traffic and drops him under the hotel marquee. The credit card works its usual magic and a mere four hours after deplaning, Pascual finds himself standing at a window in air-conditioned comfort regarding a splendid view of the distant Acropolis and a complete void where expectations for his stay in Athens should be.

He is under instructions to call Melville upon arrival, but he is inclined to interpret that loosely. He stands for a moment holding the phone Melville gave him and then tosses it on the bed. He washes his face and hands, runs a comb through his hair, and leaves the room.

He keeps an eye out for Melville as he passes through the lobby, though he has no reason to believe he will be at the same hotel. Unobserved as far as he can tell, he waves off a doorman offering to call him a taxi and starts walking downhill. He is fairly quickly sure that no one is following him. With no phone or map to guide him, he strays a few times, but gravity eventually delivers him to Syntagma Square. Here a lingering whiff of tear gas, the odd shoe or smear of blood on the pavement and a few scattered clusters of police in riot gear are all that is left of the anarchist ructions. Things have changed in thirty years; Pascual recognizes nothing and is unable to locate the café where he spotted the table full of American officers and decided to salvage his life by betraying everyone he knew.

In adjacent streets, shopkeepers are sweeping up broken glass and boarding up storefronts. In a street far enough from the square to have escaped the rampage, he gets cash from a machine and finds a store where he can buy a cheap prepaid phone and a Greek SIM card. He watches, faintly alarmed, as the clerk photocopies his passport, but he needs the phone and decides it is unlikely anyone will ever search the records. The young woman who sells him the phone has good English and manages to get him up and running with his new device.

On the sidewalk outside, he taps Sara's number into the phone. "Who's this?" she says by way of answering.

"That's a brutal way to greet the love of your life."

She sighs, perhaps in exasperation. "Where are you?"

"Athens."

"Athens. What are you doing there?"

"I have no idea. I can't tell you how long I'll be here, either. I just wanted you to know where to start looking if I go missing."

Pascual walks a few paces, phone to his ear, people brushing by him with harried looks on their faces, a few still masked in superstitious fear of pandemics. "Is that a real possibility?" says Sara.

"I don't know. Probably not. Most likely everything will go smoothly and I'll be finished in a couple of days. But you never know. Anyway, you can reach me on this phone. I can't keep it with me all the time, but I'll check it for messages. And with any luck, you'll see me in a week or two and we'll be rich."

"I don't care about that. With or without money, just come home."

"I sincerely hope to," says Pascual. "With or without."

Back at the hotel Pascual slips his new phone into his shaving kit and retrieves Melville's. On the phone Melville's voice is brusque. "We need to meet."

"Fine. Are you at the hotel?"

"Of course not. You think the agency can afford to put us all up in luxury? I'm in an apartment. Not too far from you. Take a taxi, I'll give you the address."

The address proves to be a short ride away. Pascual has a good sense of direction and an eye for landmarks, but he is quickly disoriented. The streets all look much the same; one block after another is lined with four- or five-story apartment houses ringed with balconies. In a characterless flat on the third floor of a nondescript building in an undistinguished street, Melville ushers Pascual to a chair and offers him a drink. "Did you come in on the Aegean flight?" he says, handing him a gin and tonic.

"Yeah. It was that or Volotea, and I figured the Greeks were more likely to know the way."

"All right. Now that you're finally here, we can start plotting strategy. The situation is a little unstable."

Pascual takes a leisurely pull on his drink. "Let's start with that, the situation. Maybe it's time to fill me in a little bit. I sort of lost track after you said something about the hackers being hacked."

Melville settles onto a chair. "That's exactly what happened. The Syrians got hacked, and suddenly they couldn't access the data any more than we could, and more importantly, they couldn't access the key. That's when they panicked and tried to bluff you. And apparently that's when that poor bastard Sabbagh decided he'd had enough and tried to blow the whistle. The Monaco cops have determined that he was tossed off his balcony, by the way. They're looking for two suspects, both Arabs according to the witness who saw them leaving the building."

"Can't blame them for being peeved. Who hacked them?"

Melville crosses his legs and puts on a thoughtful frown. "Have you ever heard of somebody who calls himself Zarlik?"

"Can't say I have. Who's he?"

"Zarlik is one of the more notorious hacktivists out there. You know the term?"

Pascual nods impatiently. "Hacker, activist, sure."

"At least we think he's one. Sometimes it's a collective, or a team that assumes a name. But assuming it's one guy, he's pulled off some pretty good stunts. A couple of years ago he cracked a bank in the Cayman Islands and took a hundred thousand dollars."

"So he's just a thief. What makes him a hacktivist?"

"He gave the money away. He converted it to cryptocurrency and then back to dollars and poured it into the account of a women's advocacy organization in Bangladesh. The bank's tried to get the money back, but they've come up empty."

Pascual shrugs. "So far, I think I'm rooting for Zarlik."

"Yeah, yeah, Robin Hood and all that. Terrific. He also hacked a cybersecurity firm in Germany that worked with law enforcement, making surveillance and lawful intercept tools. He put everything they had out there on the web. Nice anarchist type of move, but it was a massive security disaster that made things easier for criminals, terrorists and hackers everywhere."

"Anarchists can cause a lot of trouble."

"You're telling me. He also got into Honey Bear, which took some doing."

"What's Honey Bear?"

"It's a Russian hacking group with GRU connections. Zarlik exposed a lot of juicy stuff about ties between the Kremlin and the Russian mob."

"Well, that one at least you should approve of."

"I might, if he hadn't spent most of his time undermining western governments. Anyway, now Zarlik's jumped right into the middle of this business with the Syrians, and he's got the whip hand. Our tech guys say he locked the Syrians out of their own hack. And now he's the one making demands."

Pascual drums his fingers on the arm of his chair, frowning. "I'm struggling to see a role for me in this. It sounds like something for your tech guys to deal with. Just shoot them a few million in cryptocurrency or whatever."

"If only it were that simple. Zarlik doesn't want money. Not one red cent."

"What does he want? Information? Digitize it and have your tech guys send it."

Melville puts on an imposing frown. "What's the one thing you can't digitize? Not yet, anyway."

Pascual gives it a second or two but is short on patience this evening. "I give up. What?"

"People. Zarlik wants to swap our data for a person."

"A person," says Pascual, amused at the look on Melville's face. "Who are we talking about?"

Melville sighs and hauls himself out of his chair. He walks to the sideboard and reaches for a bottle. "Have you ever heard of a man named Ali Husseini?"

"I've probably met a few of them. That would be like John Brown or

Joe Jones in English. Which Ali Husseini would this be?"

Melville takes his time mixing his drink and then turns. "Ali Husseini is a journalist from the UAE. Some people have called him a dissident. He's made himself unpopular with the powers that be by writing about nepotism and corruption in the Emirates."

"Corruption in the Emirates? I'm shocked."

"Aren't we all. But as they are our gallant allies, we are tolerant."

"The name sounds Shiite. That would be another strike against him in the UAE."

Melville returns to his chair, drink in hand. "No doubt. Whatever he is, he disappeared about a year ago. In Yemen."

"That doesn't sound good."

"No. Yemen is not a very good place to be present and accounted for, much less missing. He was there reporting on the war for some Arabic news website. And he vanished. His wife, however, insists he's alive. She claims to have heard from a released prisoner that he's being held in one of the prisons the Emiratis are running there in Yemen."

"I thought the Emiratis had pulled out of Yemen."

"They pulled out the bulk of their troops, yeah. That doesn't mean they're not there anymore. They're doing it all through proxies now. Their spooks are running the various militias in the south. And they've still got the jails, even though they were supposedly shut down after the human rights people made all that noise a few years ago. And of course, they deny they have Husseini. And now this Zarlik says we have to produce him or we don't get our data back."

"Produce him as in confirm he's being held, or spring him?"

"We're supposed to deliver him to the custody of the UN High Commissioner for Refugees here in Athens."

"Why here? I believe that agency's headquartered in Geneva."

"That's correct. But they have a big presence in Greece now because of the refugee flow from the Mideast. And that's where Zarlik specified Husseini is to be delivered. To the UNHCR office here in Athens. We're guessing that's because Zarlik has some link to the people here."

Pascual finds that his sympathies still lie mostly with the hacker. "OK, now why you? Why would an anarchist hacker pressure the CIA to release a prisoner held by the United Arab Emirates?"

Melville shrugs. "Probably because, like a lot of left-wing goofballs, he assumes that we run everything he doesn't like. We don't, of course. But we have worked pretty closely with the Emiratis against al-Qaeda in Yemen, so we have good connections, a good working relationship. We might just be able to spring him."

Pascual considers. "What do you think? Is Husseini still alive?"

Melville downs half of his drink and scowls into the rest. "He's alive. Our man down there located him." Melville's eyes rise to lock with Pascual's. "Now all we have to do is persuade the Emiratis to let him go."

"And how long is that going to take?"

"Not long. We've got good clout with the Emirati intelligence apparatus because we helped set it up. But it has to be done on the sly, because the sheikhs back in Abu Dhabi are happy with Husseini where he is."

"How are you going to manage that?"

"Well, you remember we were just talking about corruption in the UAE. For once it's going to work in Husseini's favor. We're going to grease a few of the right palms and buy him out."

Pascual nods. "That's nice. I like that."

"It has a certain aesthetic appeal, doesn't it?" Melville grins and takes another slug of his drink.

Pascual looks out through a window into a pleasant Athens evening sky, the haze beginning to go a rosy color. The booze has begun to work on him and he knows there was a reason it was given to him. He steels himself and says, "OK, now tell me why I'm here."

Melville shrugs. "Because we need someone to go to Yemen and bring him back."

In the street a car honks. Distant voices rise, strained and querulous. Pascual stares for a long moment and then laughs. "No. I'm not going to Yemen."

Melville looks genuinely astonished for a moment. Then he frowns and says, "Not for a million dollars?"

The moment is longer this time, and as Pascual holds Melville's gaze, a sour, heavy bolus of dread settles in his stomach. At the same time, he feels his resistance fighting a desperate rearguard action against pecuniary considerations. "Why me?" he says finally. "Why anybody? Just put him on a plane."

"We don't know what kind of shape he's going to be in. Probably not good. He will need an escort. He may need medical care, he may need papers, he may need all kinds of things. Somebody will have to handle all that."

"So you've got a guy down there. Why the hell do you need me?"

"I thought that was clear. We need a representative who is not officially connected to the agency. You have deniability. That's a precious asset, and that's why we're willing to pay you for it."

"Deniability. Meaning if anything goes wrong, I'm on my own."

Melville manages a perfectly straight face as he says, "We would do what we can to assist you if you got into any difficulties. Discreetly."

"Thanks, that's reassuring."

"But we don't anticipate any difficulties. All you have to do is go and get the man. You'll bring him back and hand him over to the UN."

"Am I supposed to deliver the bribe as well?"

"We'll give you the money. And the directions. Our guy down there will give you all the help you need."

"What's my cover story? What the hell do I tell the reporters when I deliver him to the UN?"

"You're thinking. I like that. You can tell them you were approached by unnamed parties in Dubai, where, you may recall, Pascual Rose resides. Everyone who thinks about it will assume you bought his way out as a favor to somebody in Dubai. The government won't be happy, but the people who count will figure you're doing it for us, and the others won't be able to find you. As usual there will be a great deal of confusion and speculation about the mysterious Pascual Rose."

For a moment Pascual gives serious thought to bolting, simply throwing the rest of his drink in Melville's face and sprinting out the door. Monaco was a lark; Athens has its rough edges but money can still buy you insulation. Yemen is another matter.

Pascual looks at his choices and doesn't like any of them. "When do I leave?" he says.

Melville rises and goes to a desk, where he pulls a manila envelope out of a drawer. "You're booked on Aegean to Cairo the day after tomorrow," he says, handing the envelope to Pascual. "From there Yemenia will get you to Aden. After that, you take your chances on something called Felix Airways to get to Mukalla. It's still not that easy to get to Yemen, or to get around once you're there. But the airlines seem to be functioning this week. You've got a return ticket with the date open, and a one-way reservation for Husseini. Be prepared to spread some bribe money around to make sure you get seats on those flights. We'll give you some cash. That's what we had to do to get you a visa, by the way. That's in there, too. Fortunately we've got a guy at their embassy in Riyadh who has expensive tastes and will do little favors. We got you the same kind of visa the NGO people travel on. Should be bulletproof."

Pascual opens the envelope and pulls out the printed e-tickets. He scans them without enthusiasm. "The prison's in Mukalla?"

"Not too far away, according to our guy. It used to be right at the airport. The Emiratis took Mukalla back from al-Qaeda in 2016 and turned the airport into a military base with a prison for all the terrorists they scooped up, real or imagined. They handed it back to the Yemenis in 2019 and opened it for air traffic again, but they didn't release all the detainees. They let a few go, and the rest they just moved somewhere else."

"Who do I contact when I get there?"

"Our guy will meet you at the airport. He'll take care of you."

"Who's your guy? Who am I looking for?"

"He'll look for you. He knows you're coming."

Pascual gives him a lingering look but sees he is not going to get anything further on that score. "What about the money?" he says.

"That's been arranged down there. Our guy will have it for you. You wouldn't be able to get a sack full of cash through customs, believe me."

"All right. Now. One more question. How do I make sure I get the right guy? Suppose Husseini's dead and they try to sell us a ringer? How do I know the guy they give me is Ali Husseini?"

Melville blinks a couple of times before answering, and Pascual gets the impression the question has caught him off guard. "He'll have papers. They'll have been confiscated when he was arrested. Just make sure you get them back along with him. Compare him with the photo. And look online, familiarize yourself. There was some coverage of his case, with photos."

"If he's been enjoying Emirati hospitality for a year, he's not going to look much like his old photos."

"That's a point. So you make sure he comes with papers."

"It would be better to have biometric data. Fingerprints at least. That's a long way to go to have a fake palmed off on me."

"I appreciate your caution, but I think you're inventing problems. Look, our guy down there has been doing this for a while. He's on good terms with the Emiratis and he's been around the block a few times. He says he identified Husseini and sealed the deal in person with the head of the prison. I think you can trust him."

Pascual sits nodding slowly, not liking any aspect of it. "Who's the contact at the UN here?"

Melville nods at the envelope in Pascual's hand. "You've got her information there. You might want to give her a heads-up before you leave." Pascual fishes in the envelope and comes up with a paper bearing an Athens street address and phone number for UNHCR and the name *Sabine Degitz*. Melville says, "That's the individual Zarlik wants Husseini delivered to. She's German, and she's a piece of work. One of these crusading Eurocrats. Not a great friend of the United States."

"Who is, these days?"

Melville gives him a sharp look. "Presumably Degitz has been alerted that Husseini's coming, but there's no reason to think she knows about this hacking deal, so stick to your story. You're on a mission of mercy, using your clout to do a good deed."

"I'll dust off my halo."

"We're working on the connection between her and Zarlik. Sometimes these hacktivist types slip up in the real world. They cover their tracks in cyberspace but they shoot their mouths off at the hookah bar and get nailed."

Pascual slides the sheets back into the envelope. "I'm not sure your agenda is exactly the same as mine."

"The only part of the agenda you need to worry about is getting Husseini out of Yemen and back to Athens. Do that and you get paid."

Pascual frowns. "What do I tell Husseini when he asks me who's springing him from jail?"

"Tell him influential parties in Europe have exerted their influence. You can be vague. He won't look a gift horse in the mouth."

"And if I wind up hanging by my thumbs in an Emirati jail?"

Melville shrugs. "We'll see what our guy down there can do for you."

"I look forward to meeting him," says Pascual.

As Pascual expected, Sabine Degitz has gatekeepers to shield her from random strangers who obtain her agency's number, and also as expected, they speak English, after a fashion. The name Ali Husseini buys him a couple of minutes on hold, a brief conversation with Degitz, and an appointment in the glass-fronted commercial building discreetly housing the UNHCR on a boulevard roaring with traffic, not too far from his hotel. There is security in the lobby, this not being the most popular UN agency in a country unhappy with its role as a refugee catch basin, but another phone call gets Pascual up to the third floor and eventually to a chair across the desk from a woman who looks as if she could use a long vacation.

"I am not very clear on your role in this," says Sabine Degitz in smooth Euro-English. She is fiftyish, tall, blond and Teutonic, with cropped hair, sunken cheeks and the haggard look of the perpetually overworked. "How did you become involved?"

Pascual crosses his legs and strives to project gravitas. "I have business interests in Dubai and have spent a good deal of time there. I was approached by friends of a business associate and asked to intervene. I have a small amount of influence in certain quarters in Abu Dhabi, and I was able to secure Mr. Husseini's release. Now all I have to do is fly to Yemen and bring him back."

Degitz's eyebrows rise. "You're very brave. I hope you have good connections there."

"So do I." Pascual flashes a smile that is not returned. "I have a local contact who assures me there will be no difficulties."

"I think I can assure you there will be difficulties. I've been to Yemen. It is hell on earth."

"I'm aware of the dangers. May I ask in turn why I was instructed to deliver Mr. Husseini to you, rather than to your agency's headquarters in Geneva?"

Degitz receives this with a stony look that lasts a few seconds while she swivels idly back and forth on her chair. At length she says, "You must allow me to be discreet. Certain parties with whom I've worked in the past requested my intervention. I am to verify Mr. Husseini's identity and see that he receives any medical care he may require. If you can give me flight information I will arrange to receive you at the airport."

Pascual can see that neither of them quite believes the other, making a nice equilibrium. He nods. "I see. I'll notify you as soon as I've confirmed the reservations."

"Very well. I wish you luck." Her look hardens. "You'll need it."

"I'm sure. How are you planning to verify Husseini's identity?"

"His wife is coming to Athens. I am to notify her as soon as I know when he will arrive." Degitz hesitates for a moment, lips parted. "I would think that would be a question for you. How are you going to identify him?"

"He's supposed to have papers. But I'd like to have a backup. Can you get in touch with his wife?"

"Of course."

"Then do this. Have her make a short list of questions that only her husband could answer. Personal things, family things, that only he would know. What's the name of their pet cat, what color is the rug in the bedroom, that kind of thing. If you can text that to me in the next twenty-four hours or so, that would give me a valuable tool."

Sabine Degitz sits swiveling back and forth, unblinking. Finally she smiles, just perceptibly. "You have done this kind of thing before," she says.

"Not really," says Pascual, rising. "But I've been cheated by rug merchants in the bazaar. It has made me suspicious by nature."

"I'm going to Yemen tomorrow," says Pascual into his new Greek phone.

Far away, Sara says, "*Dios mío*. Pascual, you're mad."

"Probably. But that's where the job is."

"It's not worth it. It's not worth a million dollars. It's not worth ten million. Don't go, I beg you."

"I'm only going for a day or two. I'll have a simple job to do, in the more or less stable part of the country, with local help. All I have to do is locate a man and bring him back to Athens. There's no danger."

"Pascual. I read the news. I know what's going on in Yemen. You can't tell me there's no danger."

"It's a calculated risk. A big reward for a little risk. If you don't hear from me in three days, you can panic then."

"And who do I call? Who's going to help you?"

"I'm going to text you some information. You'll call Campos at *El Mundo* and pass it on to him. But odds are it won't come to that."

"*Ay, Pascual.* When will you be done with this kind of thing?"

"One week," says Pascual. "With any luck, one week."

Pascual has history with Yemen. In the early 1980s the Popular Front for the Liberation of Palestine maintained a training camp in South Yemen, the communist part of the divided country, a barren, sun-blasted dead end where an impetuous, anomic Spanish youth, poorly educated in France and the United States, estranged from family and infected with political zealotry, was turned into a trained killer. Yemen was where Pascual was turned out, seasoned, broken in, corrupted. It has taken him the best part of forty years to recover. For Pascual, Yemen always evokes a shudder, a shadow on the heart.

The shadows are short and sharply defined as Pascual shuffles across the tarmac toward the terminal, stunned by the heat and blinded by the glare. The jet's approach took it out over a shimmering sea, but here on the ground all Pascual can see are the bare jagged hills he remembers so vividly, a moonscape that always suggested to him that people were never meant to live in this place.

The past forty-eight hours have tested him. He had not traveled in the Middle East for more than thirty years, and he had forgotten the heat, the noise, the crowding, the disorder. The airport at Cairo was merely chaotic, but Aden was sinister, bullet-pocked and devoid of amenities, the concourses patrolled by men in mismatched half-military garb brandishing automatic weapons, the officials harried, hostile and suspicious. Getting from Aden to Mukalla required him to negotiate multiple reefs and hazards: delays and cancellations, the dispensing of the first bribe monies from the stash of dollars Melville provided him with, a near fistfight at the boarding gate. The only sleep Pascual has had since he left Athens was an hour's uneasy doze in a corner of an abandoned duty-free kiosk, ended by a kick from a militiaman demanding to see his papers.

Al Rayan Airport at Mukalla, capital of Hadhramaut governorate in the now uneasily united Yemen, at least appears more or less intact. The whitewashed terminal building has glass in the windows and no visible scars. The men with assault rifles are in camouflage, a minor reassurance, as the uniform suggests they may be subject to some degree of military discipline. Their shoulder patches bear Saudi insignia.

Inside the terminal, there are functioning customs procedures, uniformed officials seated behind high desks, a minimal level of courtesy. Even the air conditioning works. Pascual has begun to think the worst is behind him, but he still catches his breath as the officer casually scanning his visa freezes, shoots him a severe look and slowly lays the paper down in front of him. "What the purpose of entry?"

Pascual represses an urge to jab a finger at the line where somebody, perhaps the complaisant embassy official in Riyadh, has printed *HUMANITARIAN MISSION* in block capitals. "As it is written," he says. "I am on a humanitarian mission."

The officer picks up the visa and peers at it. "*Hyuma . . . nitriyan.* What the meaning?"

Pascual replies with a sinking feeling. "I am here to accompany a released prisoner to Europe." He does his best to meet the man's glare without provocation.

The visa goes onto the desk again for more study. The officer runs his finger down the edge of the paper until he reaches the line labeled in English *Add. of responser*, which Pascual took to mean "sponsor." This line was filled in by the same hand with *STAR SERVICES, INC.*, and Melville assured Pascual it would get him into the country. "Ah," says the officer.

The syllable hangs in the air as the man pushes away from the desk and stands, taking the visa and Pascual's passport with him. He disappears through a doorway. Pascual sags against the desk. Is he going to have to find a secluded place where he can dip into the money belt again? He straightens up and turns to apologize to the people in line behind him. There are three of them, all Yemeni and all now taking great care not to make eye contact with him.

Pascual waits. Through the open doorway he can hear voices murmuring in Arabic. The officer reappears in the doorway, visa in hand, and beckons to Pascual. "Come." Pascual stoops to grab his bag and hurries to join him. He follows him into an office where three other uniformed men lounge, one behind a desk and the others sprawled on chairs. Pascual nods at them but they merely stare as the first man lays his visa on the desk. The man behind the desk bestirs himself and pulls a hand stamp out of a drawer. He inks it on a pad on the desktop and firmly and authoritatively stamps the bottom section of Pascual's visa. The first man tears off the section, slips it into Pascual's passport and hands it to Pascual, then beckons again. Pascual follows him through another doorway and down a short hall to another office. The officer halts at the open door and motions for Pascual to enter. "Your friend," he says.

This mystifies Pascual, but he steps to the doorway.

A man sitting on a couch manipulating an Xbox controller looks away from a TV screen long enough to say, "Well, shit. I thought you'd never get here."

Pascual just stares. The man thumbs the controller a few more times and then tosses it aside and grins at him, teeth gleaming between ginger mustache and beard. "Dammit, you distracted me. Wasted again." He jumps up off the couch and sticks out a hand. "I'm Cody." The beard, the baseball cap, the camouflage pants with bulging thigh pockets and the weight-room physique stretching the T-shirt all scream former U.S. military on a private payroll, and as Pascual shakes hands he is no longer mystified.

"You're their guy down here." Pascual tries to judge whether Cody would be a first or last name and decides it does not matter, as it is likely false anyway.

"That's right. I'm the guy. You're the babysitter."

"I suppose so. I'm here to retrieve Ali Husseini."

"Well, we'll see if we can't get that done." With a hand on Pascual's arm he herds him back out into the hall. "Thanks, Abdul. You guys need anything, you holler, OK?" This last to the official, who is already retreating back down the hall. Cody leads Pascual in the opposite direction at a brisk walk. In a low voice he says, "They give you any trouble up there?"

"Not to speak of. Star Services seemed to be the magic words."

"Oh, yeah. They know if we bring somebody in, somebody upstairs has signed off on it. Now, what do you need? Food? Booze? A shower? If you flew in through Aden, you probably could use all of the above and a couple of tranquilizers to boot. I'm actually kinda surprised you made it. There aren't too many flights, and they get canceled a lot."

Pascual trots a couple of steps to keep up. "I made it on the third try. I wouldn't mind a bit of a rest and a chance to wash up, to tell you the truth, but I don't want to hold things up. What's involved in getting Husseini out, and how long will it take?"

Cody bursts through a door at the end of the hall and abruptly they are outside again. It is like stepping into an oven. Pascual squints and falters a bit. Cody points and says, "Truck's over here. I can't say for sure. What I would suggest is that after you rest up we go talk to the man who counts and show him the money."

Cody leads Pascual to a Toyota pickup parked in the scant shade of a cluster of palms. Rolling away from the terminal, Cody points to the left at a scattering of low buildings. "That's where they had the prison, when the Emiratis ran things here. The human rights people made 'em shut it down. They supposedly let everybody go, but you know how that goes. They hung on to the ones they really wanted and just shifted 'em someplace else. That's where you have to go."

"How far away?"

"Just a few miles up the road. I'll get you there. But let's get you squared away first."

The airport access road joins a highway; across the highway is a scattering of houses that might just qualify as a village. Cody tears out onto the highway, tires squealing, goes two hundred meters down and turns off into the village. "We've got a little crash pad here we use when we can't get back to Mukalla. This'll do you for a night or two."

"It may have to be longer. I've got two reservations on the plane back to Aden, but that's not till next week. Then two from Aden to Cairo, date open."

"Well, I think we can arrange something better. Reservations can be kind of theoretical around here. And getting out of Aden might be a problem. You can always try to catch a military flight, or an NGO charter or something. But you can't count on that. For that matter, you can't really count on the airlines, either."

Pascual gropes for his native sunny optimism and comes up empty. The streets of the village are unpaved and deserted; the dust cloud the Toyota raises as it passes settles on a motley collection of concrete houses, slapdash cinderblock construction with mortar seeping out of the joints, whitewashed walls with peeling plaster. A few cars are parked haphazardly in the street, baking in the sun. Cody pulls up in front of an unadorned concrete construction next to a patch of open ground strewn with rubble and garbage. "Here you go. It ain't the Ritz, but the price is right."

Pascual doesn't need the Ritz, but water to wash would be nice. Staring into a tiny bathroom with a squatter toilet in a corner and a tap protruding from the wall, he inquires. Cody explains that there is a tank on the roof but he is not sure how full it is. "Fill up that pail and grab a bar of soap," he says. "Whatever you do, don't drink any. There's bottled water in the fridge, which will be cold unless the power's conked out again. I don't know if there's much to eat here, but I can probably rustle you up a kebab from the guy with the grill down the street here. There was some beer, but I guess the last crew drank it all up."

Cody goes in search of food and Pascual sits on rumpled sheets on a cot in a tiny bedroom with pitted concrete walls, looking out through an unglazed window at the distant crags. For nearly forty years he has consoled himself at low moments with the thought that at least he will never set foot in Yemen again. He pulls out his Greek cell phone and is mildly astonished to see that it has service. He texts Sara: *In Yemen, safe. All well.* He desperately wants to talk to her but knows it would be unwise. He puts the phone away and puts his face in his hands.

Think about the money, he tells himself.

"We've talked to the Emiratis about it," says Cody, steering one-handed with his wrist on top of the wheel, the Toyota holding a steady line as it eats up the kilometers on a good asphalt road heading away from the sea toward the crags. "I don't know how many actual al-Qaeda guys they've got locked up here anymore. At this point they could probably let 'em all go and nobody would be the worse for it. We got all the guys we wanted." He gives Pascual a sidelong glance. "We didn't sit in on any of the rough stuff. Not allowed to. But we told the Emiratis who and what we wanted, for sure. And sometimes they delivered. We got some bad dudes, and we got some good intelligence."

Pascual wonders about the quality of intelligence extracted under torture but has no interest in debating the point. Somewhat restored by a splash of cold water, a skewer of something that might have been goat and a half hour on his back, he is anxious to do what he came to do. A thick envelope containing ten thousand dollars in used hundreds weighs down the pocket of his sweat-soaked cotton shirt. That apparently is the market price for a life redeemed from the Yemeni scrap heap. "So. How is this going to work?"

"Smooth as silk, I hope. We're meeting the guy that calls the shots at a gas station up ahead here. Name of Rashid. He'll take you to the prison and see that you get your man."

"You're not coming along?"

Cody grins. "I was never here. If anybody asks. This is one hundred percent an Emirati deal. Remember that. You're bribing Rashid, he's getting Husseini out of jail. I had nothing to do with it. Got it?"

"Got it. I give Rashid the money, do I?"

"Yup. There's some etiquette. I'll introduce you, you make nice, you show him the envelope and say here's something for the widows and orphans fund or whatever comes to mind, please accept it as a token of respect. You don't just shove it at him and ask if he wants to count it."

"All right. Does he speak English or are we doing this in Arabic?"

Cody's head snaps toward Pascual. "You can do Arabic?"

"If necessary."

"Well, I can't, so it's English or nothing. Rashid speaks it OK. Once you've got Husseini, Rashid will bring the two of you back to the gas station and I'll run you back to the pad and start working on your flight out. If it's gonna be more than a couple of days I'll run you out some supplies from Mukalla."

"What if Husseini needs medical attention?"

"He probably will. And he'll probably have to wait till you get back to Athens to get it."

Pascual looks at it from every angle and finds nothing at all to like about any of it. His forebodings occupy him until a geometric jumble on the horizon resolves itself into a town. Cody slows as the road becomes a broad boulevard with a strip down the middle, planted with stunted dusty palms. It has the look of a thoroughfare built for a larger town that never appeared; there is no traffic and only scattered construction on either side, with broad rock-strewn empty lots between houses. They pass two women draped in black *abayas* and a clutch of children throwing rocks at a tethered goat. A few hundred meters ahead the gas station appears, a concrete canopy sheltering four pumps from the sun, a few vehicles parked haphazardly at the edge of the lot. One of the pump lanes is occupied by a BMW SUV and the other by a couple of old men in turbans squatting in the shade. Cody pulls up behind the BMW. "Here's the man," he says. "Right on time. He's been known to make me wait, but I guess when there's dough involved he gets motivated." Cody switches off the ignition and opens the door. "Let's go talk to the man who's going to make or break your Yemeni vacation."

9

They get out into the heat. Cody saunters toward the driver's side of the SUV as Pascual lingers by the Toyota and nods at the old men, who make no response. Cody holds a brief, inaudible conversation with the driver and then beckons for Pascual to come around the front of the SUV. "This here's Rashid. He's the guy that can work miracles around here." Cody gestures at the man behind the wheel.

He is lean, hawk-nosed, angular, with the standard-issue mustache and eyes made arresting by dark circles under them. Pascual puts him somewhere in his forties. He wears a khaki shirt with shoulder straps but no insignia of any kind. He nods at Pascual and his eyes go to the envelope. Cody cocks a thumb at Pascual and says, "This is our visitor from Europe."

"Honored to meet you," says Pascual.

Rashid nods just perceptibly. "How you like Yemen?"

Pascual guesses he is not talking to a Yemeni patriot but opts for something non-committal. "I haven't seen much of it. It's hot, I'll say that."

Rashid smiles. "Yes, very hot. Very bad place, Yemen. You from where?"

"From Spain."

"Very beautiful, Spain. Very beautiful women."

Pascual merely nods, inwardly groaning at the effort that will be required to make extended small talk at this level of eloquence. "There are beautiful women in every country," he essays.

"Not in Yemen," says Rashid. "Not now." The smile vanishes abruptly. "Come, we will go to the prison."

Cody slaps Pascual on the arm. "See you back here in a while." He nods at Rashid and heads for the Toyota.

Pascual gets into the SUV and Rashid starts it. "Why you want Ali Husseini?" he says.

Pascual has been given no instructions on how to answer this, and it takes him a moment to come up with an answer. "There are people in Europe who believe he has committed no crime."

Rashid issues a single grunt of laughter, putting the vehicle in gear. "How they know?"

"I couldn't tell you. All I know is that they want him released. And they are very grateful for your cooperation in the matter."

Rashid steers out onto the street and heads toward the hills. "I cooperate with America and Europe always. Together we fight against tourists." Pascual gives him a startled glance before realizing that with his uncertain vowels and heavy trilled r's Rashid has mangled the word "terrorists." Eyes to the front, Rashid says, "What Europe will give me for my cooperation?"

Hoping he is reading the signals right, Pascual pulls the envelope from his pocket. "The people in Europe would like to make a small contribution to the good work you do here."

"Put there." Rashid points at the glove compartment and Pascual opens it and stashes the envelope. Rashid says, "If I think Husseini is al-Qaeda, I don't release him. But Husseini is just stupid man. You take him to Europe."

Pascual wants to ask him why Husseini needed to be detained if stupidity is his only crime, but senses it would be unwise. They are rapidly leaving the town. Patches of gnarled trees fringe the outskirts, half concealing isolated houses, but before long there is nothing in sight but rocks. In the distance are bare ridges, gullies scoured into them by centuries of infrequent rains. Pascual remembers gazing in despair at similar escarpments during his Yemeni ordeal years ago. Perhaps these very ones; Pascual never had a very clear idea of where he actually was, except that it was somewhere out in the Hadhramaut wasteland. The road bends east, and as the ride becomes long Pascual begins to fight off yawns.

He comes to with a start, appalled at having dozed off, as the SUV slows. Pascual jerks upright. "Good sleep?" says Rashid.

"Very tired. Sorry." Pascual is wildly trying to regain some sense of direction. From the angle of the sun he decides they are going roughly north. This does nothing to reassure him. No human activity could possibly flourish in this desolation.

Except, perhaps, banditry. The reason for Rashid's braking finally catches Pascual's attention. Someone has placed three oil drums in a row across the road a hundred meters ahead. The someone is apparently this crew of armed men emerging from a pair of Humvees parked off the road near a jumble of rocks. The full panoply of Yemeni warrior accessories is on display: turbans, berets, camo and T-shirts, here and there a long *jellaba*, the usual mix of military and unmilitary with the common theme the carelessly brandished automatic weapons. Pascual's heart leaps and he shoots a quick glance at Rashid to see how concerned he is. Rashid is frowning, concentrating on his driving as he brings the SUV to a gentle halt.

In the middle oil drum a flag is planted, with horizontal red, white and black stripes and a triangular blue field with a red star. Pascual remembers it well; it flew everywhere in communist Yemen. "Who are these guys?" he says, just above a whisper.

"Militia," says Rashid. He lowers the driver's side window and puts out his hand to give a nonchalant wave. The fighters have spread across the road, one in the middle blocking the way, two or three on each side approaching the vehicle. They all have the lean, feral look Pascual has always associated with Yemen, the product of deprivation and constant strife. Several of them have the telltale bulge in the cheek of the qat aficionado, and this does not reassure Pascual. Powerful stimulants have unpredictable effects on a man with an assault rifle.

"*As-salaam aleikum.*" Rashid greets the man stepping up to his window, this one in a uniform of sorts with a camouflage blouse and a red beret. A conversation ensues, which Pascual has trouble following.

He starts at a rap on the window on his side and turns to see a bearded specimen in a carelessly wound turban. The man grins at him, showing a couple of gold teeth, and motions for him to lower the window. Pascual complies. The man says something he fails to understand, in thick Yemeni dialect. "I'm sorry," Pascual says. "I don't speak Arabic."

The man rubs fingers in the universal gesture for money. Rashid breaks off his conversation to say, "Give him nothing. He is a dog." The man in the beret snarls something and the other snarls back but moves away from the window.

Rashid resumes his conversation. It goes on for a minute longer as Pascual tries to look casual, scanning the sullen-looking crowd for signs of imminent hostility. Nobody has racked a bolt, but the rifles are unslung. Rashid laughs, harshly, and shakes hands with the man in the beret. "We go now," he says, pressing a button to raise the window. The man in the beret barks orders and two fighters drag the oil drums out of the way, taking their time. As Rashid accelerates through the checkpoint, Pascual's friend flashes his gold teeth again, giving him a farewell grin.

When the checkpoint is a couple of hundred meters behind them, Pascual says, "What militia is that?"

"Yemeni militia. South Yemen people. They don't like Yemen government. If you not with me, they kidnap you. With me you are OK. They know if they hurt any Emiratis, or my friends, we come and kill them all."

Pascual's heart is still beating rapidly. "Well," he says. "Then I'm very pleased to be your friend."

A few more kilometers go by, the road winding and beginning to rise. Rashid slows and turns onto a gravel track and the ride becomes bumpy. The track ascends past vast reefs of pitted, sun-bleached rock. It goes around a bend and suddenly here are signs of human activity: a cluster of buildings on a mountainside, a few palm trees inside a walled enclosure, three or four parked cars. "What is this place?" says Pascual.

"Village." Rashid steers past a whitewashed house with a door painted blue. A man in a turban squatting by the side of the road raises a hand in salute and Rashid returns the gesture. Pascual cannot believe his eyes. Why would anyone live here? He sees no signs of agriculture, no fields or orchards or herds of sheep. There is a small eruption of trees in a nearby gully, so there must be water, perhaps a spring, but beyond that is only the endless rock. Rashid turns, ascends a steep grade, pulls onto a flat space surrounded on three sides by buildings, and switches off the ignition.

"We arrive." Rashid opens his door and steps out. Pascual blinks a few times and does the same. On the slope above the open side of the square is an array of solar panels, a startling anomaly but a sign somebody has reason to be here. A man has come out of one of the buildings and is advancing toward Rashid with his hand out. He wears a military uniform but manages to look distinctly unmilitary in it, balding, portly and unkempt. Pascual cannot make out the insignia. The soldier and Rashid shake hands and go through the greeting ritual as Pascual looks on, still half-dazed from sleep. Eventually Rashid turns and beckons to Pascual. "Come."

Rashid presents him to the soldier. Pascual's Arabic was learned in Damascus, but he has encountered the Gulf dialect enough to make out the gist: Here is the man who has come to take Husseini away. The soldier gives Pascual a suspicious look and grunts once. He does not offer to shake hands. He says something to Rashid that Pascual fails to catch and turns toward the building. Rashid follows, gesturing to Pascual to come along.

The building has a more substantial look than its neighbors, with blue shutters and a molded cornice, the look of a minor town hall or police station. Inside is an office of sorts, with a desk, a few ancient wooden chairs and a fan on the desk feebly stirring the warm air. Pascual slumps on a chair and watches as Rashid and the soldier go through a doorway into another room and hold a murmured conversation he cannot follow. He looks around this outpost of civilization and sees a laptop computer, a porous clay water jar of the classic type that cools by evaporation, and a plastic jerrican in a corner. He wonders how long this building has been here, if Turkish conscripts once languished here in a forgotten corner of the empire, pining for sweethearts back in Anatolia.

Rashid and the soldier come back into the room, Rashid holding a manila envelope. He beckons to Pascual and upends the envelope, spilling the contents onto the desk. "Ali Husseini. Documents. You take it."

Pascual steps to the desk and from the small scattering of papers selects the dark-blue UAE passport, embossed with the gold falcon logo. He opens it and looks at a smiling Ali Husseini, bearded and plump-cheeked, the same photo he has seen on the few websites that discuss his case. He sets it down and picks up a photo ID card certifying Husseini as a member of the UAE Journalists Association. Next is a photograph, a curled and faded snapshot. It shows Ali Husseini with his arm around a young woman in a hijab, both of them smiling at the camera, the gaudy skyline of Dubai in the background. Suddenly Pascual has to take a deep breath. Here is a man with a wife, job, colleagues, a reputation, innumerable contacts and connections, and they have buried him alive here in the desert. Pascual tosses the photo onto the desk. "Very good. Can I see him?"

"They bring him now." Rashid nods at the soldier, who saunters to the door and goes out. Pascual stands in the doorway and watches as he crosses the square, heading for a broad metal gate in the wall on the opposite side. He calls out as he goes, and a second soldier comes out of a shed at the corner of the square, nods and heads for the gate, pulling a ring of keys from his pocket. He unlocks the gate and pulls it open, then follows the first soldier through it. Before he pulls the gate shut behind him Pascual gets a glimpse of a line of stalls inside and he realizes he is looking at a stable.

"For horses," he says, unbelieving.

Rashid grunts with laughter. "Horses and tourists."

They stand in silence for a couple of minutes, and then the gate swings open and the soldiers reappear. With them is a man who ought to be in a hospital bed, judging by his gait and aspect. He is emaciated and bent at the waist, wild-haired and unshaven, limping on bare feet, dressed in trousers that were once white and a short-sleeved shirt that once had buttons but now hangs open to reveal a sunken chest crisscrossed by scars. He looks across the square at Pascual with wide feverish eyes. "Now they wash him," says Rashid. "Then we take him."

"Wait." Pascual holds up a hand. "I want to talk to him. Bring him into the office."

Rashid makes a face, wrinkling his nose. "Bad smell."

Pascual strives to keep his expression neutral. The two soldiers have halted, flanking Husseini, waiting for instructions. "All right," says Pascual. He goes to the desk and picks up the passport, then goes outside and walks across the square. Husseini watches him come, motionless. The soldiers move a couple of paces away. Pascual becomes aware of the smell as he approaches. He halts in front of Husseini and says in English, "My name is Pascual. I'm going to take you away from here."

The face he is looking into is not the one in the passport photo; starvation and prolonged stress have stripped it of its flesh. The black eyes glisten with tears. "My name Ali Husseini." The voice is a breathless croak.

Pascual takes Husseini by the arm and gently steers him along the wall to a patch of shade cast by the palms in the walled compound. Husseini grimaces as he limps, bending forward, gasping a little. Once in the shade, Pascual steadies him and looks him in the eye. In Arabic he says softly, "What is your name?"

The eyes widen. "Ali Husseini."

Pascual opens the passport and holds the photo up next to the ravaged face. Starve away the fat, allow a wash and a shave once a month, is this what you get? Pascual looks at eyes, nose, bone structure. He lowers the passport. "Where were you born?" he says.

"Dubai."

"What is your wife's name?"

"Khadija."

Pascual nods. The answers came without hesitation, and they are correct. "What color is the dress you brought Khadija back from Beirut two years ago?"

The eyes widen again. For a moment they show panic; then they seem to lose focus and close briefly. "Forgive me. . . . I have forgotten many things. Blue, I think. Yes, a blue dress I brought her."

Pascual nods again. He hesitates for a moment before saying, "What does Khadija call you when you come to her at night?"

Pascual stands and watches the tears well in the desolate eyes. They spill onto the bony cheeks and run down into the thick whiskers, and the man says, "She calls me *habib galbi*, love of my heart."

Pascual nods a few more times and then takes him by the arm and urges him gently back toward where Rashid and the soldiers are standing. It seems to take an hour to cover the scant few meters. Rashid wears a look of detached amusement. "You have problem?" His accent makes it "broblem" and Pascual wants to scream at him.

"Nothing you can't solve." Pascual gives the man at his side a gentle shove toward Rashid. "All you have to do is tell them to go back and bring me the real Ali Husseini."

10

"They are stupid men," says Rashid. "Now they get Ali Husseini."

Pascual stands rigid with anger. The two soldiers have gone back into the stables, leaving the fake Ali Husseini on the ground after felling him with an abrupt punch to the face and applying a few savage kicks to the body. He is bleeding into the dust, his blood mixing with his tears. Pascual is fairly certain that the production was a fraud rather than a mistake, and he is appalled at the consequences of his unmasking it. He is trying to anticipate Rashid's next move, acutely aware that Rashid holds all the cards. Even if Pascual could reach Cody or Melville by cell phone, which is not at all certain, he has no idea how much influence they could exert.

The gate opens and the soldiers reappear, now with a different man in tow. Instantly Pascual feels a little thrill of hope. This face is also wasted and gaunt, but it is broader in structure, closer to the face in Ali Husseini's passport photo. This man is also limping, but he is not bent like the first man; he walks erect and only drags his left leg a little. He is staring at Pascual with what looks like dazed astonishment.

Pascual turns to Rashid. "I'm going to take him into the office. If you don't like the smell, you don't have to come with us."

Rashid shrugs. "As you want."

In the office Pascual seats the new prisoner on a chair and pulls another one over to sit in front of him. "What is your name?"

In a hollow, ragged voice the man says, "Ali Ibn Ahmad Husseini al-Bahrani."

This is exactly as written in the passport. Pascual holds up the photo for comparison. Again it is difficult to be certain, but the eyes could be a match and the width of the forehead is similar. Pascual takes a deep breath. "What is your wife's name?"

"Khadija."

"And what does she call you when you come to her at night?"

The eyes widen. "You have spoken with her?"

"What does she call you?"

Pascual can barely hear the whispered answer. "She calls me *ya gamar*. My moon, she calls me."

Pascual snaps the passport shut and hands it to Ali Husseini. "*Yallah*. Let's get away from this place."

"Who are you?" The look of disbelief on Husseini's face deepens.

Pascual stands. "With luck, I'm the man who's going to get you out of Yemen. But I have a feeling we'll need a lot of it." He is looking out into the square, where the soldiers are standing over the first prisoner, who has made it to his knees and is pleading with clasped hands.

"Do you know who that man is?" Pascual asks.

Husseini shakes his head. "Another prisoner. I don't know his name. He is Yemeni, I think. Are you taking him, too?"

Pascual shakes his head. "They tried to pass him off as you." The prisoner looks toward the office, frantically searching for Pascual as the soldiers begin to drag him back toward the stables. Watching hope die out in those sunken eyes, Pascual is filled with loathing, for this world, for spies and soldiers, for himself.

Rashid turns, and his eyes meet Pascual's. They stare at each other for a moment, Pascual trying hard to keep his expression utterly blank. Rashid mutters an order and the soldiers let the prisoner fall back to the ground. Rashid beckons to Pascual, who goes slowly out into the heat. Rashid leads him a few steps away, out of earshot of the soldiers, then wheels and says, "How much you pay to take this one, too?"

Pascual gapes in astonishment. "You'll let me take both of them?"

"He is only criminal. Not al-Qaeda. You take him, I don't have to give him food. How much you pay?"

Recovering from his shock at this gargantuan venality, Pascual mentally counts the cash he has left in the money belt, wondering what he could raise on the strength of a credit card in Mukalla, whether he can sell this to Cody, how he is going to get two men out of the country. All he knows is that there is a chance he will not have to stand and watch them drag this man back into the stables. He takes a deep breath, assuming what he hopes is a businesslike frown. "Well, let's see. If this one is only a criminal, he's not worth much. I'll give you two thousand."

Rashid makes a disgusted noise. "Five thousand."

That will nearly exhaust Pascual's cash reserves. "Two thousand five hundred," he says. "And that's all I can offer. Take it or take him back to the stables." Pascual turns and makes for the office, hoping he has not misjudged his man.

"Very good, two thousand five hundred," Rashid says to his back. He looks at the soldiers and growls in Arabic that they are to release this prisoner as well. They trade a look and a shrug.

"I'll need his papers, too," says Pascual, careful to keep his tone neutral.

"I will give you." Rashid wrinkles his nose. "We will go in office and you will give me money. And they will wash them. Very dirty. My car very clean."

Pascual stands in the doorway of the office, watching two naked men washing themselves with water from a plastic tub on the ground. Their frail brown bodies are covered with scars. Scars on the back, scars on the legs, scars on the arms. Husseini's left leg is visibly atrophied; the other man cannot stand fully upright and winces when he tries. His nose has finally stopped bleeding after Rashid gave him a dirty rag to press to his face. Pascual has been contemplating the slow smolder of his outrage, knowing he cannot let it burst into flame until he is well clear of this place, of Rashid, and perhaps Yemen altogether. He wonders how many more men are back there in the stables and how much longer they will be there before Rashid decides on a whim that they can be released.

"Documents."

Pascual turns to see Rashid at the desk, brandishing another envelope. He tosses it on the desk and Pascual goes to examine the contents. There is a Yemeni national identification card with a photo that is instantly recognizable as the first prisoner; he had less flesh to lose than Husseini did. His name is given as Omar Majid Abdullah Qasim. Besides the ID card there are a driver's license in the same name and a couple of letters in scrawled Arabic that begin with a formula of greeting to *my son*. Pascual does not trouble to decipher them further. "Very good, thank you. Your cooperation is appreciated."

Rashid sniffs and goes back into the inner office, where he has been conferring with the soldier who runs the place. Pascual listens as Rashid addresses the soldier in an urgent undertone. Pascual cannot catch it all, but the Arabic for "delete" catches his ear, and Rashid finishes with the distinct admonition, "They were never here, you understand?" Pascual recognizes the sound of records being scrubbed, tracks being brushed out.

Pascual is standing in the doorway again, watching Husseini and Qasim dress themselves in the same rags they wore before, when Rashid re-emerges and brushes past him. "Now we go," he says. Pascual is reproaching himself for falling asleep on the journey here. A surreptitious look at his cell phone has established that he has no service and so no GPS location. He wonders how much Cody knows about this place. He wonders if Cody will wash his hands of the whole thing when presented with an extra man. He wonders how he allowed himself to be talked into this fool's errand.

"*Yallah*." Rashid is standing by his SUV, motioning to the two ex-prisoners. The second soldier is spreading a blue tarpaulin over the back seat of the vehicle. Husseini and Qasim shuffle uncertainly toward it, as if wary of a trap. Pascual makes a last check of the two manila envelopes and goes to join them, giving them what he hopes is an encouraging nod.

Rashid glares at them as they climb in, Husseini and Qasim in the back and Pascual in the front. Rashid climbs in behind the wheel and says, "Now my broblem finish. Your broblem start."

Pascual has no idea what Cody has done to entertain himself in the three hours he has been gone, but the Toyota is there at the gas station, now parked near the edge of the lot where the shadow of the canopy has shifted with the declining sun. Pascual has remained awake on the return journey and has determined that the makeshift prison is some twenty-five kilometers to the northwest. He hopes to be able to locate it when next he can consult a map.

Cody steps out of the cab as Rashid pulls up, scratching his belly. He grins at Rashid and touches the bill of his cap in a languid salute. "Things go OK?" he says to Pascual.

"Just fine. Better than expected."

Cody frowns as Husseini and Qasim climb out of the SUV. "Who's this, then? I was only expecting one."

Rashid has gotten out of the SUV to join the conversation, so Pascual speaks carefully. "There was a mix-up. They brought the wrong guy out first, and Rashid was kind enough to throw him into the deal."

Cody's eyes go to Rashid. "That right?"

Rashid smiles. "He is nothing, only a criminal. You give him to police, they put him in jail."

Cody trades a look with Pascual, who keeps his mouth shut. Cody says, "OK, we'll check with them. Thanks, chief." He shakes hands with Rashid.

Pascual makes a slight bow toward Rashid, hoping it does not look like mockery. "Thank you for your help."

Rashid makes no reply. He jumps into the SUV and peels out of the lot. Cody eyes Husseini and Qasim and says, "I'm afraid you guys are gonna have to ride in the back."

"They need medical care," says Pascual.

"We'll see what we can do." Cody lowers the tailgate but makes no move to assist the men. Husseini manages to climb onto the bed of the truck, but Pascual sees that Qasim will never make it; he winces as he turns his back to the bed and sits gingerly on the open gate. Pascual jumps up into the bed of the truck and he and Husseini grab Qasim under the arms and pull him aboard. Qasim grimaces and stifles a groan.

Cody slams the tailgate shut and he and Pascual get in the cab. In a minute they are rolling back down the wide, deserted boulevard. "You know about this jail they've got up in the hills there?" says Pascual.

Cody keeps his eyes on the road. "I figure that's Emirati business, not mine. I'll tell you something I didn't know. I didn't know you were gonna bring out a second guy."

"Rashid tried to pass him off as Husseini. When I called him on it, he tried to make it look like a mistake, but I don't buy it. And then his greed got the better of him and he offered me the second guy, too, at a discount. So I bought him, too."

"I hope he didn't cost you too much. He's probably al-Qaeda but probably not real hardcore. If Rashid doesn't want him, I got no problem cutting him loose. We'll see what the local cops have to say. Not that they're likely to know anything."

Pascual realizes he has already done more for Omar Qasim than anyone could have expected and will have to settle for that. "The fact that Rashid tried to swindle me says the Emiratis would be happier if Husseini doesn't make it out of the country. What can they do to stop that?"

"Shit, just about anything. Them and the Saudis pretty much run things in this part of the country. That's why we're gonna lay low till we're on the plane."

"You have a plane in mind?"

Cody grins. "That's what Star Services does, pal. That's our slogan. We do the impossible."

11

"I am sorry, my brother. They told me if I pretended to be you, I could leave with the foreigner and they wouldn't come after me. They told me what to say, told me all about you, gave me your wife's name." Qasim lies on a mattress, knees drawn up to his chest. Hands together in supplication, he directs a feverish gaze at Husseini.

"Never mind." On cushions piled up in a corner Husseini waves it all away. "In your place I probably would have done the same." There is no anger in his look, only a trace of disgust.

A cool evening breeze wafts in through an open window, along with the noise of a jet taking off from the airport across the highway. Feeble light comes from a single bulb hanging from the ceiling. Husseini and Qasim are dressed in ill-fitting but more or less clean western clothes that Cody delivered along with flat loaves of bread, cans of hummus, a tub of yogurt. The food disappeared fast and the men are beginning to look a little less like walking corpses.

"Who told you what to say?" Pascual has had difficulty understanding Qasim's thick Yemeni accent but is beginning to get used to it.

"The sergeant and the officer who brought you there. They came and got me yesterday and told me what to do."

Pascual refills the men's cups with water from a liter bottle and resumes his seat on a bench along the wall. He looks at Husseini and says, "He took a bribe to let you go but he knew his superiors wouldn't be happy if they found out."

Husseini drinks deep and sets the cup down. "Who paid money to gain my release?"

Pascual just manages to refrain from blurting out the truth. He feels absolutely no loyalty to the agency, but he decides that for a million dollars it is owed some rudimentary operational security. Avoiding Husseini's eyes, he says, "Influential parties in Europe exercised their influence."

When Husseini sees that is all he's going to get, he lets his head loll back against the wall and sighs, eyes closed. "Praise God. I thought I was going to die there."

"I think that was the intention," says Pascual. "Why were you arrested?"

Husseini spits out a bitter laugh. "They accused me of being a spy for the Iranians. But the real reason was that I did my job too well. I asked too many questions about our operations in Yemen."

Qasim stirs on his mattress. "The Emiratis don't need a reason. They arrested me because of my uncle. He let some jihadis stay in his village for a few days. So the Emiratis accused him of being with al-Qaeda. He was only doing what honor demanded. They were guests, and they hadn't done anything to us. But the Emiratis came and got him. And I was there at his house, so they took me, too. My uncle died after they broke his ribs, choking on his own blood. Me, they broke my back but I didn't die."

Husseini says, "They broke my leg and I lay in pain for three weeks before they brought a doctor. He did nothing, just said stay off it and it would heal. I suppose it has. I can walk, after a fashion."

After a heavy silence Pascual says, "The American is bringing a doctor tomorrow. We'll take you to a hospital if you need it." He pulls his CIA phone out of his shirt pocket and verifies that the service is working. He holds the phone out to Husseini. "Do you want to call your wife?"

Husseini blinks at him. "I'll call her when I'm convinced I'm actually flying out of here."

Pascual nods and looks at Qasim. "How about you? You have people you want to call?"

The thin frame shakes and after a moment Pascual realizes Qasim is laughing. "All my people are dead. My mother and my sisters were killed when a drone bombed our village. And my father and brother were killed by our blood feud enemies from another family. The reason I was at my uncle's house was because our enemies had come to my village looking for me. If I stay in Yemen I'll be killed. Can I come to Europe with you?"

Pascual puts the phone away. "I didn't see a passport with your documents."

"Don't they take emergency medical cases? They take refugees without documents all the time. Don't they?"

Pascual stares into a look of desperation and wishes he had an answer. "I don't know. We'll see what the American says."

"Not my call," says Cody. "You're gonna have to sell it to the refugee agencies." He and Pascual stand in the morning glare outside the house, where they have just seen off a Saudi military doctor who spent a half hour briskly examining Husseini and Qasim. A gaggle of children gapes at them from across the street. "I only got instructions about the one guy."

"You heard the doctor," says Pascual. "What are his prospects for getting the kind of care he needs around here?"

"Pretty bad, I'd say. Everything's bad in Yemen. But that's not really my problem. Or yours, for that matter. He's just a guy. Yemen's full of them. For what it's worth, I ran his name past the counterterrorism guys, and it didn't set off any alarms. They said he probably just got scooped up in that big net the Emiratis dragged through here a few years ago. If I was you, I'd wish him luck and be on my way. You did what you came for."

Pascual squints into the glare bouncing off houses, rubble, the dusty earth. He moves into the narrow band of shade cast by the house. He puts his hands to his face and sags against the wall. Lack of sleep and a haphazard diet have made him light-headed. "I have to go back in there and tell him I can't do anything for him."

Half a minute goes by in silence. Cody has moved to Pascual's side. He says, "Shit, we can take him on the plane. The problem will be at the other end, when you get to Athens. He can try for asylum, I guess. They'll just throw him in one of those camps. If you think he'll be better off there than here, then hell, we'll make room for him."

Ever the technophobe, Pascual is amazed that he can be standing in a lot full of rubble in Yemen and talking to Sabine Degitz in Athens. "I've got Ali Husseini," he says.

"Oh, splendid." He can hear the surprise in Degitz's voice. "I wasn't at all sure you'd be able to do it."

"Neither was I. Can I ask that you not make it public until I've got him out of the country? I think things could still fall apart if it makes any kind of noise."

"Of course. I have been doing this for a while, you know. Mum's the word. When will you be bringing him out?"

"That's yet to be determined. Soon, I've been told."

"What airline will you take? I can have someone meet the flight."

"It's going to be a private flight. I'll advise you when I know more. And there's one complication."

"What kind of complication?"

"I have a second prisoner. I was able to secure his release as well."

There is a pause. "How did you manage that?"

"It's a long story. This man is Yemeni, but he wants to get out. The problem is, he doesn't have a passport. I thought your agency might be able to help him."

Pascual imagines he hears a sigh come through the ether, faintly. Degitz says, "My agency is already overwhelmed. It would be irresponsible of me to encourage yet another migrant to throw himself on our mercy without papers."

Pascual gives it a few seconds and says, "What shall I tell him, then?"

The answer comes immediately. "I don't care what you tell him. Just don't tell me anything more. Do what you think is right and we'll respond as best we can." Abruptly the call is cut off.

Pascual stands with the phone in his hand for a moment and then goes into the house. Qasim and Husseini are dozing on their cushions but rouse themselves when Pascual enters. "Are we going?" says Husseini, awaking with a start, eyes wide.

"Not yet. The American says when we go it will be at short notice. Be ready." He looks at Qasim. "Both of you."

■ ■ ■ ■

Deep in the night Pascual is awakened by the sound of tires grinding on gravel, a vehicle drawing up in front of the house. The darkness is profound, with no artificial light inside and only a few distant lights showing through the window. A car door closes softly, quiet steps scuff toward the door, a key sounds in the lock. Pascual thrashes at the sheet and swings his feet to the floor. As he is pulling on his trousers the harsh white light of a cell phone flashlight app washes over the walls of the front room. As Pascual comes in, pulling on his shirt, Cody is prodding Husseini's prone form with his foot. "Let's go, bud," he says. "Time to get moving." The light shifts, blinding Pascual, and Cody says, "I hope you're packed. The plane's waiting."

"Jesus, you weren't kidding about the short notice."

"No but that's not the real news. Y'all need to get your asses in gear, because we're maybe five minutes ahead of the lynch mob."

Pascual freezes. "What lynch mob?"

"Either Rashid had second thoughts, or somebody blew the whistle on him. I got a text from a buddy in Emirati intel saying they're looking for Husseini. And at least some of them know about this place, so it's about as safe right now as a tree house in a tornado. Grab your stuff and let's get these fuckers on the truck."

Pascual stammers a little as he puts together a hurried summary in Arabic of Cody's message. Husseini and Qasim blink into the light and then begin to move, as fast as pain and wasted muscles will allow. Pascual feels his way back into the bedroom and gathers his few things in the dark, grateful he took care to pack before lying down. He straps on the money belt beneath the tail of his shirt but does not bother to tie his shoes.

Cody is hectoring the Arabs when Pascual passes through the room, Husseini helping Qasim to stand. Pascual throws his bag onto the passenger seat of the Toyota and then hurries back in to lend a hand. Cody lowers the tailgate and Husseini and Pascual lift Qasim onto the bed of the truck while Cody locks the door of the house. Cody slams the tailgate shut and he and Pascual jump into the cab. Cody pauses with his hand on the key in the ignition, listening. A couple of hundred meters away, a vehicle slows and turns off the highway.

"Shit." Cody starts the truck and puts it in gear, without turning on the headlights. He takes the Toyota gently down the street, ghostly white houses drifting by in the dark. Pascual looks over his shoulder and sees headlights just beginning to wash over gravel a couple of streets behind them. Cody swings abruptly left around a corner. He accelerates a little as they roll toward the lights of the airport. "Well, fuck me," he says. "They were even closer than I thought. Hang onto your hat."

There are after all a few isolated lights in the village, high on a post or glowing dimly behind blinds, just enough for Cody to navigate them back to the highway. By the time he hits the access road he is picking up speed. Pascual sees no sign of pursuit behind them. Cody turns onto the highway and hits the gas, still without lights. "I think we're good," he says. "Unless they're watching the airport. But even there we ought to be able to get around them. We fly in and out all the time, and the airport people know us." He is hunched over the wheel. There is no other traffic but not much light either, and Pascual is glad he is not driving.

"How can you see the road?"

"I can't. I'm just guessing." Cody brakes and slews left onto the airport entrance road. After a few meters he switches on the headlights. A hundred meters along, they come to a boom barrier lowered across the road and a cabin with a light inside illuminating a soldier in camouflage, slumbering with his head against the wall. Cody taps on the horn and the soldier comes awake, focuses, and puts on a look of sullen resentment before coming out of the cabin to challenge them. Cody brandishes a laminated card on a lanyard and says, "Good morning, sunshine. I hate to wake you up, but I got a plane to unload. These guys in the back are my hired help. OK?"

Pascual is unsure how much the soldier understands, but the card seems to be all he needs to see. With a glance at Pascual and then the two in the bed of the truck, he returns the card to Cody and goes back into the cabin. Immediately the barrier rises. "*Shukran, amigo*," Cody shouts, waving as he goes through. "Hot shit. That right there was my main worry. If they woulda gotten through to that dude there on the phone, we'da been fucked." He pulls a cell phone out of his shirt pocket and thumbs it as he drives, picking up speed as they roll toward the terminal a few hundred meters ahead. Phone to his ear he says, "Yo, Cody here. We're in. Get her fired up. I'll be with you in two minutes."

Pascual cannot believe it is happening. "How far is this flight taking us?" he says.

"All the way, partner. You'll be in Athens in under six hours."

Pascual is struck dumb. After contemplating days of agonizing uncertainty, suddenly here he is, looking at lunch in Athens. "That's unbelievable. I don't know how to thank you."

"All in a day's work," Cody says. He jerks the wheel to the left and they skirt the terminal, rushing past outbuildings, parked military vehicles and the control tower. Cody shoots a look over his shoulder and says, "None too fuckin' soon, too. I think they're onto us." Pascual twists and sees headlights at the barrier behind them. Cody slows, turns and rolls through a gate, and suddenly they are on a vast concrete apron, with military helicopters parked in rows and, at the far end, a sleek twin-engined executive jet. "There you go," says Cody, picking up speed. "A Gulfstream V, the best Star Services has to offer. No stewardesses, but they might be able to pour you a drink."

Pascual has had precious few moments in his life of anything that might be called euphoria. This is one of them, he thinks, watching the scant cluster of lights around Al Rayan Airport fall away behind them as the plane banks and climbs over the lightless void of the desert. This is one I will remember. My second and, let us fervently hope, final farewell to Yemen.

The interior of the aircraft is blessedly cool and softly lit. They are in the rear compartment, with plush seats disposed in pairs facing each other and a couch along one side. Pascual has hardly had time to notice it since Cody hustled him and the Arabs out of the truck and handed them over to a bearded Yank in a khaki shirt and cargo shorts who herded them up the steps and onto the plane while Cody wrenched the Toyota around and sped off. They were taxiing onto the runway before the Yank had finished strapping them in. The process was hard on Qasim, who now sits across the aisle from Pascual, grimacing, eyes closed. Facing him is Husseini, who is staring out the porthole into the night. He is gaunt and unkempt, cast-off clothes hanging loose on his wasted frame, a bedraggled alley cat in the executive suite, utterly out of place. Eventually he turns a wondering look on Pascual. "Praise God. Please tell me this is real, and not a dream."

"I'm no authority. But if it's a dream, let's hope we don't wake up for a while."

Husseini manages a smile. "I don't know whom to thank."

Pascual hesitates before answering. "I couldn't tell you. I'm just the agent."

The door at the front of the aircraft opens and the bearded Yank comes back to their compartment. He approaches and says, "You are now free to move about the aircraft." He grins. "I'm not a stewardess, so don't ask. You want a drink, you get it yourself. The bar's back there. Bathroom's back there, too." He frowns at Qasim. "What's wrong with him?"

Husseini answers in English, accented but fluent. "His back is injured. It is difficult for him to sit."

The Yank nods. "He might be better off over there." He points at the couch opposite. "Wanna move him?"

Pascual helps Husseini shift Qasim to the couch, where his grimace eases once he is lying on his side with his knees drawn up. He shivers in the chilled air and the Yank produces blankets from a storage compartment. Husseini drapes one over Qasim and another over his own shoulders.

Pascual addresses the Yank. "Will my cell phone work up here, and may I use it?"

"Knock your socks off. It'll go through a satellite. You can order a pizza and have it waiting at the gate."

Pascual pulls the phone out of his pocket and hands it to Husseini. "You never got a chance to call your wife." He turns back to the Yank. "Speaking of waiting at the gate, what are the arrangements for when we land?"

The Yank shrugs. "All's I know is, we're landing at Tatoi and you're getting off. What happens on the ground is above my pay grade."

Pascual thanks him and the Yank returns to the cockpit. Husseini is thumbing at the cell phone. Pascual wanders toward the back of the plane, marveling at the opulence: leather upholstery, television screens, spacious tables. He goes into a galley at the rear of the craft and finds an assortment of liquor bottles behind glass doors in a cabinet. It is the middle of the night and he is light-headed with exhaustion and humming with adrenaline aftereffects. He decides a drink might be in order. He finds glasses and pours himself a respectable slug of a premium cognac.

Half an hour after being roused from an uneasy doze by the sound of tires on gravel, Pascual stands cocooned in luxury with a drink in his hand, ten thousand meters above a failed state laid waste by war, watching Ali Husseini in his seat with the phone to his ear, struggling to speak between sobs.

The sea has never sparkled so breathtakingly, the rugged Attic hills have never looked so welcoming, as when the Gulfstream banks slowly to bring Athens into view. Three hours ago Pascual finally nodded off after watching the sun rise over Arabia; now he sits with dry mouth and faintly throbbing head, face to the porthole at his side.

The approach takes them over fringes of the city crowding into the hills; then the land flattens and it is just an airport like any other, roads and houses rushing up at them as they descend. Husseini and Qasim are strapped in, Qasim no longer grimacing, Husseini looking like a six-year-old boy on a carnival ride. The landing is smooth, only a mild thump, and once they are down, Husseini closes his eyes and turns his hands palms up in prayer.

A long taxi ensues. Through the porthole Pascual can see fighter jets parked outside a gigantic hangar, a long low terminal, the rocky hills rising in the distance. The Gulfstream comes to a stop a long way from the terminal. The Yank makes his way to the rear from the cockpit and says, "All right, boys, you made it to Athens. Now we wait till the Greeks find time to come and collect you." He goes back up front and busies himself with opening the hatch and lowering the steps. Pascual checks his phone and sees a text from Melville: *UNHCR meeting you at Tatoi. Second man no problem. Call when on the ground.*

Pascual hits *Call* and Melville answers immediately. "You down?"

"We're on the ground. What happens next?"

"You get cleared by air force intelligence and they hand you over to the UN people. There shouldn't be any trouble. We've brought people in through Tatoi before, and they know not to ask too many questions."

Pascual wonders briefly about the fate of other people flown by the CIA from Arab lands to military airfields in Europe. "When is my job over?"

"When we get our data. That's supposed to happen as soon as Degitz confirms Husseini is safe. She'll want to verify his identity, check his condition and so forth. God knows how long that will take. She's supposed to contact Zarlik as soon as she's satisfied, and then we're supposed to get the key. Until we do, you stay right on top of Husseini. If the UN people try to stop you, you insist. You brought him out, you're going to stay with him until you're satisfied he's safe, whatever you have to tell them. But you stick with him. And you keep the media away. Don't let the UN people put him in front of a camera or let anybody shove a microphone in his face. They want to issue a statement or something, that's fine. We get our data back, they can do what they want with him. But until then, you make sure he's not talking to Al Jazeera or the BBC or even the *Athens Free Weekly*."

"How can I stop him?"

"Look, as the guy who got Husseini out of Yemen, you'll have the clout. Just tell them your backers want it kept under wraps until further notice. They'll assume the parties behind you want to handle the media end of it and they'll go along. Understood?"

An old familiar feeling steals over Pascual: a disquieting lack of confidence in the assurances of people giving him orders. He says, "Understood" and rings off.

The wait becomes long. It grows warm in the aircraft. By Pascual's watch it is nearly half an hour before a car draws up at the steps and two men get out. They are not wearing the same uniform as the bored customs officers who stamped Pascual's passport at Venizelos Airport a few days before; one is in civilian clothes and the other in blue camouflage with military insignia. They come up the steps into the plane and shake hands with the Yank. There is a conversation in English but Pascual cannot make out more than a few words. The door to the cockpit opens and Pascual gets a first glimpse of the pilot and copilot, who emerge to join the parley. They look like squared-away military types, clean-shaven, but in casual civilian dress. They cast curious looks aft but show no inclination to come and talk to the cargo they have just delivered.

Finally the Greeks break off and come slowly back to the rear compartment. The officer is black-haired, chiseled and fierce-looking. The civilian is older, gray and grizzled. "Papers," barks the officer.

Pascual presents his own passport and produces Husseini's passport and Qasim's identity card from the manila envelopes. The officer gives them a perfunctory examination and holds up Qasim's ID card between two fingers. "This is not a passport."

Husseini and Qasim have been watching with the silent anxiety of people long accustomed to the depredations of officialdom. Qasim now shoots a look of appeal at Pascual, who says, "He doesn't have one. He is an emergency medical evacuation case, claiming asylum in Greece. I believe the UN Refugee Agency has someone here to receive us."

"Asylum." The officer glares down at Pascual for a moment. "Well, what's one more? He and fifty thousand others. I hope he likes living in a tent." He hands the documents to the civilian, who leafs through them and mutters something in Greek. The officer says, "You are lucky. You have powerful friends. Come." The Greeks stalk back up the aisle, taking the documents with them. Pascual motions to Husseini and Qasim and hastens to grab his bag from the luggage area at the rear. Husseini helps Qasim out of his seat and the three of them straggle up toward the exit.

The bearded Yank nods at them as they pass. "Guys, it's been fun. Give us a good Yelp rating, will ya?"

Pascual never expected brass bands and balloons, but neither did he expect to be abandoned in what appears to be a storage room. There are filing cabinets, shelves bearing sealed cardboard boxes and stacked traffic cones, broken chairs and derelict fax machines. There are enough unbroken chairs that Pascual and Husseini are able to sit, though Qasim prefers to squat in a clear space at the base of a wall. "They have forgotten us," he says.

"They're trying to decide how to fiddle the paperwork," says Husseini.

"They're just letting us know who's in charge," says Pascual.

Husseini laughs. "Our jailers were fond of doing that. Their methods took less time than this, but I'm not complaining." In contrast to Qasim he has been sitting patiently, looking almost happy, a man appreciating his new lease on life.

Steps sound in the hallway outside, a key turns in the lock and the door opens. An airman in blue camouflage enters and stands aside to let a young woman come in. She is tall, brown-haired and pale-skinned, athletic in bearing, lithe and sleek in black jeans and a linen jacket with the sleeves rolled up. She has arresting hazel eyes under brows just a shade thicker than fashionable for a woman, a long straight nose, a slash of a mouth. Her hair is short and combed back off a high forehead, her face devoid of makeup. "I am Nela Nachtnebel," she announces. "I'm from the UN Refugee Agency. I'm sorry you have been treated this way. The airport authorities have not been very cooperative." Her English is smooth and practiced, with a slight accent that Pascual pegs as German.

He stands. "I'm not sure they're the ones responsible," he says, managing a smile. "Anyway, we're glad to see you."

Nachtnebel extends her hand. "You are Mr. Rose?"

"I am Pascual Rose. This is Ali Husseini, and that is Omar Qasim."

From a bag hanging over her shoulder Nachtnebel pulls out the men's documents and distributes them. "Mr. Qasim has been released to our custody, which is something of a miracle. I am amazed they let him off the plane."

"We have friends in high places," says Pascual.

"I imagine they are in need of medical attention," says Nachtnebel. Husseini is helping Qasim to stand up. "We have an ambulance waiting to transport them."

"Where are you taking them?"

"To a private clinic. Your role is finished. We thank you for your part in obtaining their release." The look she turns on Pascual is cool.

He stiffens a little. "My instructions are to accompany them to their destination. Meaning their place of accommodation, not a broom closet at the airport."

"They have been delivered to the UNHCR as agreed. They are in safe hands and your assistance is no longer required."

If it were up to him, Pascual would be happy to go and find himself a taxi, but with a payday at stake he is determined to follow Melville's instructions to the letter. He makes a slight bow and says, "I'm afraid I must insist. To begin with, I would appreciate seeing some credentials. Anybody could walk in here and claim to be with the UN."

During the brief stare-down that follows, Pascual decides that if this woman is not exactly beautiful in a conventional sense, the intelligence and spirit in the long, clean-lined face reward a few seconds' close study. "Credentials," she says. "You think I could walk in here, persuade the Greek air force to surrender your passports and then to bring me back here to get you, without credentials?"

Pascual has to concede it is unlikely. He smiles and says, "Humor me."

She gives him a contemptuous look before digging in the bag again and extracting a card and presenting it to him. Under the UNHCR logo she appears in a glowering mugshot with *NELA NACHTNEBEL* below it. The card identifies her as an intern in the Geneva headquarters of the agency. Pascual hands back the card. "They must be stretched thin if they're sending interns from Geneva to meet released political prisoners."

"You can't imagine," she says, stashing the card. "Now. Can we reach an agreement? Once I have verified their identities, I am willing to give you a written statement that you have delivered these men into my custody. And then your role will be at an end."

Pascual gives this a few seconds' thought. "The people I represent gave me very explicit instructions. I am to stay with Ali Husseini until they receive confirmation from Sabine Degitz that he is safe and his needs are being met. When I am satisfied that he is beyond the reach of the government of the United Arab Emirates, I will notify them. Until then I must insist on accompanying him, and let's include Qasim while we're at it, wherever you intend to take them."

Nela Nachtnebel rises to her full height, blinks a couple of times and says "I'm not sure it's the government of the UAE we have to worry about."

"There may be others. All the more reason to make sure they're in a safe place."

"And what if I don't trust the people you represent?"

"Then you are perfectly free to appeal to whomever you think will be able to protect these men. Put them under police guard if you wish. Move them under cover of night after Degitz has confirmed Husseini's identity. But until that happens, I'm staying with them."

Pascual expects more pushback, but he sees the change in Nachtnebel's face as she comes to a decision. Her lips firm and she says, "Very well. Let's get these gentlemen to a more comfortable place."

13

"His wife recognized him at once. She didn't want to let go of him. The nurses finally had to pull her away, gently, so they could get him to a bed. It was . . . really quite moving." Sabine Degitz still looks as if she could use a good night's sleep, but witnessing Ali Husseini's reunion with his wife has lent her face what might almost qualify as a glow of satisfaction. "That's why we do this work, for moments like these." She is actually smiling as she looks at Nela Nachtnebel, who appears unmoved and merely continues to slump on her chair, arms folded.

"So what happens now?" says Pascual. They are in a cramped and dreary waiting room with scuffed sofas, cigarette-scarred armchairs and bars over the windows, all that the Diamandis Clinic is prepared to offer those attached to its patients. Pascual has been cooling his heels here for an hour since the taxi containing him and Nela Nachtnebel pulled to the curb in front of a five-story stuccoed facade on a treelined street in a western suburb of Athens, just behind the ambulance delivering two abused and malnourished patients. Shortly after their arrival, Sabine Degitz arrived in another taxi with a pretty, young Arab woman in a hijab, and they were ushered into an elevator along with Nela Nachtnebel, leaving Pascual to chat in broken English with the septuagenarian security guard manning the desk in the entrance hall.

"Now they rest and recover," says Degitz. "This is a private clinic. The agency has arranged for them to be treated here and has found money in a very stretched budget to pay for it, at least in the very short term. We've even agreed to pay for extra security for a few days, in light of some of the things that have happened to Saudi and Emirati dissidents abroad in the past. When their condition has stabilized, we will assist them in the next steps. My understanding is that they will both be applying for asylum in Greece."

Pascual nods. "Excellent. So you are prepared to notify certain parties that Ali Husseini has been released and is in your safekeeping."

Degitz sends him a cool look. "The notification has already been made."

This catches Pascual by surprise. He has been held at arm's length by both women, who have been remarkably sparing with expressions of gratitude. Pascual has no feelings in the matter to be hurt, but he judges that mere courtesy might have acknowledged the trouble he has been put to. He stands. "Thank you. Let me see what my principals say." He nods at the two women and leaves the room. On the pavement in front of the building, he pulls out his phone.

Melville answers his call without delay and says, "What's the situation?"

"They're checked in, Husseini's wife's here, everybody's happy. Degitz says she's already notified the interested parties that Husseini's safe."

"She has, huh? I don't suppose she said when I'm likely to get my data back. No, she wouldn't. Stick close. Don't let them pull anything."

"Like what?"

"Like moving Husseini."

"Why would they move him?"

"I don't know. But this is the tricky part, right here. We've delivered and they haven't. We've put the bag full of unmarked bills under the park bench and we're waiting for the bad guys to let little Tommy go. Until I get my data back, I want to be sure I know where Husseini is."

"What, so you can grab him and send him back to Yemen?"

"No, just to make this Zarlik character think I can. There are ways to complicate Husseini's life. I hope I don't have to use them. But I will if I don't get my data back. Meanwhile, you're my eyes and ears. If they try and move him, pull the alarm cord, hard."

Pascual holds the phone away from his face while he looses an exasperated breath. "When am I off duty? I could use a shower, a meal and a good night's sleep."

"Once the key comes through, you can do what you want."

"Do I still get to stay at the St. George?"

Melville laughs in Pascual's ear. "You've got the credit card, right? Stay wherever you want." His voice hardens. "Once I get my data back."

Pascual recognizes an exit line and ends the call with a brusque "Understood." He stands for a moment watching clouds high above the roofline and then goes back inside the clinic. The guard comes out of a doze long enough to wave him in. In the waiting room Nela Nachtnebel is intently thumbing her phone; Degitz has disappeared. Pascual drops into a chair, lets his head loll back and closes his eyes. When he opens them Nela Nachtnebel has put her phone away and is staring at him with faint distaste. "I'm not sure why you're still here," she says.

"I'm not either." Pascual blinks at her. "I'm also not sure why you are so hostile."

The finely sculpted chin rises a degree or two. "Because I know who you work for."

In spite of himself, Pascual is irked. It may be only an aging man's vanity, but it bothers him that this rather splendid young female so obviously detests him. "What exactly is it that you object to? I've sprung not one but two men from a secret prison and delivered them to you. I don't expect tears of gratitude, but a little civility would be appreciated."

"I'm sure you were paid."

"Not yet. In any event, whoever I work for, surely it has served a good purpose today."

The look of disdain only deepens. "We shall see."

Pascual chews on that while Nela Nachtnebel goes back to her phone. Out in the hall an elevator door opens and a few seconds later Sabine Degitz appears in the doorway and beckons to Nachtnebel, who jumps up and goes to join her in the hall. The two women hold a brief conversation in German; Pascual identifies the language but cannot make out many words. His phone goes off in his shirt pocket and he answers.

"Bingo," says Melville. "Success."

"You got your data?"

"Full access. Everything works. The key came through a couple of minutes ago and all systems are go. We did it."

Pascual wants to question the pronoun but lets it pass. "So it's over."

"Your part's over. You did a hell of a job."

Accustomed as he is to disasters and recriminations, Pascual is completely thrown by this praise; Melville sounds positively giddy. "Well, all I did was follow instructions, really."

"That's all it takes sometimes. You earned yourself a fat payday, and you did a good thing, too. You got the guy out of jail."

"Two guys."

"Ah, yes. Mr. Qasim. I'm not sure I'd have played it that way, but it seems to have worked out."

"I couldn't just walk off and leave him."

"Maybe not. Hell, he won the lottery, good for him. He may find things a little harder than he expected here in the promised land. But that's not my problem. We'll let the UN worry about him."

"I suppose he's better off destitute here than there."

"No doubt. Look, here's a thought. You got anything left in the money belt? You didn't have to spend it all, did you?"

"No, there's a couple of thousand dollars left. I was holding some back to bribe my way out of Aden if need be."

"Well, hell, whatever you have left, give it to your guy, Qasim. Give him a little leg up. He'll need it."

"You're in a generous mood."

"I got my data back. It's a good day."

"Then maybe this is a good time to discuss my fee."

"Sure. Come by the apartment when you're done there. We can discuss arrangements."

For a moment Pascual is stunned into silence. It is actually happening; there will be a payday. "What's the catch?"

Melville actually laughs. "You are a suspicious bastard, aren't you?"

"I am an experienced bastard. You mean to tell me I've actually earned a million dollars?"

"That's what I mean to tell you. Come by and we'll have a drink to celebrate. And we'll discuss how to make a million dollars available to you without being too obvious to the Spanish tax authorities."

"That sounds like a pleasant way to pass an evening. I'll come by after I check in at the St. George again."

After he rings off Pascual stands holding the phone for a moment, his mind racing. Pull the other phone out of your bag, he thinks, and call Sara. Tell her our lives are about to change.

Not yet, he thinks. Wait till you see the money.

The thought of money brings him out of his reverie. The money belt has been chafing the soft flesh around his middle for a week. He will be glad to get rid of it. He goes into the tiny bathroom just off the waiting room and pulls up his shirttail. He sighs with relief as he slips off the belt. He unzips it, removes the handful of hundred-dollar bills that remain, and drops the money belt into a wastebasket under the sink. He rolls the bills into a thick wad and stuffs it into his trouser pocket.

He finds Sabine Degitz and Nela Nachtnebel in the hall talking to Diamandis, the owner of the clinic, a morose-looking bald man whom Pascual met in passing earlier. "Still here, Mr. Rose?" says Degitz.

"I'm leaving in a moment. I would just like to say goodbye to Husseini and Qasim, if I may."

From the look that passes among the three of them an observer might think that Pascual has made an indecent proposition. "I'm not sure that's possible," says Degitz, appealing with a look at Diamandis, who merely shrugs.

"Just a word or two. I won't even shake their hands, if you're worried about infection."

"Don't let him," says Nela Nachtnebel. She is training a flat, cold stare on Pascual.

He is beginning to be annoyed. "What do you think I'm going to do to them?"

"We know who you represent and you can't possibly have their best interests at heart. If I had my way, you wouldn't even be here."

Pascual appeals to Degitz. "I've come a long way with these men. I'd like to wish them the best. For God's sake, I'm not going to harm them. Send the guard up with me if you want."

Degitz says, "When I left him just now, Mr. Husseini was sleeping. I don't think you should disturb him. He was quite exhausted."

Pascual guesses that this is a lie, but he has no desire to press the point. "What about Qasim, then? The poor man has nobody here, nothing to fall back on. Can I at least leave a few dollars with him?"

The women exchange a look. "Watch him," says Nela Nachtnebel.

"I will go with him," says Diamandis.

"Very well," says Degitz. "I don't see what the harm is. If it's all right with Dr. Diamandis, I have no objection. Nela and I have a taxi waiting, I believe. We'll take our leave now." She holds out her hand. "Thank you for your help, Mr. Rose. Whoever you represent, you have done a good thing."

Pascual shakes hands; he is not surprised when Nela Nachtnebel stalks away toward the exit. He watches the two women leave and then turns to Diamandis. "Thank you. I won't take much of your time."

They take the elevator to the fourth floor. Diamandis confers briefly with a nurse in a small office and then leads Pascual down a tiled hallway to a room at the end. The door is standing open and Diamandis raps lightly on the door frame with his knuckles. "A visitor."

Omar Qasim is lying in a hospital bed with a drip in his arm. He is still unshaven, but his hair has been washed and combed. The deep-set eyes in the gaunt face widen a little when he sees Pascual.

"How are you?" Pascual steps to the bedside.

It takes Qasim a moment to find his voice. "Better. They have given me drugs."

"That always helps."

"Yes. They say I need an operation. An operation to fix my back."

"I'm sure it can be arranged."

"I don't know who's going to pay for it."

"Don't worry about that. If you get asylum, the United Nations will help you."

"And what if I don't? Will they send me back to Yemen?"

"I don't know. Listen." Pascual looks over his shoulder and sees that Diamandis has drifted away from the door and is talking quietly to the nurse in the hall. He slips his hand into his pocket and pulls out the wad of bills. "I can give you something that will help a little. It's not much, but it will give you a start." He presses the wad into Qasim's hand. "There's about two thousand dollars there. It will buy you some clothes, maybe a place to stay."

Pascual is prepared to fend off fulsome expressions of gratitude, but he is not prepared for this look of frozen shock that seizes Qasim's face. The bony hand tightens around the bills and the lips work silently for a few seconds. "As you wish," Qasim says.

Pascual wants suddenly to laugh. There are not going to be any fulsome expressions of gratitude tonight, and he does not deserve any. Two thousand dollars are not going to solve Omar Qasim's problems, and a million dollars are only going to cement his own status as an expensive errand boy for political gangsters. He is filled with self-loathing. "I wish you luck," he says, and turns away.

■ ■ ■ ■

"There are a number of options," says Melville. "You've got the financial infrastructure already set up to make Pascual Rose wealthy, and it can all be accessed fairly discreetly. Now, if you want Pascual March to come into money, there will be more issues with the taxman."

Pascual nods absently. He is standing at the open door to the balcony, drink in hand, looking out into a cooling Athenian evening with the murmur of the great chaotic city rising from below, wondering why he feels so little satisfaction at what appears to be a radical change in his fortunes. "I want it to be legal," he says.

Behind him Melville laughs softly. "That's going to reduce the net quite a bit."

"I don't care." Pascual turns and comes back into the room. "I don't need to be rich. I want enough money to be able to live comfortably with my wife, have something to pass on to my son. I don't want to have to worry about taxmen or forensic accountants poking into my affairs. The sooner Pascual Rose expires, the better."

Melville raises his hands in surrender. "Have it your way. We can pay Pascual March and make it one hundred percent kosher. We can make it look like business consulting services, or whatever you wish, in euros if you still believe in the euro. I believe we have your banking information already. I can put the transaction through tonight. As for Pascual Rose, I'm afraid he's too useful to expire."

"I thought that was part of the deal."

The look Melville gives him instantly shows Pascual the depth of his childlike naivety. "The deal was, we don't let anybody prosecute you or kill you. In return, every once in a while you get to be Pascual Rose again and stay in nice hotels. And you get paid every time. I don't see that that's such a bad deal."

Pascual stands motionless, knowing he might win this stare-down but will never win the game; his hand is too weak. He drains his drink and says, "All right. I'm at the St. George again tonight. I hope to fly out tomorrow or the day after." He sets the glass down on the sideboard. "Anything else?"

Melville says, "Just the phone. You won't be needing it. You'll need the passport to fly out, but you keep it with the understanding that if you ever use it again, it will only be on agency business. I think we'll probably be able to find you again if we need to."

Pascual hands the phone to Melville and makes for the door. "You'll excuse me if I try not to make it too easy for you."

"Pascual."

Pascual pauses with his hand on the doorknob and turns slowly to face Melville, who is regarding him gravely from his chair, legs crossed and drink dangling casually from his hand. "What?"

"If the money doesn't mean anything to you, think about the two guys you got out of that hellhole down in Yemen. You did that."

Pascual blinks at him a few times. "Yes. I did that. I did that for you. Why does that make me uneasy?"

"I'm out of Yemen," says Pascual, his Greek phone to his ear.

"Thank God," says Sara at the other end of the Mediterranean, venting a sigh. "You don't know how I've worried. You even made me start praying again."

"You can stop praying. I'm in Athens again, and tomorrow or the next day I'm flying back to Marseille. I'm just going to collect my things and then I'm coming home."

"Home? I'm not sure where that is anymore."

"Wherever you are."

"I'm in Barcelona. I'm staying with Nuria, singing at Los Tarantos for the next month."

"I'll come to Barcelona, then. We'll get a hotel room. Unless you've got some young buck paying court these days."

Sara's laughter raises Pascual's spirits instantly, bouncing off satellites and into his ear. "*Imbécil*. Who would have an old woman like me, except an old man like you?"

Tell her about the money, Pascual thinks, but something stops him. "*Vida mía*. I long to be with you."

14

Pascual's eyes rise from the phone in his hand to the splendid view of the Acropolis and beyond it the distant sea from the sixth-floor restaurant terrace of the St. George Hotel. He gazes at the luminous horizon for a moment and then looks down at his phone again, half-convinced the hallucination will have passed.

And yet here it is: *€882,936.24*, staring him in the face.

Lingering over coffee at breakfast, he has managed to download the banking app for Pascual March's CaixaBank account on his Greek phone, hardly daring to look at it but finally overcome by curiosity. The sight of an account balance swollen by the euro equivalent of one million dollars has left him stunned.

He stares at the figure for a moment longer and then begins to laugh softly. There is going to be a reckoning with the Agencia Tributaria. There are going to be multiple complications, time spent with financial advisors, lawyers, bankers, people of the sort Pascual has sneered at all his life. He will, finally, have to become what he has always resisted: thoroughly *aburguesado*.

He will have to revise a deeply fatalistic view of life; he will be able, finally, to assure a future for the only two people he loves.

Pascual puts his phone away and drains the last of his coffee. He has booked a seat on a flight to Marseille leaving in the late afternoon, and he will have time to contemplate the reversal of his fortunes at leisure, culminating in a pleasant lunch, before scheduling a taxi to Venizelos. He is absorbing the magnificent view again, with new eyes, when two men approach his table after a consultation with the waiter.

Pascual is fairly sure they are the police before they reach him; robust-looking young men with this air of owning a place when they walk in are generally either cops or criminals, and if they were hotel guests they would dress to a higher standard. In jeans and untucked shirts these two could be a couple of young bucks on a bar crawl. The dark one has a neatly trimmed beard and a high and tight haircut, and the fair one sports a couple of days' stubble. "Mr. Pascual Rose?" says the bearded one.

For a few seconds Pascual is too busy running through disaster scenarios to do anything more than blink stupidly. Somebody at Interpol flagged his passage through Greek customs; Pascual Rose's credit card activity set off some distant alarm at the Europol financial crimes bureau; somebody at Tatoi blew the whistle on foreign intelligence services sneaking in undesirables. "That's me," he manages finally.

The bearded one is showing him an ID card. "Inspector Karvelas, Hellenic Police." His English is smooth and practiced. "This is Inspector Markopoulos."

Pascual nods, assuming the concerned look of a man with a clear conscience, anxious to be helpful. "What can I do for you?"

"We would like to ask you some questions about a crime that took place last night."

Pascual's expectations vaporize. "What kind of crime?"

"A homicide, I am sorry to say."

A slow freeze creeps through Pascual's belly. "Who's dead?"

"There are four victims. At a clinic in Peristeri. You were there yesterday."

"They killed his wife, too?" Pascual is stunned.

"And the nurse. Don't forget her. Stabbed to death, all of them." Karvelas is sending him the cop look across the table, the look that says go ahead, lie to me and see how far it gets you.

Recovering from shock, Pascual is finally putting some order into his thoughts. He was shown into this room with gray walls in the bowels of a massive modern building in central Athens, after a ride in the back of an unmarked Citroën, Markopoulos at the wheel and Karvelas refusing to answer questions. He has shown his passport to attest to his identity and refused an offer of more coffee. "Who did it? Do you have somebody in custody?" he says.

"Actually, Mr. Rose, you are here to answer our questions, not the reverse." Karvelas has taken the lead, presumably because of his English, though Markopoulos is taking notes and so presumably understands it. "But no, we do not have anyone in custody."

Pascual waits for more but only gets more of the look. "I thought they were supposed to be guarded. There was supposed to be extra security."

"Why would they need to be guarded? Perhaps you can tell us."

Pascual has achieved one clear thought, regarding the extent of his responsibility to Melville and the agency: it is null. Nonetheless he sees no need to bring them in until prompted. "Because the government of the United Arab Emirates would not be happy to hear that Ali Husseini had been released."

Karvelas's eyes narrow slightly. "Yes. I was told that there was a political element in this. But I am not at all clear about your role. Do you work for the United Nations?"

"No. If you've talked to Sabine Degitz, you know I don't. I assume it was she who gave you my name?"

Karvelas concedes with a nod. "Though she didn't know where you were. We had to call a lot of hotels. So, why are you here?"

"I accompanied Ali Husseini and Omar Qasim from Yemen, where I was able to get them released from a secret prison run by the United Arab Emirates. The government had Husseini locked up because of his criticism of the regime. I was able to get him out by bribing a prison official. If the government then found out he had been released, they would not have been pleased."

Karvelas looks skeptical. "So they sent somebody to kill him? Why didn't they just kill him when they had him in custody?"

"Maybe they saw him as a potential asset. A prisoner with a constituency can always be used as a bargaining chip. But once he got out, they knew they couldn't let him tell his story."

Karvelas isn't buying it, to judge by his look. "Why you? You have a Maltese passport, which shows your residence as Dubai. Are you involved in UAE politics?"

"No. I stay out of politics as far as possible."

"So why are you involved? Who sent you to Yemen?"

Pascual takes a deep breath and leaps. "An American named Melville, who offered me a million dollars to do the job."

This is something Karvelas did not know, to judge by the very slight change in his expression. "Who is this Melville?"

"That is almost certainly not his real name. He is an officer of the

American CIA."

Karvelas has lost the cop look and is looking distinctly interested. "And why would he pay you a million dollars to do this?"

"Because I am deniable and expendable."

"Please explain."

"I do occasional jobs for the agency because they are in a position to make my life difficult. My position is much like that of a man in debt to a criminal organization. When they ask him to do something, he does it."

Karvelas and Markopoulos exchange a look. Karvelas says, "Where will I find this man?"

"If he's still in Athens, you might find him at this address." Pascual pulls out his wallet and produces the scrap of paper on which he wrote the address of Melville's apartment. He hands it to Karvelas, who looks at it and passes it on to his partner. "But you'd better hurry. Once he hears about the murders, I doubt he's going to stick around."

Karvelas turns to Markopoulos and mutters a couple of sentences' worth of Greek. Markopoulos snaps his notebook shut, stands and hurries out of the room. Karvelas frowns into space for a moment and turns back to Pascual. "Now. Why did the CIA want this Husseini to be released?"

Pascual is not sure what stops him from disclosing the full story to an Athens police detective; perhaps only fatigue and an aversion to involved explanations. Or perhaps a vestige of the reflexive discretion he developed in his years underground. Whatever it is, he says merely, "I'm sure they had their reasons. I imagine Mr. Melville can tell you all about that."

Karvelas appears to accept that. He leans forward a little, intent.

"Let me ask you this. If the Emiratis sent somebody to kill these people, how did they know where they were?"

"That's a very good question," says Pascual, coming at last to the reason why he is sitting in this room. "There aren't too many candidates for the role of Judas, are there? And I would be at the top of the list."

Karvelas sits perfectly still for a long moment. "Who was this Qasim? Why did he come with Husseini from Yemen?"

Startled a little by the abrupt shift, Pascual says, "He was a prisoner in the same jail as Husseini. At first the Emiratis presented him as Husseini, hoping I would be deceived. When I exposed the deception, they produced the real Husseini. But they agreed to let me take Qasim, too, for another bribe."

Karvelas stares for a moment longer and then leans back on his chair, exhaling. "So Qasim was not expected to come with Husseini. He was there only because you insisted to bring him out of Yemen."

Pascual feels the slow chill beginning to seep through his core again. He can see Karvelas waiting for him to work it out. It doesn't take him long to get there, and when he gets there he doesn't like it at all. "How were they killed? What happened?"

Karavelas's look goes perfectly blank. "Omar Qasim killed them. He came out of his room in the middle of the night and took a pair of scissors from the nurse's desk. He killed her with them when she tried to stop him. Then he went to Husseini's room and killed him and his wife. A nurse from another floor heard the screams. When she got to Husseini's room, she saw Husseini and his wife bleeding on the floor and Qasim standing there with the scissors. Then she watched Qasim cut his own throat. The poor girl had to be sedated."

The windowless room in which he has been alone for the past hour is just big enough for Pascual to step off eight paces in one circuit around the table. Having determined this to his satisfaction, he has given up pacing and returned to the chair. With his face in his hands he returns to contemplation of his probable futures, all of them dire. He looks up at the sound of the door opening to see Karvelas returning. The policeman gives him an opaque look and closes the door softly behind him. "Your Mr. Melville has disappeared," he says.

"I'm not surprised." Pascual folds his hands on the table and waits.

Karavelas sits heavily, fatigue showing. Pascual realizes he must have been hard at work since the wee hours of the morning. "Nobody has heard of him at that address."

"He probably left shortly after I did, last night. He took back the phone he'd given me, too. I imagine the credit card will have been canceled as well."

"So. He has abandoned you."

"So it would seem."

"Leaving me to decide what to do with you."

"Any ideas?"

Karvelas makes him wait for an answer, drumming fingers softly on the table. "First I have to decide if you're telling the truth."

"If I had anything to do with these murders, why would I have stayed in Athens? Why wouldn't I have been the one to disappear? Instead of hanging around to be questioned, with such a weak story?"

"Criminals give me weak excuses all the time. But I agree, in this case you look like the . . . what do they say? The fall guy."

Pascual raises his hands. "All I have to prove Melville exists is the cell phone number he gave me. Even if he's discarded the phone, it will tell you something. You'll be able to trace the movements of whoever had it, won't you?"

Karvelas shrugs. "Perhaps. I'm not sure it's worth my trouble. There's no doubt who killed those four people last night. If Sabine Degitz hadn't told me about you, I would probably have completed my report this morning. A mentally disturbed refugee slashed two fellow refugees to death along with a Greek nurse and then killed himself. I could write it up now, and all that would happen would be that there would be another demonstration tomorrow against the flood of migrants into Greece. Nobody would question it. Nobody's questioning it now, in fact. We gave the press a statement and only one journalist asked why these refugees received such special treatment. I told him to go ask the UN refugee commissioner. I don't know what Sabine Degitz has told him."

"Sabine Degitz should corroborate my account. She knew they were coming, she knew the Emiratis would not be pleased. I discussed this with her before I went to Yemen."

Karvelas nods. "She was very careful when she spoke to me. Despite her shock. That makes me think she knows more than she said. But she confirmed what you told me. Except she said that you never mentioned a second man. Qasim was not supposed to be there, and it was you who brought him."

"That's right. But I didn't know he was a killer. I can't prove that, of course."

"And if you're lying and planned the killing yourself, I can't prove that." The look on Karvelas's face is shading to disgust. For a moment he and Pascual just stare at each other, and then the policeman says, "They planted him, didn't they?"

Pascual nods. "Like a magician forcing a card, they forced Qasim on me."

"Your man at the prison takes the bribe, but he makes sure Husseini will never have the chance to talk, to embarrass the regime. Very clever."

"Extremely. Are you going to charge me with anything?"

Karvelas laughs, a little puff of disdain. "What can I charge you with?"

"Stupidity? Credulity?"

"Association with criminals, perhaps." He sighs and pushes away from the table. "No, I'm not going to charge you. I'm going to write my report as I told you and refer further questions to the UN. As for you, I have been asked to hold you a little bit longer."

Pascual does not like the sound of this. "Asked by whom?"

"By a man who has finally called me back after a great deal of time wasted on the telephone talking to people at the American embassy. You would be surprised how difficult it is to contact the Central Intelligence Agency. They don't list their telephone number. But they are sending someone to talk with you. He should be here shortly."

"You're lucky he believed you. I bet cops deal with lunatics claiming to be with the CIA all the time." The man from the embassy is not what Pascual expected. Rather than another generic Caucasian, this one is Black, impeccably groomed and dressed to the nines in a summerweight linen suit and maroon tie, no doubt to forestall the usual bigoted assumptions due to the mahogany hue of his skin. His hair is shaped in a modest flattop and his mustache is a trim chevron. The look he is sending across the table at Pascual is scathing.

"I didn't claim to be with the CIA," Pascual says. "I claimed that the man who sent me to Yemen claimed to be with the CIA."

"And did the man who sent you to Yemen give you permission to broadcast that association?"

Pascual has had enough. "Cut the shit, will you? I was hired to do a job and I did it. Then the thing blew up in my face. I wasn't going to lie to the cops. That's Melville's job. Where the hell is he, anyway?"

"I don't know anybody named Melville. If you mean the officer in charge of the operation you participated in, he has left Athens and is probably back in the States by now. As far as he knew, the job was over. It should be over. The only reason it isn't is that you let the Emiratis play you for a fool."

"Is that what happened?"

"I think that's pretty clear, isn't it? If the way you told it to me is the way it went, I'd say they planned it from the start. Did you really think they'd just toss another al-Qaeda detainee into the deal like that? Right there, all your alarm bells should have gone off."

Pascual remembers Qasim bleeding into the dust, hands clasped, pleading. "Well, they didn't. All I saw was a man in distress, and I thought I had a chance to help him."

"Well, you helped him all right. You helped him do what he was ordered to do. The Emiratis probably were holding his father or somebody as a hostage. Kill these people or we kill your father. That's a pretty classic way to operate. Your guy Rashid pocketed the money, and he made sure nobody would hear from Ali Husseini again, too. Pretty slick work."

Pascual finds no comment to make. "What happens to me now?" he says.

"Regrettably, nothing. We just see if we can make you go away and keep your mouth shut. I can probably get you out of here without going through the media swarm down there on the sidewalk, but after that you're on your own. I'd get the fuck out of Greece tonight if I were you. And let me make clear, you really are expected to keep your mouth shut. My job is to make sure this massacre doesn't go down in history as a CIA fuckup. And step one is, make clear to you that if you ever talk about this to anyone, we will come down on you like a ton of bricks. Do I need to remind you of the ways we might do that?"

Pascual does his best to look contrite. "No. You don't. You can count on my full cooperation."

Pascual is pleased to find that the credit card Melville gave him has not yet been canceled, allowing him to retrieve his things from the St. George and pay his bill. The clerk at reception is apologetic about the need to charge him for a second night, but Pascual airily waves it off. It is not his money. He has missed his plane, but the idea of fleeing to the airport and grabbing the first available seat heading west still has a certain appeal. Instead he stands uncertainly for a moment under the hotel marquee before allowing a flunky to summon a cab for him, and when one appears he tells the driver to take him to the central railway station.

This proves to be an unimpressive structure that looks more like a bus station, but it has what Pascual is looking for: first a cash machine and then, separated from the station by several lanes of traffic and a small plaza, a modest-looking hotel. Pascual squats in a sheltered corner of the waiting room and digs into his bag to pull out his zippered toilet pouch. From this he extracts an envelope containing his Spanish passport in the name of Pascual March and his CaixaBank card. He stuffs Pascual Rose's passport into the envelope and replaces it in the pouch.

The cash machine displays his suddenly immense cash balance and obligingly coughs up a hundred euros. Pascual makes the short hike to the hotel and takes a room. As the sun begins to approach the hills to the west, Pascual stands on the balcony outside his room and considers his needs. Food first of all; he has not eaten since his idyllic breakfast. After that a plan, something better than fleeing to the airport.

On one hand, Pascual wants desperately to get out of Greece and be back on familiar ground. On the other he is beginning to feel a slow combustion of anger, like a peat fire smoldering deep in the earth. He has been played for a fool, and he has been given a million dollars to ensure that he remains a contented fool.

His long-standing habit of memorizing phone numbers stands him in good stead, and he taps Sabine Degitz's number into his Greek phone. He gets her voice mail and says simply, "Please call me. I know who ordered the killings at the clinic." Then he leaves the hotel and finds a hole-in-the-wall restaurant where he downs a souvlaki sandwich and a glass of Roditis, watching foot traffic and reviewing everything he knows.

■ ■ ■ ■

His phone goes off as he is ambling back to the hotel in the cooling evening air, street lights coming on, aimless transients drifting past wary locals on the pavements. Pascual sees Sabine Degitz's number and answers the call. "Anything you know you should communicate to the police," she says without preamble.

"I've just spent the day with the police. They know who did the killing and that's all they want to know. What's behind it, they don't care about. Not enough to pursue, anyway. The only person who wants to pursue it is me."

There is a silence. Pascual strolls, an aimless transient, phone to his ear. "Why would you want to pursue it?" says Degitz. "You work for them."

"You don't know who I work for. If you mean that I was the instrument they used, you're right. That doesn't mean I share their agenda."

"And what is your agenda?"

"My first agenda is to contact the person who knows the most about Ali Husseini and what he knew. The reason I'm calling you is that I want to talk to Zarlik."

Pascual has reached the corner where his hotel sits. He steps out of the way of his fellow strollers and stands at the curb, watching traffic rush by, watching the people waiting for buses in front of the station, waiting to hear if he has guessed right. "I don't know who that is," says Sabine Degitz.

"I think you do. Your hesitation betrays you. I think you know who Zarlik is, and I think I do, too. I think I met her yesterday."

Pascual waits. At length Degitz says, "What makes you think that?"

"When I asked you if you were going to notify our counterparty that Ali Husseini was safe, you said you already had. You might have made a phone call when I was not present, but when you weren't in my presence you were with Husseini and his wife or with the clinic personnel, and I didn't think you would have made the call then. But your intern was with you the whole time. Nela? Is that her name? I knew that there was a personal link between you and Zarlik. That's why we were to deliver Husseini to you. Oh, yes, and I looked up the name Zarlik. In Turkic mythology Zarlik is the goddess of justice. Female. So I'm guessing your Nela is the hacker who calls herself Zarlik."

The silence this time goes on long enough that Pascual begins to wonder if the call has dropped. He is about to ask if Degitz is still there when she says, "I will call you," and the line goes dead in Pascual's ear.

16

When the buzzing of his phone wakes him, Pascual cannot think for a moment where he is. A hotel room, a cheap one, to judge by the smell of insecticide and the clattering of the decrepit air conditioner, but where? By the time he has kicked free of the covers and laid his hand on his phone, he has remembered. Who is calling him in Athens at two o'clock in the morning? "What?" he growls into the phone.

"You wanted to talk to me."

This is not Sabine Degitz; it takes Pascual a moment to pin the voice to Nela Nachtnebel's face. "Yes," he says after a moment spent gathering his thoughts. "Though I was hoping to be awake when I did."

"You can take a nap later. Where are you?"

"At a hotel near the train station. Where are you?"

"You'll know when you get here. Give me the name of the hotel and get dressed. You're going to get a tour of Athens by night."

Pascual has a feeling this will have little to do with dance clubs and after-hours bars. He manages to recall the name of the hotel and gives it to her. After a brief pause she says, "They can be there in ten minutes. Wait for them in front."

Who "they" might be is another intriguing question. Pascual ponders it while he dresses. No longer groggy but with lead in his step, he takes the elevator down to a deserted lobby and nods at a startled night clerk as he passes the desk. "Can't sleep," he says with a rueful smile. The desk man merely stares.

Outside the hotel, the cool night air revives him a little, as does the approach of an African prostitute in a miniskirt, tube top and not much else. When Pascual declines her offer she totters away on her stiletto heels with a look of infinite sadness. The only other attention he attracts comes from furtive male figures conferring on the corner across the street, and by the time the Toyota Yaris slews to the curb Pascual is beginning to wonder who will get to him first, his ride or the muggers.

The man in the driver's seat is a villainous-looking character with a beak for a nose and a black mustache and goatee. "Get in," he says. Pascual stoops to see inside the car and makes out two other figures, one in front and one in back. He opens the rear door and gets in, coming face to face with the man in the back seat, this one considerably larger than he is, bearded and broad in the beam, a heavyweight wrestler, with a shaven head that gleams dimly in the faint light. Pascual barely has time to close the door before the driver jams it in gear. As they lurch away from the curb the man on the passenger seat in front twists to talk to Pascual. This one is thinner and has hair, black and curly. "Give me your phone," he says with an accent that Pascual pegs as Arabic. "I give it back to you after."

Pascual hands it to him. The car screeches around a corner and pulls to the curb just long enough for the Arab to jump out and slam the door. As the car accelerates again Pascual watches out the back window as the Arab recedes, Pascual's phone with him. Pascual turns and says to the driver, "You'll want to search me, won't you? There's more than one way to track a person, and for that matter, I could be carrying a weapon."

"We will search you," the driver says. This one sounds Greek. "And maybe we have weapons, too."

Pascual lurches toward his massive seatmate as the car takes another turn on two wheels. He raises his hands. "Peace." They speed along a main thoroughfare, deserted in the dead of night. Pascual has only the most rudimentary awareness of Athens geography and could not begin to say where they are. They enter a stretch overhung by trees on either side, and then there is a long building beyond a fence on the right, perhaps a museum. The driver slows and steers into a narrower street. "Where are we going?" says Pascual.

"Safe place," says the driver.

"Safe from whom?"

"From police."

Balconied facades rise into the dark on either side. Pascual sees shop fronts and apartment entrances, old construction and new, all slightly down-at-heels, the whole overlaid with an extravagant encrustation of graffiti. A right turn, a left, another left, a complicated intersection where the street forks, and Pascual has lost all sense of direction. They are climbing now, the ground rising. Another turn brings them into a wider street, and suddenly the Toyota pulls over at the foot of a broad flight of steps ascending a hillside through a gap between buildings. The driver points. "You go up the stairs. At the top you go left. You walk till you see a basketball court. There you turn right and walk through the park. Walk to the end and wait. Understand?"

Pascual repeats his instructions and gets out. The Toyota speeds away and he begins to climb. The climb is not trivial, more than fifty steps, and Pascual is panting by the time he reaches the top. Here a narrow road runs along the hillside. Pascual rests for a moment, looking up and down the poorly lit lane, trying to anticipate. He decides this is most likely a test to see if he is being followed. He walks a hundred meters or so, goes up another short flight of steps, and there is a fenced enclosure, unlit, in which he can just make out two opposing basketball hoops. A road paved with flagstones leads uphill to the right.

Pascual walks. It soon becomes very dark. The road commences to wind, and flights of steps and smaller paths branch off to either side. Around him, as far as he can make out against the glowing urban sky, is the usual Mediterranean grab bag of cypresses, pines, eucalyptus. There are lamps on high poles at intervals but the intervals are very long.

Pascual stops to listen. He would be surprised if he were alone; an urban park in a distressed city in full economic and demographic crisis is certain to be full of people sleeping rough. Soft steps scrape on the hard ground somewhere not too far away, and Pascual hurries on. Soon the path begins to descend and lighted windows gleam through the trees. A final hairpin turn delivers him to a ramp leading down into a narrow street. He stops at the foot of it and stands with his hands in his pockets, listening to the murmur of the vast city. Twenty meters down the street, the Toyota starts up, flashes its headlights, and pulls away from the curb to draw even with him. The driver motions for him to get in the back; the wrestler has moved to the front.

"Did I pass?" Pascual says as he settles onto the seat.

"You are maybe a spy," says the Greek, "but you are alone."

The ensuing drive is not long. Plunging back into the neighborhood at the bottom of the hill, the Toyota makes several more turns and comes to a stop in front of a recessed entryway in a stuccoed facade. Wooden shutters with missing slats cover the windows. The driver parks and everyone gets out. "Now we search you," the Greek says. "Put your hands on the wall."

Pascual complies and the wrestler pats him down. "No weapon." The Greek hands him his wallet after perusing the receipt from the St. George Hotel and a Marseille bus card. "You are French?"

"I'm an international citizen. No borders, right?"

The Greek is not amused. "For poor people they have borders."

"And always will," says Pascual.

The wrestler puts his fingers in his mouth and whistles once, looking up at the top floor. He waves at a figure who appears on the balcony and shortly thereafter the buzzer on the street door sounds. Pascual follows the Greek into the building and up a narrow flight of stairs to the top floor. The Greek knocks once and leads Pascual into a small entryway that gives onto a living room softly lit by a single floor lamp.

For a moment Pascual is transported back to his student days in Paris; here is the same jumble of found and improvised furniture, the same strident prints on the walls, the same smell of incense and unwashed dishes.

The same layabouts draped over the furniture, too: the male one with stringy fair hair and tattoos covering his arms, the female one the person Pascual has come to see. It takes him a moment to recognize her because in place of the nicely turned-out intern from Geneva is an anarchist Amazon. The black T-shirt proclaims *NO GODS NO MASTERS*. The jeans are ripped at the knees. Uncombed, the hair now stands in spikes. The severe look in the hazel eyes is unchanged.

"Well," she says. "We meet again. I did not expect to."

"I didn't either. Then things happened."

"You could say that." She takes in the three other men with a look and says, "It's all right, thank you." The tattooed man stands, gives Pascual a dubious look, and follows the other two out of the room. She waves Pascual to the vacated chair and he sits.

Nela Nachtnebel waits a beat, staring at Pascual. "So, what's this nonsense about Zarlik?"

"I don't think it's nonsense. I don't think I'd be here if it was."

She stares for a long moment, conceding nothing. "Why the fuck does an ex-terrorist informer and CIA stooge want to talk to Zarlik?"

The sudden crudity in the smooth, practiced English is mildly shocking. Pascual crosses his legs, folds his hands in his lap and frowns. "Googled me, did you? Good for you. But don't believe everything you hear about CIA stooges. Not everybody who does things for governments does them because they believe in the mission."

"No, I'm sure there are mercenaries as well. How much did they promise you to help kill Ali Husseini?"

"Plenty. But they didn't mention the killing. And the money's not why I got involved. You know the expression carrot and stick?"

"Of course. What's the stick?"

"They have a box full of them. But let me answer your first question."

"Please do."

"I wanted to talk to you because you know what they're up to. And I want to help you expose it."

A faint breeze coming in through the open windows stirs the air. The skeptical look on Nela's face deepens. "Oh, dear me. A change of heart? Another one?"

"Not a change of heart. Just the reaction of a man who's been lied to and manipulated. Even a CIA stooge can be disgusted. They think they can buy my complicity. They're mistaken."

A few seconds go by as she looks down her nose at him. "You're telling me you had nothing to do with it?"

"I'm telling you I didn't know Qasim was a plant. They played me. They counted on my sympathy for a man in distress and exploited it. And now, if there are any repercussions they're going to blame me. The story they're prepared to sell is that the Emiratis set up Husseini to be killed. But I know it wasn't the Emiratis."

"Who was it?"

"It was the Americans. It was all set up so that Qasim didn't act until after you had released the data. My handler had to make sure he got that first. Then he flipped the switch. He did that by calling me. I was the one who gave Qasim the signal to kill. I put the money in his hand."

Pascual holds Nela's gaze as she considers this. "I knew it. I told them not to let you go upstairs."

"They should have listened to you."

Nela stares at Pascual for a long moment and says, "What do you want?"

"I want to join your team."

"I don't have a team. I work alone, and I get help when I need it. What kind of help can you offer?"

"Money, for one thing. I assume you have some operating expenses. And you've probably used up your credit with Sabine Degitz."

Nela frowns. "Sabine should have been more discreet. But then she doesn't have much experience in this kind of thing."

"How did you get her to cooperate with you?"

"I asked her. And I'm not going to tell you anything more than that. I've compromised her enough." Nela stares some more, and after a time a faint smile stretches the thin lips. "Money. Well, I suppose everyone has their price." Her eyes narrow. "I will need some time to think about this. You will stay at the same hotel?"

"Unless you can recommend someplace better."

"Stay there. We will return your phone tomorrow. I will contact you again tomorrow night." She stands abruptly and strides from the room. Pascual sits frozen until the wrestler appears in the doorway. "Come," he says. "We take you now. Bedtime."

17

Pascual rises late, awakened by the chambermaid's knock. He mumbles at her through the door and sits on the side of the bed, groggy, half-convinced the events of the wee hours were a dream. When he descends to the lobby the desk clerk calls to him. "A man returned your mobile phone. An Arab, I think. He said you left it in his car."

"Careless of me," says Pascual, duly thankful. He goes out into the sunshine and finds a place that serves him strong coffee and fried bread. He revives and begins to think. He finds that what seemed urgent in the dead of night looks rash and ill-considered in the light of day. He takes out his phone and stares at it. He can drop everything and be in Sara's arms tomorrow.

The smile on Ali Husseini's face, flying to Athens to be with his wife, comes vividly to mind. Pascual awakens the phone and taps Sara's number. "I'm staying in Athens for a few days," he tells her when the small talk is done. "I'll keep you informed."

He ends the call and sits with the phone in his hand, watching traffic and second-guessing himself. He is startled when the phone begins to vibrate angrily with an incoming call. The number is not one he has ever seen. Nela Nachtnebel with his marching orders? He answers. "Mr. Pascual Rose?" says a man's voice in his ear.

Pascual freezes. There is no benign explanation for a stranger who knows Pascual's name to have this number. "I'm afraid you have a wrong number," he says, knowing it is a futile gesture.

"Then Mr. Pascual March, perhaps. I might have mistaken the surname."

Pascual has a feeling that playing dumb will do nothing but postpone the interview. "Who are you?"

"My name is Khalid al-Mansouri. I must apologize for disturbing you, but I think you will find it to your advantage to speak with me." His English is smooth and lightly accented, the English of an Arab educated in Britain.

"How did you get this number?" Pascual says.

"You may remember that Inspector Karvelas of the Athens police recorded the number of your mobile phone when he detained you. He was good enough to pass it along to me."

"I see. And why do you wish to speak to me?"

"I am very interested in talking to you about Ali Husseini."

Warning lights begin to flash in Pascual's head. "In what capacity?"

"I am an officer of the State Security Directorate of the United Arab Emirates."

Pascual resists the urge to fling the phone away and run for it, mostly because he has no idea where he would go. "Hello?" says the voice in his ear.

"Still here. How do I know you're who you say you are?"

"I will be very happy to show you credentials. Can we meet?"

"You're in Athens?"

"Of course. May I suggest we meet at my country's embassy? You'll find it at . . . My God, these Greek names. I believe it's pronounced . . ."

He enunciates slowly. "Marathonodromon, Number 73."

The bottom drops out of Pascual's stomach. When he recovers his voice he says, "You'll forgive me if that doesn't appeal to me very much."

A soft chuckle sounds in his ear. "Quite understandable. Those Saudi scoundrels made sure nobody will ever feel safe walking into an Arab embassy again. Let us find a neutral site."

"Excuse me, but I'm having trouble understanding why it would be to my advantage to talk to you in the first place."

"Because you are about to be made the scapegoat for Ali Husseini's murder. And I don't believe it."

Pascual chews on this. "The police released me."

"It's not prosecution you have to worry about. It's notoriety. You have spent most of your life trying to avoid it. But every time something like this is attributed to you, your notoriety increases. You are in danger of becoming something that is extremely useful for any intelligence agency."

"What's that?"

"A professional scapegoat."

Pascual has been lied to many times, and has told more than his share, but he is still capable of recognizing the clear bell-like tone of truth. "Yes," he says. "I'm aware."

"The role can be well paid, but it does have its risks. Sooner or later it exposes one to retaliation."

Pascual sits with his phone to his ear, weighing indisputable truths against unknowable risks. "What do you propose?" he says.

"First, just a talk. I think it's to your advantage to have somebody like me in your corner. And I'd very much like to know what you know, because I was looking forward to speaking with Ali Husseini."

If you are going to cut and run, now is the time, Pascual thinks. He says, "Where do you suggest we meet?"

"We are in Athens. Where else but the Acropolis? I can meet you by the main ticket office, at the western end. We don't have to actually visit the thing, as it's expensive and we'd have to stand in line. But it's completely public, so you'll be quite safe. I'll be the Arab gent waiting in the shade. Shall we say one o'clock?"

The taxi driver who takes Pascual to the Acropolis advises him that it is folly to enter the Acropolis by the main entrance. "Many people, you wait two hours. I take you to special entrance, no waiting." When Pascual explains that he is meeting a friend, the driver shakes his head and lapses into a sulk. Pascual overtips to avoid fussing with change. A flagstone roadway leads through a grove of trees to a ticket kiosk where tourists stand in a long queue, sweating in the sun. A man rises from a stone bench in the shade of an olive tree and waves at Pascual.

In person Khalid al-Mansouri is much as Pascual imagined, tall, dark and if not handsome at least well-turned-out in a sky-blue jacket, tieless. His haircut, mustache and erect bearing are vaguely military. "How do you prefer to be addressed, then?" he says, shaking hands. "Are you Mr. Rose or Mr. March today?"

"Pascual will do. I thought Pascual Rose was dead, but he's been resurrected."

"Yes. You are a known quantity in the intelligence world. One of those figures who are referred to in the media as 'murky.' With no apparent fixed loyalties."

"Much against my will."

"I'm sure. Shall we walk a little? Just to gain a little separation from the crowd." He gestures with a brochure he is holding. "We may find a shady place to sit."

They find it a few meters farther on, where the path turns uphill. Ticket holders trudge past them, looking at the climb ahead like Sherpas at the foot of Everest. "I find I am quite content to appreciate the marvels of the Acropolis in printed form," al-Mansouri says, briefly opening the brochure with its pictures of the Parthenon and other monuments. He refolds it and his look goes serious. "I was quite distressed to hear of Ali Husseini's death."

Pascual looks into a pair of shrewd, very dark eyes. Ever since his phone buzzed he has been frantically wondering what to make of this wildcard he has suddenly been dealt. "You got here in a hurry."

"I was already here when Husseini was killed. I knew he was coming."

"How could you know that?"

"I was alerted by the men who failed to stop your plane from taking off at Al Rayan. Not directly, of course. I am the last person they would want to know that they were holding him. But I have my sources."

Pascual strives to make sense of this. "I'm sorry, you're going to have to give me a little background."

"Why don't I start with my credentials?" Al-Mansouri reaches inside the jacket and pulls out a leather ID holder, which he opens and presents to Pascual.

The falcon logo of the UAE crowns a card with text in Arabic and English: *United Arab Emirates – State Security Directorate – Colonel Khalid Muhammad al-Mansouri*. In the photo al-Mansouri stares at the camera, chin raised, a man who recognizes no obstacles.

Pascual hands back the wallet. "Why were you so interested in Ali Husseini?"

"Because he had information."

"About corruption in the Emirates?"

"That, and other things."

Pascual waits; when nothing further comes he says, "What I heard was that the powers that be in the Emirates were happy to have Husseini out of the way."

"No doubt some of them were. He had made himself a nuisance."

"And what makes you different? I would consider a member of the Security Directorate an element of the powers that be."

"Yes, but even the powers that be are expected to police themselves, in places that aspire to become world financial centers. When international bodies such as the Financial Action Task Force began to talk about gray-listing Dubai for its failures to police money-laundering, it got our attention. I had been looking for Ali Husseini for some time."

This strikes Pascual as plausible, but any good intelligence gambit will come cloaked in plausibility. Mind racing, he says, "If you'll excuse my saying so, you couldn't have been looking too hard. He was being held by your own army."

"Not exactly. When we withdrew our troops from Yemen a few years ago, certain functions were delegated to local forces we had trained. That included custody of prisoners taken in the fight against al-Qaeda. And those forces did not always keep reliable records."

"That's a wonderful formula for evading responsibility. If you'll excuse my saying so."

Al-Mansouri concedes the point with a nod. "Be that as it may, I sent men to look for Husseini and they failed to find him. When one of my informants received a report three nights ago that he was on a plane that had just left Al Rayan, having filed a flight plan for Athens, it was the first I'd heard of him in three years. I arranged to fly here myself. I arrived a few hours after you and Husseini did. But I was unable to find out where he had been taken. He was killed before I could arrange to speak with him."

Pascual looks at this from various angles, the urge to accept a proffered hand contending with a suspicion born of long experience. This man has neither threatened him nor offered him money, which puts him in a class of his own. "You've spoken with the police. So you know who killed him."

"Yes. But I don't know who put him up to it."

Pascual has a decision to make. More than one, in fact; he has to decide whether he can trust this man, and he has to decide how much to tell him, because he now has other confidences to protect. Al-Mansouri is staring placidly out across the park, evidently in no hurry. Pascual has a feeling the easygoing manner conceals other qualities without which a man does not rise to a high position in state security. Pascual comes to a decision, feeling like a diver stepping off the high platform. "The CIA killed him."

For a dramatic pronouncement, this has surprisingly little effect on al-Mansouri. He merely nods and says, "The CIA flew him out. You must have been in contact with them. You had no idea they were planning to kill him?"

"None."

Al-Mansouri waits for more and doesn't get it. "Who sent you to Yemen? Who gave you your orders?"

"He told me his name was Melville. He approached me in Marseille and met me in a safe house here. He paid me off and disappeared before Husseini was killed. The police couldn't find him. I also spoke with an officer from the embassy here, after Husseini was killed. He told me to keep my mouth shut."

"And what were your instructions? What did this Melville tell you?"

"I was supposed to go and negotiate Husseini's release. The agency wanted him freed."

"Why?"

"I was told that they had suffered a ransomware attack, and the price for getting their data back was to deliver Ali Husseini."

"To the UN?"

"That was the demand, yes. And they manipulated me into bringing Qasim out as well. To make sure Husseini didn't talk. But not until they had retrieved their data."

"How did they manage that?"

"They told me to give Qasim money, to compensate him. I believe that was the signal to kill."

Al-Mansouri's eyes narrow. "That was clever. That was . . . diabolical." His gaze lingers on Pascual for a moment. "There was another brutal crime just a few days ago that attracted a good deal of attention. In Monaco."

Pascual's stomach flutters. "Yes."

"It attracted my attention because the victim worked for a hedge fund known to serve Syrian interests." Al-Mansouri flicks something off his trousers with the brochure. "I made inquiries and was told that you were there."

"You are very well informed."

"I try. Why were you there?"

"Because Melville sent me. I was to be the broker in a disguised ransom deal. The man who died was killed because he questioned the transaction."

"I see. Was the ransom for Ali Husseini?"

"No. It was a ransomware attack. The Syrians had hacked the agency's computer system. And then they got hacked in turn. And the second hacker's demand was to free Ali Husseini. That's why I went to Yemen."

"You amaze me. Who was the second hacker?"

Pascual shrugs, judging a gesture is not quite explicit enough to be called a lie. "Evidently somebody who shares your concern with Husseini. And now you know as much as I do."

Al-Mansouri nods. "Except for one thing."

"What's that?"

"Why are you still in Athens?"

Pascual smiles to cover the fact that the question has caught him completely off guard. "Because I have nowhere else to go," he says. "I was living in genteel poverty in Marseille, and getting tired of it. The CIA paid me handsomely for my trip to Yemen, and I now have the luxury to choose where to go next. I decided to take few days to make the decision."

Al-Mansouri just looks at him, smiling faintly. "Well. I wish you luck. Did you talk with Husseini before he was killed?"

"Some, yes."

"And did he tell you anything about why he had been detained?"

"We didn't discuss that. He was just happy to be released. He was looking forward to being reunited with his wife."

Al-Mansouri assumes a mourning look. "Yes, I can imagine. Such a tragedy." He stands. "So you can tell me nothing more about the mysterious Mr. Melville?"

"Not much." Pascual rises reluctantly. He would rather go on sitting in the shade for a while. "I could give you a description."

Al-Mansouri begins to walk slowly uphill. "You have no way of contacting him?"

"He took back the phone he had issued me. I memorized his number, for what that's worth."

"Not much, probably." Al-Mansouri walks a few paces in silence, frowning, and then halts and turns to Pascual. "I have good relations with the CIA. I shall have to try to exploit them." Abruptly he reaches out and stuffs the brochure he has been holding into Pascual's shirt pocket. "I pass this along to you. I'm going to stroll a little farther and think about all this. You've been very helpful, thank you." He shakes hands and makes a slight bow.

Shambling back downhill, Pascual is struck by the oddity of al-Mansouri's gesture with the brochure. He pulls it out of his pocket. It is a standard tourist brochure, with full-color photos and semi-literate descriptions of the archaeological wonders in five languages. At the bottom of an inner fold a phone number is written in ink followed by the words *Don't hesitate to call me.*

Pascual goes in search of a taxi, wondering who al-Mansouri thinks may have been listening.

18

The buzzing of his phone at two in the morning does not awaken
Pascual this time for the simple reason that he has been unable to fall
asleep, expecting the call to come. He rolls wearily to grope for the
phone and when he puts it to his ear Nela says, "Christos and Tawfiq
will be there in ten minutes. Leave your phone at the hotel." She hangs
up before Pascual can reply.

Christos the driver is Greek; the wrestler is Tawfiq. Pascual tries
out his Arabic on him only to be informed brusquely he is Afghan.
Christos speeds back into the same area as the previous night, again
disorienting Pascual with a series of turns. The Toyota brakes abruptly
in the middle of a block, coming to a stop in front of a building Pascual
would have pegged as derelict, boarded up at street level with plywood
panels, a scabbed facade of plaster peeling off brick rising two stories
above it, pipes protruding from the plaster and running across the face
of the building with the look of a hasty amateur plumbing job. Graffiti
covers the front of the building: *FUCK ALL POLICE, NO BORDERS,
CLASS WAR.* Slogans in Greek, the anarchist A in a circle. And
here, *NO PASARAN*, the accent missing but nice to see somebody
remembers the history.

Everyone piles out. Tawfiq pushes through a metal door in a corner of the building. Christos motions for Pascual to follow. A flashlight app comes on and Tawfiq leads him up a flight of chipped concrete steps, Christos bringing up the rear. They go up two flights, the light washing over scarred cinder block walls with more of the endless graffiti, the heat increasing as they ascend. On the top landing Tawfiq pauses and turns to Pascual. "Quiet now," he whispers. "People sleeping." He leads Pascual through a broad doorway, stepping softly. Light coming in through cracked windows from the street is enough to show Pascual a vast, dark room, the building's structural columns running down it in ranks. Tawfiq trains his light on the floor to guide Pascual on a path through the maze of sleepers on the floor, some on mattresses and some on flattened cardboard boxes. An electric fan mutters near an open window, to no perceptible effect. As they make their way through the room, a child stirs and cries out, and a woman murmurs softly.

At the end of the room is another doorway and beyond it a short hall with doors opening off it, all of the locks torn out. Tawfiq goes to the end of the hall and around a corner and leads Pascual up a flight of narrow steps. Suddenly the air is cooler. At the top of the steps is an open window and a closed door with an intact latch. Tawfiq raps softly on the door, then opens it and motions for Pascual to enter. He goes into a long room with windows opening at the rear of the building onto a roofscape, beyond it lights rising up hillsides in the distance. Pascual judges that this once was an office, but it is now someone's home; there are bedclothes on an air mattress at the far end, water bottles and cooking gear on a small table, multiple electric cords spiderwebbing walls and the ceiling, all softly lit by a single lamp standing on a wooden crate.

Sitting cross-legged on a pile of cushions against a wall, Nela

Nachtnebel stabs twice at the keyboard of a laptop and then sets it on the floor beside her. Tonight she has softened the look: a loose tank top bares shoulders and arms; flowing *salwar* pants cover the long legs ending in bare feet.

Behind Pascual the door closes softly and he turns to see that his two escorts have left them alone. "Nice place," he says. "Reminds me of home."

Her look hardens. "Mock it if you want. For the people that live here, it's the only home they have."

"I'm not mocking. I've spent a lot of time in places like this."

One eyebrow rises slightly. "Have you? Not quite like this one, I think." She waves him to a folding chair, the only one in the room. "This district is called Exarcheia. It's a people's quarter. The anarchists have always been strong here. For a long time, the police didn't even try to enter."

"I think I read about some disturbances."

"Yes. A couple of years ago the new government decided they had to clean it up. What they meant was, close the squats, round up the migrants, chase out the poor and let the property tycoons buy up all the flats. So the rents have doubled, and most of the squats are gone. But not this one. They try to keep a low profile, and so far they have been left alone. If they weren't here they'd be in a camp on Lesbos, or someplace worse. There are more than fifty people living here. They've been kind enough to let me stay here for a few days. They have next to nothing, but what they have they share."

"Nobody is more generous than the poor. So the place last night was a decoy?"

"Of course. If it had been raided following your visit I wouldn't have been there. But I'd know you betrayed it."

"Good test, simple but effective. And Nela Nachtnebel is not your real name, I'm guessing. Night and fog, very dramatic."

"You can call me Nela. That much is real."

"I'm going to make another guess. I'm guessing you heard my conversation with that Emirati security officer today."

She shrugs. "Of course. Why do you think I wanted your phone overnight? By the way, while I was installing my application I checked it for other malware, and there was none. But anyone who has the number can track you if they can pressure the service provider, which police and intelligence agencies can and do. That's why I had you leave it at the hotel."

"I'm aware of the possibility. So you heard what I told him. I kept you out of it."

"Yes. So, what exactly do you hope to accomplish by collaborating with me?"

That, thinks Pascual, is an excellent question. "Ideally I'd get some justice for Ali Husseini and his wife. But if I've learned one thing, it's that intelligence agencies are very good at evading justice. So I suppose the next best thing would be to expose what they're doing. And that seems to be the kind of thing you do."

"When I can. Why don't you just go to the media?"

"I'd like to, but number one, I don't know the whole story, and number two I've been warned explicitly against that, and they have permanent leverage over me in the form of an implicit threat to my family. So my fingerprints can't be on this anywhere. But I can help you. Why don't you start by telling me the whole story? You've got the parts I don't know."

The look on her face tells him that the whole story is not something she hands out for free. "What are the parts you know?"

"I know some Syrians hacked the CIA and tried to ransom their data. Then you hacked the Syrians. And took their place. But instead of money, you wanted Ali Husseini. I don't know why."

"What did they tell you when they sent you to Yemen?"

"They told me he had written about corruption in the UAE."

"He had done that, yes. Then he went to Yemen. That's where he found the really bad things."

"And what were those?"

"Murder. Extrajudicial killings. Torture, illegal imprisonment, as you saw."

"That's bad, all right. But it wasn't exactly news. I don't think Ali Husseini was the only one who reported it."

"No, he wasn't." She hesitates. "But he had the bad luck to find out about something nobody else did."

Pascual sighs gently. If it killed Ali Husseini, you don't want to know it, he thinks. "And what was that?"

The hazel eyes narrow. "Why do you think the Americans wanted Husseini silenced?"

"Because they were implicated."

"Well, of course. The Americans and the Emiratis worked together against al-Qaeda in Yemen. The Americans trained the Emiratis, advised them, supplied them. I don't have a problem with that. I don't like jihadis any more than anyone else. But those drone strikes that killed all those al-Qaeda people also killed a lot of innocent Yemenis. And some of those Emirati death squads pulling men out of their homes in the night weren't one hundred percent Emirati."

"That would be a sensitive topic for the Americans, I can see."

"Yes. But a few extrajudicial killings weren't the real problem for them. The real problem was the Mukalla money."

Somewhere far out in the murmuring night a motorcycle accelerates with an angry roar that trails away into silence. "Tell me about the Mukalla money," says Pascual.

Nela frowns, concentrating. "In 2015 al-Qaeda captured Mukalla. When they took the city, the Mukalla branch of the central bank held more than a hundred million dollars in cash."

"Aha."

"Yes. Not surprisingly, when the Emiratis took back the city a year later, the money wasn't there. The whole operation was slightly . . . fishy, I think the word is. The Emiratis claimed they had fought a battle and killed a lot of Al Qaeda fighters, but some accounts said it wasn't much of a fight, more in the nature of a gentleman's agreement to let the jihadis leave town. The dirty little secret is that in the process of liberating the south, the Emiratis just co-opted a lot of al-Qaeda fighters and sent them off to fight the Houthis. They're all good Sunnis, and they don't like Shiites any more than they like Americans. Anyway, the cash from the bank just vanished. Depending on who you ask, the jihadis got away with something between one and two hundred million dollars."

"And what happened to it?"

"Well, that also depends very much on who you ask. The Yemeni government, or what's left of it, claims they located it. One of their special antiterrorist units trained by the Americans tracked the money to a fortified complex near Say'un, north of Mukalla. Al-Qaeda's still got a presence in that area. There was a fight, and the Yemenis were able to seize the money. They radioed their headquarters in Mukalla with the news and loaded the money on trucks. That's where the stories begin to diverge."

Pascual's lips tighten in a grim smile. "I've noticed that large amounts of money exert a force on memories, like gravity."

"Yes. The detachment was ambushed as they were en route back to Mukalla. There was another fight, and this time the Yemenis lost. The attackers killed most of them and made off with the money. The account that was made public said that it was al-Qaeda reinforcements, coming to rescue their money. But one of the Yemeni survivors had a different story."

She pauses, a flair for the dramatic asserting itself, and Pascual says, "What did he see?"

"It's rather what he heard. He lay hidden under a wrecked truck and listened as the attackers organized their escape. He said all the Arabic he heard was in the Gulf dialect."

Pascual frowns. "Not conclusive, in my opinion. Al-Qaeda has fighters from lots of different places."

"Including the United States?" She smiles at Pascual's startled reaction. "Yes. He said at least two of the attackers were Americans, speaking English."

Pascual sags back on his chair, exhaling. "My God."

"Yes. You can see why they wouldn't want the story to get out. Americans and Emiratis attacked elements of the Yemeni military, their allies, and stole a hundred million dollars?"

Pascual sits listening to myriad soft night noises, human and mechanical, near and distant. He wishes he could go back to sleep. He looks at Nela and says, "You're very well informed. How do you know all this?"

"I spoke to the survivor. His name was Muhammad Khamis. When he recovered from his wounds he decided it was time to get out of Yemen. While he was in Aden trying to arrange that, he spoke to Ali Husseini and told him the story. Husseini promised him he would investigate and publish. But he never got the chance."

"And what happened to Muhammad Khamis?"

"He managed to get out of Yemen and made it all the way to Germany. I spoke to him at a refugee center in Bamberg. I'd become interested in the situation in Yemen and was interviewing refugees."

"Well, you have him to testify, at least."

"Sadly, we don't. He never made it out of Bamberg. He died of the coronavirus in 2020."

Pascual sighs again and rubs his face. "So the story dies with Husseini."

"Until we find another eyewitness who's not afraid to talk. And who knows how long that will take? That's why I've decided to change my focus."

"To what?"

"To the money. I think it's recoverable."

Pascual has spent a good deal of time tonight meeting Nela's high-intensity stare, and he is beginning to find it hypnotic. He smiles. "You found it, didn't you?"

Nela nods. "I knew the CIA worked closely with the Emiratis in Yemen. That gave me a place to start. The Emiratis' security was weak, and I was able to get access to a privileged account on an archive server and look at their e-mail accounts. Their correspondence with the Americans was, of course, in English. That gave me an idea of what entities, if not what people, were involved. And I just started exploring. The CIA has fixed a lot of vulnerabilities, but I was able to get inside the firewall and into the DMZ. I got elevated privileges that gave me access to their Syslog server. And the first thing I saw was the Syrians."

"Ah, yes, the Syrians. Where did they come in?"

"I don't know exactly. They'd probably been working on the CIA for some time. They and the Iranians, probably working together. Anyway, I could see them trying to find a way into the CIA systems. And I could just sit and watch. I watched for a week and then they managed to find an out-of-date firewall and virtual private network system. The old story—some CIA employee had failed to install a software update. The Syrians got access to a whole range of accounts. They even beat the two-factor authentication, with a man-in-the-middle attack to hijack the sessions. They cracked the account and there it was."

"What? The money?"

"That's right. Not the cash. That, they probably shipped to Dubai and laundered right away. But the Syrians had found what looked very much like what I would have converted a large amount of stolen dollars to if I wished to hide it."

"What's that?"

In the soft lamplight Nela's hazel eyes are almost luminous. "Cryptocurrency."

Pascual begins to laugh, shaking silently. "Cryptocurrency, of course."

"You're familiar with it?"

"I have a passing familiarity with the concept. So the data my CIA guy was so concerned about was actually a stash of cryptocurrency?"

"It was an account on a crypto exchange run by the Turkish stock exchange."

"And the Syrians were able to break their security?"

"Probably by exploiting somebody's carelessness. The system was set up using a private blockchain, not a public one, like most cryptocurrencies use. In a public blockchain, everyone can see every transaction, and transactions are publicly validated. That makes it more secure. With a private blockchain, you have to be granted access. But if you can crack the security of someone who has been, you're in. And that's what the Syrians did."

"What did they do, lock up his wallet?"

"That's right."

"Why didn't they just steal the crypto?"

"They tried. But to actually get the key to a wallet you need a really disastrous security failure by the owner. They could see what was in the wallet and block access to it, but they couldn't actually siphon off the crypto."

Pascual frowns. "So they monetized it by demanding ransom? But what incentive does the CIA have to pay? It makes no sense to pay money just to get your money."

"Unless the ransom demanded is significantly lower than the amount that's locked up. You pay us ten million to regain access to your hundred million in cryptocurrency."

Pascual whistles softly. "You think that's what's in the wallet?"

"I know it is. I could see it. That account holds crypto worth something over a hundred million dollars. Approximately what was stolen in Mukalla. I know, money is fungible. Is it the same money? I don't know. But it's equivalent, and the people who are holding it are probably the ones who stole the Mukalla money. So I think I'm justified in trying to recover it."

Pascual shakes his head in wonder. "Recover it? How? You unlocked the wallet in exchange for Ali Husseini, didn't you? They've got their money back."

"They've got access to the wallet again. But that's not the end of the story. Not yet, not if we move fast."

"You're already moving too fast for me. First of all, are you sure the crypto is still there? If I had just fought off an attempt to steal a whole lot of money, I think the first thing I'd do would be to move it someplace safer."

"It was there as of this morning. I checked."

"You can do that?"

"Yes. When I restored their access to the wallet, I left a back door which they haven't detected yet. I can still see the account. Yes, they are probably going to move the crypto at some point. Maybe very soon. But I don't think they'll do anything hasty with a hundred million dollars, and that probably means enough delay for us to have a chance. Anyway, we lose nothing by trying."

"There's that. So how do you recover a hundred million in cryptocurrency?"

Nela stirs from her cross-legged position, stretching long legs out across the floor. Frowning in concentration, she is a cat sizing up the entrance to the mouse hole. "This is not ordinary cryptocurrency."

"What's so special about it?"

"This is crypto backed by gold."

Pascual gives it a couple of seconds' thought. "Whose gold?"

"Turkey's, mostly. Turkish banks, to be precise. Now made available to investors via cryptocurrency. A Turkish bank developed a blockchain-based system to digitize gold assets. Each unit of crypto represents a gram of gold stored in the vaults of the Turkish stock exchange in Istanbul. The bank can issue new tokens if more gold is deposited, and as the gold price has risen over the past few years, a great deal of gold has been deposited. The system allows tokens to be transferred, bought and sold. About three months ago the wallet we're interested in was created. It seems the CIA has decided that asset-backed crypto has a future."

"All right. I'm waiting to hear how you can recover any of it."

"Well, until you walked in here and offered to help me, I wasn't sure I could. It will require funding."

"How much?"

"Difficult to give you a figure. But there are always expenses. Logistics. But mostly it will require . . . I think the word is audacity."

That would be the word, Pascual thinks, admiring the force of personality in those hazel eyes. "I can supply the money. I'll leave the audacity to you. So you think you can succeed where the Syrians failed? Swipe the crypto?"

"No. That would be too hard. There's a better way. As I said, every unit of this currency is backed by a unit of physical gold, held in a vault in Istanbul. And if you choose, you can redeem your crypto for actual gold."

She pauses, as if making sure Pascual is following. He says, "Hang on. You want to switch an electronic asset that can be moved around the world at the touch of a button for a physical asset that sits in a warehouse."

"For a document signifying ownership, actually. If you choose to redeem your crypto, you are given an account with the gold transfer system set up by the banks. And every account comes with an electronic vault warrant, a certificate issued by the warehouse that tells you the specifics of the gold you own, weight and serial numbers and so forth, and entitles you to take possession of it at any time. Most people, of course, choose to keep their gold in the warehouse and trade the contracts."

"So . . . you redeem your gold and get the electronic warrant. What do you do with it? Sell the gold?"

Nela's eyebrows rise, as if in surprise at his obtuseness. "No. That would require us to execute a transaction on the gold transfer system, completely transparent and trackable. It would exchange the gold for a more portable asset, certainly, but it would also be a completely traceable asset. We would have to launder the money. That is doable, but it's time-consuming. Who would you have them send the proceeds to? Do you have a nice anonymous account ready to receive it?"

"Actually, I do. Several, in fact. But the CIA knows all about them."

"So then what we need is to get the gold off the radar, fast. And there's only one way to do that. I would simply take the metal off warrant."

"What does that mean?"

She gives him an impatient look. "That means I notify the exchange that I wish to take delivery of the metal." She blinks a few times as Pascual digests this, and finally she vents a hiss of exasperation and says, "Yes. Very simple. I want to steal the gold itself."

A silence follows, during which Pascual gapes in disbelief and Nela waits impatiently for a reaction. "The actual physical gold," Pascual says. "You want to steal a hundred million dollars' worth of gold bars."

"That's right."

"From a vault in Istanbul."

"No." Nela leans forward and clasps her hands, assuming a look of saintly patience, like a preschool teacher dealing with a particularly dim child. "Getting it out of the vault is the easy part. All we have to do is take it off warrant. We do that electronically. The gold will be removed from the vault and delivered wherever we want, as long as it's inside Turkey. We have to provide an address in Turkey."

"And do you have an address in Turkey?"

"No. That's where you and your money come in."

Pascual finally sees it. "You want me to go to Istanbul and find a place to store the gold."

"Not for very long. Just to take delivery. Then we would send the gold wherever we decide it should go. We can ship it, like any other commodity. By truck, by ship, by air freight. You just need to pay the shipping company. That's what you're going to pay for, with your money."

Pascual squeezes his eyes shut, fingers to his temples. "Wait a minute. You want to redeem the cryptocurrency for gold. Then you want to arrange to take delivery of the gold. All this is something you do online, right? In the cryptocurrency account? And won't all this be visible to the account holder?"

"It would be, if he's looking. He might not be. I can turn off any notifications that may be activated. And I can set up a spoof page that looks like the account interface and redirect him there when he logs in. It will look normal but won't reflect any activity on the account."

"I don't think a fake page will fool him for long."

"Of course not. But it should give us a window in which to work. One other advantage we have is that the system provides two methods to request delivery of the physical gold, perhaps as a backup in case of system failure. You can click on a printable form, fill in the details such as the delivery address, and fax it to the exchange. And that won't be traceable."

"How long a window do we need?"

"That depends on how fast they can deliver the gold. We will verify all the procedures and the delivery date before we begin the process. If we prepare properly, by the time the CIA realizes what's happening, the delivery process will be underway. Then it will be a race between their efforts to get information from the exchange and the lorry taking our gold from one building to another in Istanbul."

Pascual is beginning to feel lightheaded, perhaps from fatigue. "I still think it's insane."

"Why?"

Pascual sighs and resettles himself on the chair. "Number one, gold bars are very heavy. And bulky. You'll need a truck, several trucks."

"It's an interesting logistical problem, but it's manageable. Can you follow some basic arithmetic?"

"If you don't go too fast."

"We are talking about roughly a hundred million dollars. At the current gold price, that's the value of about fifty thousand troy ounces of gold. There are of course different shapes and sizes of bars, and I don't know what form our bars will be in. But the one-kilogram bar is not uncommon. A one-kilogram bar contains about thirty-two ounces. Do the math and you will see we'll have something over fifteen hundred one-kilogram bars. That type of bar is about the size of your mobile phone. I should think one medium-sized lorry would be able to move fifteen hundred mobile phones. Perhaps even a small one."

"If the shock absorbers hold out. That's a ton and a half of gold. It will attract a hell of a lot of attention, too. You may get it off the online radar, but it will hop right on a different radar. What do you think will happen when you walk into a shipping office in Istanbul and tell them you want to ship a hundred million dollars' worth of gold somewhere? The news will be all over town in an hour."

"So we do it privately. We buy our own truck. Money's good for that sort of thing."

"Who's going to load and unload the truck, drive the truck, guard the truck against hijackers? Bribe border officials and customs inspectors, for that matter? Or are you planning to stay in Turkey? Just what were you thinking of doing with a hundred million dollars in gold bullion?"

"I have a destination in mind. You'll forgive me if I keep that to myself for the moment. Basic security."

"Fair enough. Can I run a couple of thoughts by you?"

"Please do."

"I'm assuming you're not in this to get rich."

"Of course not."

"You want to make a statement."

"A political statement, yes."

"Then if I were you, the last thing I would want would be to take possession. I certainly wouldn't rent a space that would be traceable to me and tell somebody to deliver the gold there."

She bristles, just perceptibly. "All right, what would you do?"

"I'd have the gold delivered where it makes a statement just by showing up."

"Such as?"

"Oh, I don't know. The Yemeni embassy? That's who it belongs to, right? You could send an explanatory note along with it."

"I actually considered something like that. But Yemen is in chaos. Is there a legitimate government in Yemen to take possession?"

"All right, how about the office of the Turkish newspaper with the largest circulation? Let them figure out where it came from and what the story is. That would ensure maximum exposure, if that's really what you're after. In any event, I'd stay well out of its way. I wouldn't go near the stuff. You can do everything you want to do remotely, can't you?"

Her look goes very thoughtful. "Of course. There's only one problem."

"What's that?"

"I've already promised it to someone."

"At the destination you mentioned?"

"Yes."

"And they have to have the physical gold? They can't handle cryptocurrency?"

"That's not the issue. As I explained, converting the crypto and taking the gold is our only option. We can't steal the crypto, but we can steal the gold."

"Great. Have it delivered directly to your beneficiaries, then."

"Easier said than done. They are not in a position to take delivery, not now. And the theft has to happen fast. That means taking the gold ourselves, before the crypto is moved. We'll hide it and then work out the logistics."

Pascual has run out of ammunition, at least for the moment. "So you want me to go to Istanbul . . ." He leaves it hanging in the air.

"Immediately. Is that a problem?"

Pascual shakes with quiet laughter. "Not at all. I'm sure I can get to Istanbul fairly easily. The problems start when I get there. I don't speak Turkish, I don't know the city. I wouldn't know where to begin to rent a warehouse."

"Don't worry. I speak Turkish." Nela smiles. "And I'm coming with you."

Pascual is vividly reminded of the time he was persuaded by older children to sit in a gardener's handcart, which was then promptly shoved down a steep hill. Remember how that ended, he tells himself. Aloud he says, "I will need to go and collect my things from the hotel."

20

The sky has begun to lighten when Pascual comes out onto the sidewalk, following Tawfiq. "I call him," says Tawfiq, pulling out his phone. Pascual gives in to a massive yawn and stands for a moment with his eyes closed, enjoying the cool dawn air. Tawfiq is muttering into his phone. Pascual takes a couple of aimless steps and his gaze goes off down the street. The window of a car parked on the opposite side of the street twenty meters away rises noiselessly, slowly obscuring the driver's face with a reflection of the building opposite. Pascual turns back toward Tawfiq.

"He come now," says Tawfiq, putting away the phone. "Very soon."

Pascual nods. Who was that man? For an instant he is sure he has seen that face before; then he dismisses the idea. A common type, thickset with a shaved head, glowering at the world, no doubt because he has lost his hair. Or because he has to go to work at five in the morning.

Tawfiq is pointing. "He come." Pascual sees Christos's Toyota speeding up the narrow street. His eye falls on the parked car. The reflections on the windshield hide the man behind the wheel. The Toyota stops in front of him and Pascual nods his thanks to Tawfiq and walks around to the passenger side of the Toyota. He gets in, taking one last look at the car twenty meters away. It has not moved. Pascual frowns as the Toyota starts with a lurch. He is suddenly concerned by that face he saw disappearing as the car window rose. He is certain he has seen it before. Somewhere recently, in Athens no doubt. At the police station? He saw officers in a big room with many desks, officers poking their heads into the interrogation room. That would make sense, Pascual thinks. Still suspicious of his role in the killings, the Athens police have sent someone to watch him.

Or does it make sense? Why here? Was he followed from the hotel? Or are the police watching the squat? The Toyota takes a corner, shooting onto a main boulevard, free of traffic in the early morning. Suddenly Pascual's heart is thumping, his sleep-deprived mind starting to work again. Whoever the man is, the fact that a face Pascual knows has appeared in front of the building where he has just spent two hours talking with Nela Nachtnebel aka Zarlik, cannot possibly be good. Where have I seen that face before? He closes his eyes, recalling it. The round hairless skull, the jowls, that frown.

When he remembers, Pascual swears aloud, startling Christos and drawing an angry look. "What?"

"Stop. Go back." Pascual gropes for the right words. "Please. You have to go back. That man."

Christos puts his eyes back on the road and corrects his course with a swerve. He has not even slowed. "What? What man?"

"The man in the car." Pascual pounds the dashboard. "Stop. Just please stop, pull over here." He motions to the curb. "Stop, please." Pascual slaps at his shirt pocket for his phone and remembers he left it at his hotel. "Danger."

"Danger, where?" Christos is finally braking, veering to the curb, shooting an alarmed look at his mirror, then scowling furiously at Pascual. The car comes to a halt with a screech of tires.

"Back there. At the squat. Call Nela on your phone, please."

"Who?"

"Nela, Zarlik, whatever you call her. Call her on your phone. She's in danger." He motions frantically, mimicking a phone to the ear.

Christos pulls out his phone in slow motion, scowling at Pascual. "What danger?"

"That man I saw. In the parked car. He's dangerous. Just please call her."

Christos shrugs extravagantly. "I don't have her number."

"Whose number do you have? Back there, at the squat."

"Tawfiq."

"Call Tawfiq. Tell him not to let anyone in. And go back, please." He flails, motioning for Christos to turn around.

Christos growls something in Greek but does what he is told, thumbing his phone and putting it to his ear. After a moment he says, "Look out for man in car. Don't let him come in. We come back. OK?" He is already cranking the wheel and wrenching the car out onto the boulevard in a U-turn. He responds to whatever Tawfiq says with a grunt and stuffs the phone away, driving one-handed. "Who is this man?"

"A Syrian criminal. He's probably not alone. They killed a man in Monaco last week." Pascual can see the man so clearly now, in the office of Zenobia Capital, in his motorcycle jacket, telling Pascual that the key has been sent. And here, in a car, two minutes ago. As the Toyota squeals around a corner, Pascual strives to order his thoughts. If the Syrians are here in force, he stands no chance; nobody does.

The return trip seems to take forever, the Toyota avoiding parked cars by centimeters as it shoots up the one-way streets. Christos is muttering things Pascual cannot understand. Pascual is quelling panic. The only hope is that the man he saw is an advance party, here only to watch. As he forms the thought Pascual realizes that even in that case the situation is desperate. He orients himself, and as the Toyota slows for the final turn he says, "All right. Slow now. If we're lucky they're just watching. But you may have to call the police."

Christos glares. "No police. You crazy? What's the danger?"

"Just drive." Pascual grips the door handle as the Toyota goes around the corner. Ahead nothing is happening. Parked cars line both sides of the street, a quiet block just after sunrise, nobody stirring yet. At the far end of the block the pitted facade of the squat looms over the street. Pascual looks for the car the Syrian was in. He failed to note the model; it was dark blue.

And what are you going to do when you see him? Pascual has no answer.

"Slow now." Here is the car. Reflections are not an issue at this angle and Pascual sees that it is empty. Twenty meters further up, on the other side of the street, the door to the squat is ajar. "Stop." Pascual leaps out of the Toyota and crosses the street at a trot. He crosses the sidewalk in two strides and pushes the door open. Light from the street illuminates the concrete steps and the glistening tendrils of blood that have almost reached the bottom step. Halfway up, Tawfiq lies unmoving with his eyes open, the gaudy smears of blood testimony to his efforts to climb the stairs as he bled rapidly to death from a cut throat. A cry comes down the stairwell, a woman's cry of alarm, followed by an angry murmur of multiple voices.

You need to go up there, Pascual thinks. You need to defend these people, defend Nela.

His limbs refuse to move. There is nothing you can do, he thinks. You will only get your throat cut like Tawfiq. Above him men are shouting. You are a coward, Pascual thinks.

Frantic peals on a car horn behind him startle Pascual out of his paralysis. He stumbles out onto the sidewalk to see Christos standing by the Toyota, motioning frantically, phone to his ear. "Come!"

Pascual dashes to the car and they both get in. "Tawfiq's dead. They're attacking the squat."

"Yes. We meet Nela behind. Come!" Christos has the car in gear and accelerating before Pascual can close the door. They tear past the squat. At the end of the block Christos goes left, the wrong way up a one-way street, and floors it.

Pascual is bewildered. "Where's Nela?"

"Coming." Christos takes a left into a wider street, a thoroughfare. He jams on the brakes and slews to the curb. "Here." He points at the buildings opposite. "Up there."

Pascual understands. He jumps out of the car and stands, heart pounding. The roofline is sharp against a sky growing lighter. Suddenly Nela is there, at the edge of the roof three stories up, a cloth bag over her shoulder, teetering over a twelve-meter drop. Pascual waves, but despairs as he does so; he can see no way down. The building on this side is also derelict, with a boarded-up shop front covered with graffiti and handbills and a blank facade above, offering no handholds.

Nela is thinking faster than he is; she is already moving toward the adjacent apartment building with its balconies. Before Pascual can draw breath to shout, she has leapt from the roof onto somebody's third-floor balcony. While he watches, holding his breath, she slips over the rail and lets herself down to hang for a moment before swinging onto the balcony below it. Now there are no more balconies and still a five-meter drop to the sidewalk, but there is a utility pole standing a mere two meters from the balcony.

Nela leaps like a monkey and latches onto the pole, then slides down to the street. Pascual can only stand and watch as she runs across the street to join him. Her face is drawn with terror. "They're fighting. The men are fighting them."

"They killed Tawfiq. We need the police."

Nela's face goes hard. "Fuck the police. They won't come. Those people will fight. Me, I need to go far away." She is already moving toward the car. "You can come with me if you want. But no police."

Pascual watches her get into the Toyota, and then he comes out of his daze and goes to join her.

"I was wrong. The police are there." Nela ends the call and hands Christos's phone back to him. Her own was last seen sailing over a wall into a patch of greenery after she flung it out the car window, speeding away from Exarcheia. She slumps back on her chair and closes her eyes for a moment before fixing Pascual with a haunted look. "Tawfiq is dead and one of the Africans was taken to a hospital. The attackers ran away. They weren't expecting to find a room full of people ready to resist them."

Pascual says, "You never saw them?"

"I heard them. I was upstairs in the office. I heard them shouting at people, demanding to know where I was. Then things got very confused. There was a lot of screaming. One of the women came running upstairs and told me to go out the windows in back. She called Christos."

They are in a flat somewhere on the other side of the hill that looms over Exarcheia; the thin, nervous bottle-blonde who opened the door to them apparently lives here, and perhaps also Christos, who takes his phone and retreats to the kitchen with the blonde, leaving them in a parlor filled with scuffed furniture and drooping plants.

Pascual strives to order his thoughts. "Somebody may have told the police that just before he was killed, Tawfiq went to pick me up at the hotel. I can probably identify the attackers. Can you give me a good reason why I shouldn't talk to the police?"

"What can you tell them? You say you can identify them. Do you have their names? Do you know where to find them? Did you actually witness the attack?"

Pascual shakes his head. "No. All I can tell them is why."

"Then it would be useless for you to talk to the police. And dangerous to me." Nela scowls. "I was too hasty, throwing away the phone. They couldn't have found me by tracking my phones. I only ever turn them on when I need to make a call, and anyway the tower data only locates approximately, not like GPS. For that you need tracking software, and I can guarantee there was none on any of my phones. Somebody betrayed me. Was it you?" She turns a blazing look on him.

Startled, Pascual stiffens. "I was the one who warned you. Why would I warn you if I set you up?"

"Maybe it was your phone they were tracking."

Pascual shakes his head. "Nobody knew about that phone. I bought it here in Athens. Anyway, I didn't have it with me. It's still at my hotel. I'd think hard about the people at the squat. Can you trust them all?"

"If somebody there had betrayed me, the attackers would not have been surprised to find the place full of people. They would have waited for me to leave."

"They must have tracked back your hack somehow."

"They still had to locate me." Nela works on it, frowning. "There are devices that can detect mobile phone signals at short range. They could have picked up signals from the few times I turned on a phone to make a call. But they would have to know the number, the IMSI or the IMEI or both, and I only use prepaid burners. No, somebody betrayed me." She closes her eyes, sagging back on the chair. "Or I made a mistake somewhere."

Pascual gives her a moment to rage at herself, eyes closed, before he says, "What are you going to do?"

The hazel eyes snap to his. "What do you think? I'm going to Istanbul. Are you coming with me?"

Pascual is sluggish with fatigue and post-adrenaline letdown. "I'm going to have to give that some thought."

"Think fast. I'm leaving as soon as I can arrange transport."

Pascual stands and walks to the door to the balcony. He looks out at laundry on a rooftop clothesline, thin clouds in a pale blue sky. "And if I don't come with you?"

"Well, I'll have to look for another source of funds, won't I?"

"How much will you need?"

"Impossible to say until I get there."

"Could I wire you the funds?"

"Not if you're worried about your bank activity being tracked. I'll understand if you don't want to risk it." Nela rouses herself, stands and strides toward the door. "So I leave you to think about it while I go to the bathroom. Then I leave, with you or without you."

Pascual stands at the window and looks out at his choices. Cooperation with the Greek police will mean unforeseeable complications, for him and for the only person who is in a position to document the crimes he has abetted. Going to Istanbul means committing to an undertaking he would have thought was mad even in his wild youth.

There is a third choice, he reflects. He can take his money and go home. A million dollars will allow Pascual March to set up housekeeping somewhere tranquil and welcoming, not too far from his wife and son. There he will be able to stagnate, refusing to think about crimes in savage places and enjoying his hush money, at least until the next Melville comes knocking.

Pascual decides that the best way to deal with decisional paralysis is to let chance dictate the outcome. If the police are waiting for him at the hotel, so be it. If not, he will rendezvous with Nela. In any event, he needs his toothbrush.

When Nela comes back into the parlor Pascual says, "Give me a place where I can meet you in one hour."

21

The woman behind the desk at the hotel gives him an inscrutable look as he passes her on his way to the elevator. Up in his room it takes Pascual less than a minute to pack, looking longingly at the bed. When he comes back down to check out, the woman is on the phone speaking quietly in Greek, but either the call is innocuous or she is an old hand at reporting guests to the police; she rings off calmly and asks him in English if he has enjoyed his stay.

Outside the hotel Pascual turns right and walks. For the first block or two he expects to hear sirens at any moment or feel the clap of a hand on the shoulder. After a few hundred meters he realizes that the police are not going to make the decision for him. His momentum keeps him walking until he reaches a corner where a big intercity bus is parked in front of an office with a sign lettered in Greek and below it in English: *Athens – Thessaloniki – Athens*. A couple of youths with overstuffed backpacks are blocking the entrance to the office. Squatting in the shade of the overhang, back to the wall, bag at her feet, is Nela Nachtnebel. She watches expressionless as Pascual approaches and sets down his grip, sweating lightly from the hike. "Here you are," she says. "I didn't expect you to show up."

"Neither did I," says Pascual.

"Do you have your phone with you?"

"Of course. But it's turned off. You need to use it?"

"No, I bought a new one, prepaid, a burner. I want you to take the SIM card out of your phone and throw it away. You'll need a new one in Istanbul anyway. Then go in and buy a ticket to Thessaloniki. One-way. It will cost you thirty-five euros. The bus leaves in twenty minutes."

"Remember, my fingerprints can't be on this anywhere. If I leave a financial trail in Istanbul, there's a risk they'll find it. They found me in Marseille by going through my bank."

Pascual has been watching Nela's profile as she stares gloomily out the window of the bus. Departure was half an hour ago and the bus is still nudging its way through Athens traffic. Nela has barely spoken since they boarded. At first he thinks Nela has not heard or is ignoring him, but at length she turns her head toward him and says, "Then you get some cash, or some prepaid debit cards. You can do that in Thessaloniki. If anyone gets interested enough to request records from your bank again, they'll see you realized some cash, but they won't be able to track where you spent it."

"How are we going to get across the border without leaving a record?"

"In Thessaloniki we'll find someone to take us. It's easy. People do it all the time. There is a network."

"What kind of network?"

"Friends, allies. Activists, advocates, anarchists. That's why I was in Exarcheia. Because I know the people who run the squat. I've hosted some of them in Berlin. I've stayed in squats in London, Paris, Barcelona, Milan. We all help each other when needed."

"Saves on rent, I suppose." Pascual can see Nela does not appreciate the joke. She gives him a contemptuous look and turns back to the window. Chastened, he says, "I'm not knocking it. Do you have a permanent home somewhere?"

He watches her fine profile until he decides she is not going to answer. "You don't need to know that," Nela says.

"No," says Pascual. "I suppose I don't."

What Pascual knows about Thessaloniki is mostly that its old and thriving Jewish community was shipped en masse to Auschwitz and exterminated; he once sat and listened to an enthusiastic account of the affair by a Palestinian UN official over drinks in Sofia. Perhaps because of that, he has never felt drawn to the place, but ancient cities on the wine-dark sea have always cast a spell on him, and he is glad to add another one to his collection. With his first glimpse of said sea as the car swings onto a long waterfront boulevard, he revives a little from the stupor induced by a six-hour bus ride.

The car belongs to an acquaintance of Nela's summoned via her new phone to the bus station on the outskirts of town. The acquaintance is angular, dark and bearded, Panagiotis by name, occupation unknown, sympathies clearly in line with Nela's and his English just as good. Pascual has no idea what she told him on the phone, but he seems enthused by the need to stow them somewhere for a couple of days, no questions asked. "I'll take you where nobody will find you," he says, weaving from lane to lane past cars on less urgent missions.

"We're not staying long," says Nela. "Maria in Athens says you can take us into Turkey."

"You want to go to Turkey?"

"I know it's not the direction most people go, but yes."

"Actually, a lot of people are going back to Turkey now. They're finding out Europe is not paradise."

"We could have told them that and saved them the trouble. So, yes, we want to go to Turkey. Without showing our passports."

Panagiotis nods in approval. "No borders, no passports. The guy I know who takes people across is in Sweden now, but he'll know somebody who can take you. You can swim?"

It takes Pascual a moment to realize the question was addressed to him, Panagiotis watching him in the mirror. "Me?" he says with a sinking heart. "Oh, yes. I can swim."

Panagiotis laughs. "If we can't find a guy, you can always swim to Turkey. Across the river."

"Terrific. Sounds like fun." Watching a succession of inviting café terraces race by on the seafront, Pascual feels his feet growing colder by the second. Panagiotis turns away from the waterfront and takes them through a dense city center with bustling boulevards and leafy squares, then up a long avenue climbing away from the sea, past a sprawling university campus and finally off the thoroughfare into a hillside quarter where suddenly the streets are narrower and the houses smaller. Again Pascual loses all sense of direction as the streets wind, and when Panagiotis comes to a halt before a battered wooden door in a pale yellow facade with blue shutters, Pascual is uncertain which way the sea lies. "Here we are," says Panagiotis.

The house is small even by local standards, two narrow stories with the shuttered windows overlooking the street and a balcony on the side overlooking a tiny garden. Erupting from the garden is a tall and unprepossessing plane tree that overshadows the house. "Charming," says Pascual.

Panagiotis gives him a suspicious look. "The owner is in hospital. Probably she will die. Her son and daughter are in Germany. Until they come back, you can stay here." He pulls a large, old-fashioned iron key from his pocket and offers it to Nela. "I'll call you tomorrow about Turkey."

The house is much as one might expect from the exterior: cramped, musty, decrepit. On the ground floor are the kitchen and a room for living, dining, and everything else, crammed with knickknacks, photos of people long dead, an icon on the wall; at the top of a rickety staircase are a single bedroom with a double bed and a toilet and shower. Pascual dumps his bag on the floor of the bedroom and goes to stand on the balcony. The garden below him has a bench in the shade and dead leaves piled along the base of the wall. He wants desperately to talk to Sara and wishes he had thought to do so before disposing of his Greek SIM card.

He turns at the sound of Nela coming up the stairs. She comes into the bedroom, notes the bed, shoots Pascual an inscrutable look. "I'll sleep on that couch downstairs," Pascual says.

She shrugs. "There's room for two. I doubt we'll be in it at the same time. And if we are, I don't think you are going to try anything. Am I wrong?"

Pascual takes the full force of her challenging look for a moment and then laughs. "No. I won't try anything."

"Good. There's no food here. Why don't you go and look for some while I set up my computer? I have a lot of work to do." Nela spins on her heel and goes back downstairs.

■ ■ ■ ■

Pascual leans on the balcony rail listening to night sounds and wonders what the hell he is doing here. A variety of answers occur to him, none of them convincing. But at least there is this gentle breeze in his face, hinting at gardens and the distant sea, and there is this cheap Greek brandy to restore his native optimism. He lifts the glass to his lips and drains it.

The brandy was a lucky find, procured along with a plastic bag full of provisions in a sweep along the small strip of shops he was relieved to discover at the end of a long downhill trudge through a charming residential quarter devoid of commercial establishments. The walk back up the hill was much longer. Nela turned up her nose at the souvlaki but devoured the salad. Pascual ate both sandwiches and went upstairs to drink, leaving Nela at the table where she has deployed her laptop and a portable Wi-Fi device.

Pascual comes in off the balcony, weaving a little. He negotiates the stairs carefully and goes into the kitchen to place the glass in the sink. He is astonished to see how much of the bottle has been consumed. He puts it out of sight in a cupboard and goes into the main room. Here he drops into an ancient dusty armchair and sits blinking at Nela, who is staring at her laptop screen. Eventually she looks at him and says, "Yes?"

"What are you working on?"

"I'm trying to figure out how the Syrians found me, what do you think?" Her look goes stony. "You're drunk."

"Not quite. Don't worry, I'm through for the evening. I thought I would come and talk to the person I've decided to commit my time, my money and possibly my life to."

The look softens as the seconds pass, and finally Nela smiles. She taps at the keyboard, closes the laptop and sits back on her chair, arms folded. "That's very dramatic."

"So is stealing a hundred million dollars in gold."

"We're not stealing it. We're restoring it."

"I'm sure we'll be able to persuade the judge of that."

"Judges don't concern me. Justice concerns me. What about you? Are you with me?"

"I've been thinking about that all day. And I've decided it depends very much on what we do with the gold, presuming we can get it."

"What would you like to do with it?"

"My preference would be to identify some legitimate authority subject to international law and deliver it to them."

"Your faith in international law is much greater than mine. All I know is that a hundred million dollars means real power, and for once the person making the decision about what to do with it will not be a banker or a politician. It will be me."

"Most likely it will be whichever gang of bandits winds up with the truck. I think you've seriously underestimated the dangers."

"It's a logistical problem. And a security problem. I'm used to handling those kinds of things. Look, I quite understand if you're having second thoughts. But you're the one who offered to fund this."

"That was before I was aware you were planning to steal a ton and a half of gold."

"Well, now you're aware. If you want out, say so."

Pascual strives to concentrate. "I don't know that I want out. But I certainly don't want to wind up hiding under a wrecked truck trying to place the regional accents of a handful of gunmen. A ton and a half of gold is a heavy responsibility, literally and otherwise. I don't know that I'm prepared to shoulder that responsibility."

Nela vents a little puff of exasperation. "All right, your responsibility will end with funding the project. All of the logistics will be my concern. I'll keep you entirely out of it if you want. All you need to do is keep the cash coming. I'll provide a detailed accounting if you wish. You can spend your days touring Istanbul. The Topkapi Palace is supposed to be quite interesting."

Pascual considers this, his efforts to focus somewhat attenuated by the brandy. "I'll give it some thought," he says. "Meanwhile, I think I know how the Syrians found you."

He has gotten her attention, Pascual sees; now he only hopes he is sober enough to explain himself. "The Syrians didn't find you on their own. They needed help. You were right. Someone betrayed you."

"Who?"

"The CIA. They gave you to the Syrians."

The hazel eyes widen a little. "How?"

"Through Sabine Degitz. Once you designated her as the contact, they looked for connections between the two of you. I'd bet they started tracking her phone immediately. They'd have to lean on the Greeks to do that, but I imagine they can. They did it before, some years ago. There was a scandal."

"I remember. The NSA tapped the phones of a lot of Greek politicians." Her look goes distant. "And if they were monitoring Sabine's phone, they would see my calls to her. From three different phones, but one of them was the one I used to send the key."

Nela shoves violently away from the table, the chair toppling. "*Scheisse!*" She takes a few steps, halts in the doorway with her back to

Pascual, hands to her head, fingers clenched in the spiky hair. She turns to face him, hands dropping to her sides. "I was an idiot."

"You had no reason to think Sabine's phone was monitored."

Nela stalks back to the table and collapses onto the chair. "I should have suspected it. I made just enough calls that they could locate me in Exarcheia. Not as accurately as with GPS, but with a few readings they could make an educated guess about which building."

"And they tipped the Syrians. And all they had to do was send in the gorillas to sit and watch. When they saw me come out, they knew for sure."

"Why? Why would the Americans give me to the Syrians?"

"It was easier than prosecuting you. And they like to keep their hands clean. They outsource the dirty work when they can."

"God. And I always thought it was just prison I was risking." Nela sits staring at nothing for a moment and then puts her face in her hands. When she takes her hands away she looks exhausted. She directs a haggard look at Pascual and says, "May I have some of your brandy?"

Pascual laughs. "Help yourself. Kill the bottle if you want. I'm going to bed."

Pascual wakes with wool in his mouth and a feeble bass drum beat in his head. Through the slats of the shutters he can see the sky beginning to lighten. He rolls, suppresses a groan, throws back the sheet and grunts gently as he swings his feet to the floor. Sitting on the edge of the bed he contemplates his condition. Not too bad, he decides; only moderate damage considering the quantity and quality of the booze he put away. His bladder, however, is a pressing matter.

It is only when Pascual stands and turns that he becomes aware that he was not alone in the bed. At some point while he was unconscious, Nela inserted herself next to him and now lies on her side with her back to him, legs tucked up in a fetal position. In throwing off the sheet he has left her uncovered.

He has wondered when she sleeps; she dozed a little on the bus from Athens but apparently works through the night by preference. She is sound asleep now, to judge by her breathing. In any event she has not stirred since he awoke.

Pascual walks to the other side of the bed and gently pulls up the sheet to cover her up to the shoulder. Asleep she looks much younger and completely vulnerable. He resists the temptation to tuck the sheet around her chin and goes to grope his way to the toilet.

When Pascual has finished there, he goes back into the bedroom and grabs trousers, shirt and pillow. He makes his way downstairs and lowers himself onto the old creaking sofa in the main room. More or less comfortable, he tries to drift off to sleep again, firmly suppressing the image of Nela Nachtnebel's complete and splendid nakedness next to him.

22

"All I know is what Butros in Sweden said. The guy is supposed to meet us here." Panagiotis tosses off the last of his drink and slaps the glass down on the table.

The here in question is the terrace of a roadside café in a town four hours east of Thessaloniki, a succession of whitewashed houses with red tile roofs strung out along the highway. The drink is either raki or ouzo; Pascual was unable to follow Panagiotis's lecture on the distinctions, and to him it just tastes like pastis. After his binge of the previous evening he is sipping with maidenly self-control. To their right the late afternoon sun is sinking toward distant hills.

Pascual spent the morning at a succession of banks in Thessaloniki, turning some of his dirty CIA money into five thousand euros in prepaid debit cards and cash. A tiny fraction of that went to the new money belt now accenting his middle-aged waistline. On the long drive Nela dozed on the back seat while Pascual made idle talk with Panagiotis and watched the land flatten, mountains giving way to this expanse of featureless farmland stretching to the horizon. Somewhere a few kilometers to the east is the river and beyond it Turkey. Pascual is ill at ease. As they neared the river they passed several police posts on the highway, uniformed officers lounging by parked SUVs with police lights and insignia. The town is a wide place in the road, devoid of charm. The woman who served them the drinks was barely civil. Pascual is dreaming of air-conditioned express buses and wondering again if all this subterfuge is necessary.

"So you don't know him," says Nela. She has been sullen and tight-lipped all day since rising late in the morning. Panagiotis's call snapped her out of a sulk, and now she is challenging the Greek with her high-wattage glare. "This is not somebody known to you?"

"He is a friend of a friend. If Butros trusts him, you can trust him."

Nela does not look convinced, but she does not press the point. "And does he want money?"

Panagiotis is watching a car pull over in front of the café. "I think this is him. You can ask him yourself."

The car is a Peugeot and the driver stepping out of it is a man in his twenties, olive-skinned with a mushroom cloud of brown hair above shaved temples, in torn jeans and a black T-shirt, trim and athletic. He makes for their table. "Panagiotis?"

"Kamal? You found us."

Kamal joins them and introductions are made. Kamal is an Arab with passable English. The woman emerges from the interior and takes his order with ill grace. "Butros says you can take people across the river to Turkey," says Panagiotis.

"Yeah, sure. How many want to go?" Kamal gives Pascual a brief glance and trains an intense and appreciative gaze on Nela.

"Two," she says, leaning back on her chair, arms folded. "As soon as possible."

Kamal shrugs. "Tomorrow?"

"How about tonight?"

"Tonight cost you more."

Nela blinks once and turns to look at Panagiotis. "What happened to the network? The lifeline, Maria called it. Taking people across, no charge, no questions. No borders."

Panagiotis shifts on his chair, avoiding her eye. "That was Butros. He told me now it's Kamal you deal with."

Kamal says, "Butros have money. No problem for him. Me, I am poor refugee. This my job, take people across the river."

Nela meets this with a hard flat stare. Pascual says, "How much?"

"Two hundred euros. For one person. For two, four hundred euros."

Pascual and Nela trade a brief look. Nela says, "Too much."

Kamal shrugs. "This my price."

Pascual says, "How do we cross the river?"

"I have boat. Perfect boat, no problem. You don't get wet feet. Very good boat."

"But it's no more trouble to take two than to take one. It's all one trip, right? And the Evros is not exactly the Mississippi. We'll pay you for one trip across. A hundred euros for both of us."

Kamal dismisses that with a puff of contempt. "Nobody take you for a hundred."

Pascual shrugs and looks at Nela. "We can do better. We'll swim it if we have to."

Kamal laughs. "And the Turks catch you. You have to know the right place, where Turks don't look. You need guide."

"All right, for your expertise, we'll give you a hundred and fifty. For both of us."

"Two hundred fifty."

Pascual holds Kamal's insouciant stare for a moment and then looks at Nela. "Let's go back to Thessaloniki and do a little market research."

Kamal laughs. "You waste your time. And his petrol."

Pascual pushes away from the table, looking at Panagiotis. "We'll pay you for the gas. But we're not going to be cheated." He stands up.

Panagiotis is irked, but his appeal to Nela meets only a shrug. "All right." He and Nela rouse themselves.

"Wait." Kamal is scowling at Pascual. "Two hundred euros, OK."

"For both."

"For both. You pay now."

"We give you a hundred now. The other hundred when we reach Turkey."

Kamal glares for a moment longer, then shrugs. "Show me the money."

"You think he'll come back? Or has he just abandoned us here?" Nela waves mosquitos away from her face with an irritated swipe of the hand. "He could get rich just taking a hundred euros each time and leaving people in the woods."

She and Pascual are sitting with their backs to tree trunks in a strip of brushy bottomland along the Evros river, a few kilometers from the town where they concluded their deal with Kamal. After taking leave of Panagiotis they were driven to a spot along the highway where they were dropped and instructed to hike along a tree line between cultivated fields to the river and wait. The hike was longer than Pascual expected, the ground rougher. Night is falling and Pascual's spirits with it. Bugs, mud and hunger have never improved his mood, and stray bits of clothing, remnants of campfires and scattered litter testify to the desperate people who have passed this way before. "It wouldn't be a very good business model," he says. "Word would get around. And I think he wants the other hundred. He'll be back."

"I'm not sure why we need him," says Nela. "I think we could easily swim it." The river here is perhaps fifty meters wide, tranquil with only a slight discernible current. Thick woods on the other side mask whatever might lie beyond.

"We probably could. Keeping your laptop dry might be a problem. And by the time we're across it will be dark. We'll have to avoid the police and find the nearest town. I'm not prepared to camp in the woods all night. We'll need guidance. Presumably that's what our two hundred euros buy us."

Nela pulls her knees up to her chest, frowning fiercely. "I know, I know. This was all my idea. I still think it's the right way to do it." She cranes to look over her shoulder back toward the highway. "You think those police ever come down here?"

"Not at night, I wouldn't think. I think they're mostly there to pick up people with wet feet and luggage coming up from the river."

"I hope you're right."

Pascual swats at a mosquito on his arm. "Not nearly as much as I hope you're right."

A few seconds pass. "About the gold?"

"Yes."

Nela does what he least expects: she laughs. "So do I."

The crackle of brush sounds from the direction of the highway. They both turn to look. Someone is coming through the trees. The footsteps halt, and a sudden electronic tinkle startles Pascual as Nela's phone goes off. She fumbles for it and then her face is illuminated as she answers. "Yes. Yes, we're here. We see you. Yes, all right." She ends the call and punches at her phone until the screen lights up. She trains it in the direction of the highway and the footsteps in the undergrowth resume.

Kamal enters the clearing, stepping carefully over the rough ground. He has put on a denim jacket over the T-shirt. He gives them an appraising look, lingering on Nela. "Very good," he says. "Now we go to Turkey."

"You said something about a boat," says Pascual.

"The boat come now." Kamal steps to the river bank, thumbing at his phone. He mutters into it in Arabic, looking upstream. He thumbs again and the screen lights up. He raises the phone and waves it a couple of times.

A low sputtering noise becomes audible. Pascual and Nela pick up their bags and go to join Kamal. There is a steep bank dropping a couple of meters to the water. On the open water there is enough light to see a boat approaching, a couple of hundred meters upstream. It lies low in the water, less than a meter wide and maybe three meters long. A man in the stern is steering with the small outboard motor that is producing the sound.

They watch as the boat draws near, slowly. "We're not going to break any speed records, are we?" says Pascual.

Kamal laughs. "You will be in Turkey before morning." He slides down the bank as the motor cuts out and the boat eases into shore. The boatman tosses a rope to Kamal and he pulls the prow of the craft up onto the mud. "This my friend Ahmad," says Kamal.

Ahmad is darker than Kamal, bearded, about the same age. He nods at Pascual and gives Nela a reverent head-to-toe examination. "Come," says Kamal, beckoning, holding out his hand.

Nela slides down the bank, ignoring Kamal and stepping carefully into the boat, unaided. It wobbles a little and Ahmad puts his hand out to grasp hers. She regains her balance and then shakes off his hand and sits, her back to him. Pascual goes down the bank on the seat of his pants, dragging his bag, and lets Kamal steady him as he steps on board and takes his place in front of Nela.

Kamal pushes on the prow of the boat to clear the bank, then expertly steps aboard and sits in front of Pascual as it swings out into the river, keeping his feet dry without swamping the boat. With four people on board there are perhaps five centimeters of freeboard. Ahmad starts the motor and the boat laboriously swivels away from the bank and heads for Turkey, fifty meters away in the twilight.

Pascual laughs softly. "What?" says Nela behind him.

"I was worried about high seas and contrary winds."

After the stress of the long day, the crossing of the Evros is an anticlimax. On the Turkish side Kamal leaps onto the bank holding the rope and hauls the prow onto firm ground. "Now you in Turkey," he says. Pascual accepts a hand on his arm to help him disembark, but again Nela disdains help. They scramble up the bank and stand in a patch of Turkish wasteland brushing dirt from their trousers. Kamal comes up after them. "Now you pay," he says.

Pascual frowns. "Before you show us the way? For another hundred euros I want to know how to get to a train station or a bus stop. Before the police pick us up."

Kamal makes an impatient gesture toward the east. "I show you. Very easy. You walk to the road and go left, go north. Two kilometers to village. Turks don't see anybody at night."

Pascual trades a quick look with Nela, who has joined them. She makes the slightest of shrugs. "All right." Pascual moves a few steps away from the bank, into the gloom under the trees, and drops his bag. He has already stashed a hundred euros in the pocket of his trousers to eliminate having to brandish the wallet or expose the money belt. He produces them and offers them to Kamal. "Here you are. Now. Show us a way through the woods here."

Kamal takes his time, counting the bills, folding them, slipping them into the side pocket of his jacket. He is frowning slightly, as if giving thought to the best route. Pascual looks beyond him to see that Ahmad has come up the bank from the river, and the first faint alarm bells go off. "First you pay tax," says Kamal.

Pascual stiffens. Kamal must have detected the bulge at his waist. "Let's go, Nela." He stoops to grab his bag from the ground and motions with his head. "We're leaving."

Pascual is prepared for bluster, intimidation, fisticuffs. What he is not prepared for is Kamal pulling a switchblade from the same pocket in which he has just put Pascual's money, flicking it open and putting it to Nela's throat as he grabs a handful of her hair. Ahmad has come creeping up behind her and now he smiles, brilliant white teeth bright in the gloom. "You can go," he says. "She have to pay first."

That makes everything clear to Pascual; everything, that is, except what he is going to do about it. He looks into Nela's hazel eyes, now wide open with fright, and finds nothing to say. Kamal says, "She have to pay tax. I give you special price to cross, but now she pay tax."

"How much?" says Nela through a constricted throat, and Pascual wants to weep at the desperate innocence of the question. Kamal and Ahmad laugh, and in Nela's eyes Pascual can see that she finally gets it.

"Not much," says Ahmad. He grasps Nela's arms and pulls them behind her back. "But you have to pay Kamal and you have to pay me."

Kamal has taken the knife from Nela's throat and now he is waving it in Pascual's direction. "You go," he says. "You find the road, that way. You wait for her. Maybe ten minutes."

Pascual is utterly paralyzed for a moment, his heart pounding, and then he takes a deep calming breath. He looks at Nela and says, "Well, it looks like you don't have much choice. I'm afraid they won't accept payment from me. Just remember, you're the one who wanted to go to Istanbul." He watches the look in her eyes change, fear mutating to something harder. "I'll wait for you at the road," he says, and turns and begins to march over the uneven ground.

Behind him he hears a snarl from Nela, thrashing, a blow, muttering in Arabic. He forces himself to walk, scanning the ground, his mind racing faster than his heart. Here is a twisted branch, too rotted to do any good. There is a single abandoned shoe, useless. What he needs is a club, a stone, anything to use in a fight.

Something like this abandoned paddle lying in the brush, jettisoned by an arriving boater. Pascual sets his bag down and picks up the paddle. A meter long, made of good sturdy wood, with an edge to the blade that ought to get a rapist's attention.

Pascual turns. The trick will be to get in range without alerting them. His disgust with himself is great enough already, but he fears he will have to make Nela suffer a little longer. He begins to walk as quietly as he can back toward them. The twilight has become his friend; he can make out his targets but they will not see him creeping through the trees until, he hopes, it is too late.

Kamal has forced Nela to her knees; he has the knife to her throat and a firm grip on her hair with his other hand. Ahmad has unzipped his jeans and is maneuvering into position, stroking himself. Nela has begun to cry, softly. Don't startle the man with the knife to her throat, Pascual tells himself.

At the last he will just have to count on speed and surprise, but he will need something to get him over the last couple of meters into striking range. They have heard him coming, and Kamal twists to look over his shoulder. Pascual steps out of the brush, holding the paddle against his side, and says, "Actually, I was wondering if I might watch. You don't mind, do you?"

Kamal laughs. "You only want to watch?"

Pascual gets two steps closer before Kamal looks away. Nela has turned her head to the side, and Kamal forces it back with the point of the knife. Ahmad is intent on what is happening just in front of him. Kamal takes the knife away from Nela's cheek and Pascual lunges.

Kamal turns in time to see the paddle scything toward his head but has no time to react and takes the edge of the blade across his nose with a satisfying crack. He topples, Nela screams and Ahmad stumbles backward, suddenly busy with his trousers. He raises his hands to protect himself a second too late, and Pascual delivers a glancing blow to his head that drives him to the ground. He twists away, giving Pascual a chance to hack at the back of his head with the paddle, karate style. Ahmad goes limp instantly and Pascual turns to see Kamal rolling on the ground, hands to his face, groaning, spitting blood. Pascual steps over to him and waits until he presents a convenient angle, then brings the paddle down on his skull as hard as he can. Kamal spasms and goes still.

"Don't kill him," says Nela. She is sitting on her haunches, wiping tears with her hand.

"He deserves it." Pascual straightens up, panting, and goes to look at Ahmad.

"We don't want to talk to police about a murder," says Nela, scrambling to her feet. "Let's just get the fuck out of here." She retrieves her bag and begins to run, blindly, away from the river. She has gone ten meters when she trips and sprawls headlong. Pascual drops the paddle and hurries to her. Already rising, she bats his arm away. "*Lass mich!*"

Pascual stands watching as Nela disappears into the undergrowth.

"So," says Nela. "Was that a case of finding your courage, or was it a clever stratagem from the start?"

Pascual has been gazing into the fire, but now he turns to find Nela staring at him. In the firelight he can see a little swelling by her eye where she was hit and the tiny laceration on her cheek made by the point of the knife. "I knew I had to divert attention from myself and get them focused on you if I had any chance of helping you. I couldn't think of a better way than to pretend I was abandoning you."

He can see she doesn't quite believe him, and he knows he is going to have to live with that. She says, "I hated you worse than them, until you came back."

"I don't blame you."

After a moment she says, "Whichever it was, thank you."

"Please. Forget it." Pascual looks beyond the campfire to see four people staring at them with concern: the gaunt Syrian man and his wife, son and daughter, all hoping to cross to Greece tomorrow, whose fire drew Pascual and Nela across the fields at the end of a blind, exhausting trudge through the dark. Nela refused to approach them until Pascual determined that the group included women; when they gave her food, water and a blanket, she wept.

"Tomorrow," says the father. "You can take bus in Uzunköprü, near to here. Tomorrow you will be in Istanbul."

23

Pascual's introduction to the haunted space where Byzantium, Constantinople and the seat of the Ottoman caliphate once lay is a sprawling multilevel bus terminal off an eight-lane highway slicing through a megalopolis that could be anywhere on earth. Pascual has traveled enough to know that arrival is always a letdown, but he still has to fight off a flutter of disorientation and dismay as he trails Nela across a wide plaza, uncertain where she is taking him.

Nela has been brooding and silent since rising from beside the dead campfire at dawn. The Syrians had stolen away an hour before. Uzunköprü proved to be a sizable town, well worth the two-hour hike it took to reach it. There Nela procured in quick succession lira, breakfast, SIM cards and bus tickets, deploying fluent Turkish. She dozed on the long bus ride through the flat countryside of European Turkey while Pascual stared out the window at passing towns that looked much like the ones he had seen in Greece except for the pencil-thin minarets punctuating the skyline. In the last hour these gave way to high-rises, shopping malls and truck depots stretching to the horizon.

"Where are we going?" Pascual says as Nela pauses in front of the system map posted at the entrance to the Metro.

"We are going to Kadiköy."

"And where's that?"

"That's on the Asian side of the Bosporus. There's a squat there."

"Ah."

She gives him a sharp look. "If you don't think you'll be comfortable, you are free to find a hotel. You're the one who said you didn't want to leave any traces here."

Pascual smiles. "I can rough it with the best of them."

"We won't leave traces, and there are people there who can help us. I just need to get directions." Nela is already tapping at her phone. "Go and buy us two transit cards. The machine will have instructions in English."

Pascual obeys and puts himself in Nela's hands. In something under two hours he is footsore and weary but more or less comfortably installed on a sheet-draped couch in a room with bare brick walls, chaotically appointed with jury-rigged bookshelves, scavenged furniture, bedding, bicycles and the odd guitar. A dozen or so people are lounging about the room, talking in three or four languages. He has been given food and beer and is beginning to recover from the long slog on Metro, bus and foot.

The squat is a partially finished building in a quarter teetering on the edge of slumhood, little more than a shell, the concrete ribs showing, orange brickwork filling in the spaces, pirated electricity humming through cables snaking through an unglazed window. After Exarcheia the aesthetic is familiar to Pascual. The company is multilingual, multinational and multigendered, and no doubt because transients are routine here, they have stopped paying attention to him, allowing him to observe quietly. He has seen this crowd before, with its sartorial badges of authenticity and earnest disdain for comfort; Pascual has rediscovered his youth. Certain flats in the Onzième in Paris in the early eighties looked just like this and smelled the same, incense overlaid with hashish.

He takes a sip of beer and watches Nela across the room. He has been watching her all day, looking for signs of stress and trauma, and until they arrived here he has seen nothing but her steely resolve. Now he is seeing something different: complete absorption in the man leaning close to her on the sofa. He is a Che Guevara lookalike, without the beret but the hair and beard and soulful look much the same, though redeemed occasionally by a brilliant smile. It was clear to Pascual instantly that he was the reason they are here.

He was introduced as Afran; the name is Kurdish, but the language in which he and Nela are murmuring is German. Pascual has been watching eyes and body language, trying to gauge the status of this relationship. Intimate, he thinks, though probably not of long standing and possibly not exclusive. There is evident mutual passion beneath a layer of cool. On one hand it is fascinating to see Nela succumb to human weaknesses, and on the other the timing is not ideal. To him Afran looks like a huge complication. Pascual wonders how much Nela has told him.

Pascual finishes his beer and with some effort rises from the couch. He searches for a way to dispose of the bottle and finally sets it in a corner with some others and goes to stand at a window. The sky is darkening above the rooftops and with it his mood. What he most desires is to talk to Sara. He now has a working phone but is wary of contacting her with it. For all he knows, her phone could be monitored, and if there is one thing he does not want, it is to alert anyone that he is in Istanbul.

"Pascual." He turns to see Nela beckoning. She and Afran have left the couch and are making for the door. "Let's go for a walk," says Nela. The hazel eyes are luminous, the fine lines of the face a little taut, the cheekbone where she was struck faintly bruised and slightly swollen. Twenty-four hours ago she was preparing to be raped and now she is proposing a leisurely stroll. Pascual marvels at the resilience of youth.

In the street evening is drawing on, women in headscarves hurrying home, shopping bags dangling from their fingers, idlers smoking in doorways. The air has cooled and the streetlights are coming on. They amble slowly, three abreast, Nela between the men. Pascual is feeling dazed, dislocated. The signs are in Turkish, full of umlauts and cedillas. For Pascual with his six languages, the experience of being in a place where he cannot even decipher the signs is almost unprecedented and deeply unsettling.

The street leads gently downhill toward the sea, the neighborhood becoming more prosperous and peopled, a cheerful hubbub spilling from brightly lit cafés. At the end there is a wide plaza and the seafront, ferries loading passengers for the Golden Horn and the horizon going orange over the Sea of Marmara. They gravitate to the water's edge and find a vacant bench to sit on. "So," says Nela. "We need to discuss our business, don't we?"

Pascual has been waiting for this. As casually as he can, he says, "And what is Afran's role in our business?"

"You remember I said I had promised the gold to someone? Afran is the someone."

Afran looks completely at ease, a handsome lad with not much on his mind. He grins. "Not me personally. I don't need so much money."

His English is German-accented, fluent but not quite as tip-top as Nela's. "But I have an idea about where it should go."

"And where's that?" says Pascual.

"You know where Rojava is?"

Pascual cannot say he is surprised, but his heart sinks nonetheless. "In northeast Syria."

"We call it Rojava, the west. The western part of Kurdistan."

"I thought the Syrians had reconquered it."

"They have . . . reclaimed it. There's a difference. Assad's troops are there, but they haven't killed the revolution. It's only sleeping."

"And you want to send the gold there?"

"No. I want to send the gold anywhere I can sell it and put the money in a bank. But for Rojava, not for me. A revolution needs money, and a hundred million dollars is a lot of money."

"A hundred million dollars is a lot of gold. Who do you think is going to buy it?"

"That we will worry about when we have it. We can take it to Dubai, to Mumbai, to Singapore. Somebody will buy it."

"And when you get there, if you get there, somebody will have a record of the serial numbers of the bars that were taken out of a warehouse in Istanbul. And you'll be arrested."

"We will melt it and make new bars. We can do that in Mumbai. The first thing is to get it."

"Who's going to take it to Mumbai?"

"People I trust."

"How many people know about this?"

"Now? You, me, Nela. That's all. I'm not so stupid to tell people."

Perfectly calm as Afran bristles, Pascual says, "I just want you to be clear on what you're proposing."

"You don't think it's possible."

Pascual gazes out over the water. "It's probably possible. It's also the best way I can think of to attract attention. I wouldn't want to try it."

"Then you don't have to be involved. We will find somebody else to pay."

There is a brief standoff, Pascual looking into a face full of youthful confidence and possibly a touch of ruthlessness. That, he reflects, may be what counts the most. "I have agreed to fund the operation of obtaining the gold and transporting it to a secure place," he says. "But I don't know if that will stretch to Mumbai or Singapore."

Nela has been watching, intent. Now she says, "It doesn't have to. Afran knows a man who has a secure place where we can take delivery. Once that has happened, you will have done what you agreed to do. Your obligation will be at an end."

Pascual finds the prospect appealing, but suddenly here is a fourth conspirator. "I thought you said only we three know about this."

Afran nods. "He doesn't know about the gold. I only asked him if I can leave some goods at his place for a short time. He has a logistics company, and the company has a warehouse."

"Who is this man?"

"He is a friend of my uncle. I can trust him."

Pascual has known men to betray their brothers for a lot less than a hundred million dollars. "Where that much gold is concerned I would trust nobody. What have you told him?"

"I've told him you will pay him a thousand euros to use his warehouse for one or two hours."

"How curious is he?"

Afran smiles. "He wasn't curious enough to ask me what will be on the truck."

"He'll know what's on the truck. They'll deliver the gold in an armored car. That much gold, they may send a squad of policemen with it. He'll know it's not soap."

"He will give me the key. He will not want to know. He will think we are sending medical supplies to PKK fighters in Iraq. This is something I have done before."

To Pascual this all sounds too good to be true. "I'd like to talk to the man before we commit."

Afran says, "Tomorrow. We'll go see him tomorrow."

"Dortmund was a hard place when I lived there, for an immigrant anyway. I was happy to make my pile and come back here." The man behind the desk is middle-aged, graying, gaining waistline and losing hair, compensating with a luxuriant mustache. His name is Mehmet, and his German is heavily accented but fluent. The desk is at the rear of a long narrow room crowded with desks bearing computer monitors, keyboards and multiple phones, several of them with men murmuring into them. The sign over the door outside is decorated with images of jet planes and long-haul trucks and the inscription *KARGO*. What Afran grandly described as a logistics company, Pascual realizes, is in reality one of a dozen or so freight brokerages lining the narrow street along with a couple of storefront markets and some cheap hotels, all a stone's throw from the Yenikapi port district on the European side of the Bosporus.

"I don't know Dortmund well," says Pascual. "I passed through there once or twice. Mostly my business was over toward Frankfurt." Pascual and Mehmet have been trading reminiscences of Germany over glasses of tea since it was established they had a common language. Afran has mostly watched, idly stroking his beard.

"So," says Mehmet. "You need a place to take delivery of some merchandise."

Pascual nods. "For a very short time. We need a *Gefälligkeitsadresse*, an accommodation address. Just a transshipment point, really. We would immediately load the goods onto a second truck and ship them out."

Mehmet considers, swiveling back and forth on his chair. "What quantity of goods are we talking about?"

"No more than a small truckload. Perhaps even a large van."

"I see." Mehmet's expression has gone carefully neutral. "And can I know the nature of these goods?"

The fewer lies the better, Pascual knows from experience. "If you wish. Though in my experience, if there is ever a problem with the taxman or the police inspector, genuine ignorance is better than feigned. Will you accept my assurance that the material is to benefit your compatriots in difficult circumstances? Afran will direct it to its destination."

Mehmet shifts his gaze to Afran. "No weapons," he says after a moment. "That's not worth the risk. They'll kill you for that, and I'll go to jail for twenty years."

Afran puts a hand over his heart. "Absolutely not. Humanitarian supplies. As before."

Pascual watches Mehmet deciding whether or not to embrace willful ignorance, and he is not sure which way it is going to go. Finally

Mehmet turns back to Pascual. "Afran mentioned money."

Pascual's tension eases instantly. When the discussion shifts to the price, he knows the battle has been decided, and prudence and principle have lost. "Yes," he says, reaching inside his jacket for an envelope. "Will a thousand euros be sufficient?"

The warehouse is a short walk from Mehmet's office, around a corner and under a railway viaduct into a large asphalted lot filled with cars and trucks, with a handful of low buildings and some trees around the edges, situated on a busy six-lane boulevard. There is one entrance from under the viaduct and another giving onto the boulevard to the right. The warehouse is a two-story stone construction with big double doors painted blue, a smaller entry door set in the left-hand door, padlocked. An adjacent office has a separate door and front windows that have been paneled over. "There is nobody here most of the time," says Afran. "This is for his, what do you call it, his side business. Sometimes he buys and sells things. He will trust me with the key and we will wait for the gold. Who will see us?"

Pascual sweeps the area with a casual look. Anybody who happens to be here, he thinks, looking at all the convenient observation points. Aloud he says, "It could work."

24

"Tell me about Afran," Pascual says. The food has arrived, a lavish vegetarian platter for Nela and a lamb kebab for Pascual, and Nela is tucking in with enthusiasm. Pascual has finally secured a chance to speak to her alone by luring her out with the promise of a feed; communal dining arrangements at the squat are on the haphazard side. The restaurant is a hole in the wall near the waterfront, filled with promising smells, full-color pictures of the dishes on offer helpfully posted on the walls and the real thing in steaming pots arrayed behind a counter.

"What about him?" Nela shoves a forkful of eggplant into her mouth.

"How did you meet him? How long have you known him?"

She chews and swallows, frowning at him. "Why this interrogation?"

"Because a hundred million dollars are at stake and suddenly there's a new face."

She avoids Pascual's eyes, poking at her plate. "All right, I can understand that. I met him in Berlin last spring. I was staying in a housing cooperative in Kreuzberg. He was there for a few days, with some people who were organizing tenants being evicted. He had just come from Syria. We talked about Rojava. He was very ... passionate."

She forks another mouthful. "About Rojava, I mean."

"Of course."

"And I became interested. When I decided to try to take the gold, I thought of Rojava. I contacted Afran and he said he would meet me here, in Istanbul."

"I see. He was able to just drop what he was doing and rush off to Istanbul?"

"Just as I was, yes." She is giving Pascual her severest gaze. "You don't trust him?"

"I don't know him. That's why I'm asking. I don't know you, for that matter. I've put my freedom and maybe my life in your hands, and I don't really know who you are."

She shrugs. "What would you like to know?"

Everything, Pascual thinks. The more the better. He says, "Where you come from, to start with. Having heard you speak, I'd guess your German is native and your English is the product of some time in Britain. I can't rule on your Turkish, but it doesn't seem to give you much trouble."

"It shouldn't. I learned it as a child."

"So you're originally Turkish?"

She takes her time answering. "That depends on who you ask. My father and mother were born here and went to work in Germany in the eighties. I was born there. I heard Turkish at home, German everywhere else. My real name isn't Nachtnebel, as you probably guessed. It's a common Turkish surname which I'm sure you'll forgive me for not revealing. And I'm not really Nela, either. I picked that when I was a schoolgirl because 'Zeynep' made my classmates laugh. To the Germans I'll always be a Turk. And I've spent enough time here in the land of my ancestors to know that to the Turks I'll always be a German. I finally decided I would be just a human, and to hell with nationalities."

"I know the feeling."

Nela raises an eyebrow. "Do you?"

"You're looking at a half-Catalan, half-Yank, raised in Barcelona, Paris and New York. Oh, and my father was Jewish."

"And how do you identify?"

"I don't. I leave that to others."

"I think that's wise." She spears a stuffed grape leaf. "So. Satisfied?"

"Still curious. How did you become a world-class hacker?"

"The way anybody becomes a hacker. I learned how to write code and started experimenting. I studied computer science at university because I wasn't supposed to. Most of what I've done since I was twelve years old is because my father didn't want me to do it."

"I see. The old story, strict immigrant father?"

"And stupid, brutal older brothers. I decided early that I wasn't going to be like my mother, married young and sentenced to a life of drudgery."

"And the politics?"

Another shrug. "I detest politics. Anarchism is a rejection of politics. You want to argue about that?"

Pascual has to smile, watching her bristle. "I share your detestation. My early life was catastrophically blighted by politics and it took me years to recover."

She chews, peering at him. "You are referred to as a terrorist in some descriptions I have seen."

"That's accurate. Though I never pulled the trigger, I was an accessory to more than one killing. I have been attempting to atone ever since."

"Is that why you're helping me?"

Pascual pokes at his food. "I'm not actually sure why I'm helping you. Maybe just because I'm angry about the way I was manipulated. Maybe because when I look at you I see myself forty years ago and I want to help you avoid catastrophe. Where do we stand with our little project, by the way?"

Nela polishes off the pilaf before answering. "I'll show you when we go back."

"It's a little more complicated than I thought," says Nela. Here on the top floor of the squat she looks like a spider at the center of a web of electrical cables, cross-legged on a threadbare carpet laid over the concrete floor, with her laptop, a couple of unidentifiable electronic devices and three cell phones arrayed about her.

"I'm glad to hear that," says Pascual. "In matters like this, I mistrust simplicity." There is no chair in sight, so Pascual tries to make himself comfortable on the floor, grimacing as his knees creak.

"It's perfectly feasible," she says. "But there is a little more work to do. The exchange requires that the account owner have KYC documents on file. You know what those are?"

"Know Your Customer."

"Yes. And physical delivery can be made only to the registered owner, who must present photo identification. Which must, of course, match the KYC information on file."

"Perfectly reasonable. But I think I see the problem."

"Yes. We have to either provide you with the owner's identity documents, which I think is probably impossible, or we have to go in and change the name and information of the account owner."

"You can do that?"

"I can do that. The account is numbered. The KYC information associated with it can be changed, if you can access it. And I am looking at it now. Contact information, proof of address, scan of ID document."

"That's amazing. Who is the registered owner, just out of curiosity?"

"This person. Do you know him?" She turns the laptop so he can see it and shoves it toward him.

Pascual leans to look at the screen. It shows a scan of a U.S. passport with the name Roland Emery Pearson; the photograph beside it is instantly recognizable as the man who told Pascual his name was Melville.

Pascual swears softly. "The son of a bitch. Yes, I know him. That's the man who sent me to Yemen."

Nela reclaims her computer. Pascual shakes his head. "I wonder if that's his real name."

Nela says, "Well. Whoever he is, we have to decide who is going to take delivery of the gold."

She sits looking at Pascual expectantly. He gets the message and says, "Not me, if that's what you're thinking."

"Who else? Your Pascual Rose identity is still operative. I have even retrieved your KYC file associated with one of your shell companies."

"Good God, how did you do that?"

"A lot of financial firms use third-party providers to process KYC data, and sometimes their security is weak. Would you like to see your file? I can pull it up."

"No, I'll take your word for it. I told you, I can't be identified with this."

"You can tell them the identity was stolen. That's perfectly plausible, I've just stolen it. There are a lot of ways a hacker could obtain the data. They'll never be able to prove it was you."

Pascual shakes his head. "This is your caper. You put your name on it."

"I would never qualify. I have no fixed address, no bank account, none of the things that they require. I have lived entirely off the grid for two years now. If you are going to propose Afran, I think his situation is much the same. I'm afraid you are our best option."

"Find a beard."

"What?"

"A beard. That's an old American gangster term. A front man."

"Where are we going to find a front man? How much time will it take to prepare him? And produce documents for him? We are pressed for time. And you have the identity ready to use."

She is right, Pascual sees, as he meets her imperious gaze. If they are committed to this undertaking, he is the ideal beard. "You are going to be the death of me," he says.

"Not if we're careful."

Pascual heaves a great sigh and slumps back against the wall. "Let me propose something. You have all the information you need to publish a devastating exposé of this affair. You can lay out for the world the nature of the crime, the identity of the criminals, the location of the money. It will be a major international scandal, a feather in your cap. And you won't have a ton and a half of very physical, very real trouble on your hands."

"If I expose the affair before I redeem the crypto they'll make it disappear. At the first hint of publicity they'll shift it and it will never be found. To secure the gold we have to carry out the whole operation."

"Fine, take the gold. But don't try to take it to India. Don't try to take it anywhere. Dispose of it instantly and publicly. Dump it on the doorstep of the nearest Interpol office. Or better yet, notify Interpol in advance. Have a couple of officers waiting when the gold is delivered from the exchange. Maybe a couple of reporters, too."

Nela stares at him with an incredulous expression. "Invite the police? You're insane."

"Why? That will expose the crime and retrieve the money from the thieves."

"And give it to the state. The whole point is, we don't want the state to get it."

"Then some bandit will get it. India's a hell of a long way away. You'll be hijacked before you get out of Istanbul, most likely."

"It's a logistics problem. You'll be out of it, what do you care?"

"I don't want you to get killed."

Her look hardens. "They'll kill me anyway. They wanted to kill me in Athens, remember? I won't be in any more danger after stealing the gold than I am now. That's my choice. Risk death with the gold or risk death without the gold. Which do you think I would prefer?"

"Well, I can tell you which I'd prefer. I'd prefer not to be implicated in the theft of a hundred million dollars."

Nela gives him a long, thoughtful look. She sighs, uncoils, stretches out her legs, scoots to lean against the wall near him. "Very well," she says. "You have veto power. You are choosing to exercise it. I don't blame you." She folds her arms and lets her head fall back against the bricks.

A couple of minutes pass, a distant babble of voices, music and passing cars coming up from the street, Pascual wondering why he cannot simply stand up, walk out and go home to Sara. He says, "All right, you win. I'll be your beard. After that, you're on your own."

Tradecraft was never Pascual's strong suit, even in the days when he was dodging the security forces of half a dozen countries all over Europe. Documents forged to the highest Soviet standards, a reliable network of collaborators and his natural linguistic and thespian talents were the main assets that kept him alive and active during his days underground. What practical skills he acquired were oriented toward evading surveillance rather than maintaining it.

His experience in that area, however, has given him some sound principles to go on when planning how best to ascertain what a young Kurdish German anarchist might be up to in Istanbul on a sunny weekday afternoon. Change your appearance at intervals, don't get too close, try to anticipate. A couple of hats, sunglasses, a sport jacket for instant respectability, a newspaper, a bag to carry it all in which can itself be slung over the shoulder or gripped like an attaché case. Pascual has no idea if he can pull this off, but he has nothing else on his agenda today.

Nela is secluded in her top-floor lair, working at making him the registered owner of an account with a hundred million dollars' worth of cryptocurrency in it. The other residents of the squat have decided he is harmless and uninteresting and are ignoring him. Afran has been in and out and when in has pointedly avoided him. Pascual takes up station on a couch in the ground-floor common room with a view of the street door. When Afran slips out again, Pascual notes which way he turns and gives him twenty seconds, resisting the urge to dash after him. Then, as casually as he can, he picks up his bag and follows.

It is a splendid day, summer drawing to a close with benign temperatures and high clouds over the sea, bustle and cheer in the street. Pascual follows Afran down to the waterfront boulevard and nearly gives up when Afran heads for the files of buses pulled up on the other side. If Afran gets on a bus, this little escapade will be over. But Afran goes on past the bus stand toward the ferry terminal. By the time Pascual reaches it he has lost his quarry, but he spots him again, heading for the ferry at dockside, in time to duck inside and get his own ticket. Pascual dons jacket and sunglasses and goes aboard, locating Afran near the bow on the upper deck and taking a seat on a bench twenty meters away.

The ride across the Bosporus is exhilarating. Sunlight on the water, sea air and far horizons are an antidote to a claustrophobia Pascual was barely aware he was suffering. With the turn into the Golden Horn, domes and minarets adorning the skyline, he feels that he is at last arriving in Istanbul. He is distracted enough that he nearly loses Afran in the crowd upon arrival and has a panicked moment before spotting him striding away from the terminal.

Here he is in tourist Istanbul, the quay lined with restaurant terraces under awnings, tempting but not what Pascual is here for. What he is here for is to follow Afran as he strides away from the sea through narrow lanes, up ancient stone steps, emerging into a broad, busy street and then ducking into the maze again, turning uphill. Pascual has to close the gap so as not to lose him, pausing once in a doorway to shed the jacket and don the dusty beret he found abandoned on a shelf in the squat. Wasted effort, perhaps, as Afran never once looks back. He makes Pascual work, but after a strenuous fifteen minutes they have arrived.

Afran slows, pulls out his phone and consults it, and then steps to the door of a restaurant and goes in. Pascual continues to trudge, on the opposite side of the street, trying to look casual as he takes in the sign above the door, the glimpse of white tablecloths and wineglasses through a window, the venerable stone facade of the building. He goes on past and then fifty meters on pauses and turns for a last look, making sure he has noted the place correctly.

Finally he wanders on, taking in the sights, musing, wondering how concerned he should be about the fact that Afran is patronizing a Russian restaurant in the middle of the afternoon.

"They commit to deliver the gold within twenty-four hours of confirmation. I can complete the entire process of redeeming the cryptocurrency and requesting delivery of the gold within hours. We should be ready to take delivery the following day." Nela looks as if she has just crawled out of a cave after a wrestling match with a bear, gaunt and pale, hair askew and hazel eyes alight. She has come down from the top-floor nerve center in the first light of day to rouse Pascual and Afran and convene a meeting in an isolated corner of the common room. From the kitchen come sounds of other early risers arguing listlessly over access to the coffee maker. "The owner of the account is now listed as Mr. Pascual Rose," Nela concludes.

"So the clock is ticking," Pascual says.

"Possibly, yes. If the real owner should try to access the account today, he will be unable to carry out any operations and will no doubt contact the exchange. So we need to move fast."

"I can get the key to the warehouse at any time," says Afran. "We can take delivery tomorrow if you want. I'll call Mehmet today."

"Don't call him until tomorrow," says Pascual. He is still rubbing sleep from his eyes, but he is already focused, thinking about the theft of a hundred million dollars about to be attributed to him. "The less time for people to notice and think about things, the better."

"We'll need a truck," says Afran.

Pascual gives him a startled look. "I thought your friends were supplying the truck."

Afran shakes his head. "They will drive it to China if they have to. But they don't have papers to rent a truck. They're refugees, without money. You have to rent the truck."

Pascual shrugs. "All right. I might need you to interpret."

"I can do that. We'll go today."

"Very good," says Nela. "Now. We have to think about security. You have been careful with your phones?"

Afran nods. "Always off when I'm anywhere near here, or the warehouse."

Nela nods and looks at Pascual. He says, "Off. I haven't even called my wife."

"Excellent. It's unlikely anyone is tracking, but you never know. After Athens I'm paranoid. You've not seen anything strange? Or anyone familiar?" She is looking at Pascual.

He shrugs. "Ask Afran about the Russian restaurant."

There is a frozen moment. Nela looks at Afran, who is gaping at Pascual. "What Russian restaurant?" Nela says.

"The one he went to yesterday afternoon." Pascual turns to Afran. "Yes, I followed you. It's a good thing I'm not a cop. You didn't spot me?"

Afran's look goes from stunned to affronted. "I didn't have any reason to look."

"From now on, you do. You're about to give every cop and every crook in Turkey a reason to follow you. If you don't start getting paranoid, you won't get the gold out of Istanbul, much less to Mumbai."

Afran sulks for a second or two, then nods. "All right. Understood."

"What about the restaurant?" says Nela. Pascual is reassured to see that the look she is giving Afran is completely businesslike.

Without hesitation Afran says, "One of these guys who will help move the gold, he works there, washing dishes. You know him actually, Hassan that was with me in Berlin. I had to talk to him. So I went in the afternoon, before he got busy."

"What did you talk about?"

"I told him to be ready to leave his job and leave Turkey when I contact him. That's all. He doesn't know about the gold." Afran and Nela commune silently for a moment and then Nela breaks it off. "All right." She turns to Pascual. "I know this Hassan. All right?"

Pascual shrugs. "All right."

"The redemption has been confirmed," says Nela. "I have notified the exchange that the delivery request will be coming by fax." She hands Pascual a sheet of paper. "I was able to find an internet café with a printer. Do you think you can find a fax machine somewhere?"

Pascual takes the paper. It is a printed form, bilingual in Turkish and English, headed *Request Form for Physical Redemption*. Pascual scans: *Delivery Instructions . . . NOTE: DELIVERY MUST BE TO A COMMERCIAL ADDRESS (PLACE OF BUSINESS OR BANK)*. Nela has filled in the blanks with careful block capitals.

"The warehouse has a separate address from Mehmet's office," says Afran. "It is owned by him, but the company name is different."

Pascual nods, idly noting what this tells him about Mehmet's business practices. He sees his name, *Pascual Rose*, on the line marked

Carrier Contact. "This is for delivery tomorrow?"

Nela nods. "If it is received before noon today."

Pascual glances at his watch. "I'd better get moving, then." He takes a deep breath. "This is the first thing that pins us to a location. This tells our opponents where to find us."

Nela says, "If they can access the information. If they happen to check the account today, if they detect the spoofed interface, if they are able to contact the exchange directly and someone there is able to sort out the confusion. All of that will take time."

"More than twenty-four hours?"

"Who knows? If all of that happens, probably what they will do is simply cancel the delivery."

"And send police to the warehouse."

Afran says, "If it worries you, there's a solution. I will be at the warehouse. You will be nearby. When the gold arrives, I will call you, and you will come and sign the papers. If the police arrive instead, I have never heard of you and know nothing about any gold shipment."

Pascual looks at Nela. "And where will you be?"

"I haven't decided yet. Maybe with you. Maybe with him."

It still seems wildly risky to Pascual but it has the merit of leaving him out of it should things go south. "I'll go send this, then."

Pascual finds a copy center in a street sloping down toward the sea, across from a facsimile of a British pub. He is tempted to go in and down a pint or two for courage first, but he fears a drink would weaken his resolve. He can hear the clock ticking.

The young woman who handles the fax for him glances at the order but does not seem to pay it any special attention; at any rate the words *a ton and a half of gold* do not appear anywhere on it, and she is unlikely to note his name. She gives Pascual a pleasant smile as she returns the sheet to him and apologizes for her poor English.

In the street again, Pascual gives the pub another look but turns resolutely back toward the squat. He has just irrevocably committed himself to the grandest of grand larceny and there is business yet to do.

"Tell him it has to be able to carry a ton and a half of bricks." Pascual has been watching Afran go back and forth with the owner of the yard, a disreputable-looking fireplug of a man with uncombed gray hair and a three- or four-day growth of beard. Pascual's ignorance of Turkish has made him an impotent bystander, and he feels a need to remind Afran who is paying. The yard is a fenced-off half acre of asphalt with a metal shed in one corner, located in a zoning committee's nightmare: a labyrinth of narrow lanes linking residential, commercial and industrial construction, all of it shabby, a mere kilometer or so up the road from the warehouse where a ton and a half of something other than bricks is due to be delivered on the following day. The fleet of battered trucks and vans from which Pascual and Afran hope to select a suitable vehicle is parked along the fence beneath a row of drooping, dusty trees.

Afran breaks off to look at Pascual. "Of course. Don't worry. He is a friend of Mehmet, he will give us a good truck, good price. He wants to know how you will pay."

Pascual shrugs. "In cash. Ask him if he'll take euros."

There is another brief exchange in Turkish. Afran says, "Dollars would be better. But he will take euros. He asks to see your residence permit."

"I don't have a residence permit."

"Ah, he says you must have a valid residence permit to buy a vehicle in Turkey."

Pascual frowns. "I suppose you don't have one, either."

"No. What are we going to do?"

Pascual makes a snap judgment about the proprietor of this lot based on the quality of his premises and merchandise. He produces his passport from inside his jacket. From another pocket he pulls out the roll of euros he prepared for this expedition and peels off two hundred-euro notes. He slips them inside the passport and hands it to the Turk. "Tell him this is all the permit I have."

The grizzled eyebrows rise and the man examines the passport, making the bills disappear with practiced skill. He hands back the passport with a muttered comment.

Afran says, "He wants to know what you want to do about registration."

Pascual has a feeling he knows where this is going. "What am I supposed to want?"

After further consultation Afran says, "You must go to a notary to register the vehicle. He has to give you a document about the sale. And you must have insurance. Then you have one month to get your license plate. You have to go to the police station to do that. With more documents. But he says if you don't want to do these things, he can get you some license plates."

"I see. Would they be legal?"

That is a thorny question, Pascual can see as the Turk explains matters to Afran. Eventually Afran turns to him and says, "He says the police won't bother you. Nobody is looking for these plates."

"That's a relief. And how much will they cost me?"

"He says five hundred euros."

"I'll give him two-fifty."

The Turk's expression darkens, Afran's likewise. "He says the price cannot be negotiated."

"And we haven't even looked at a truck yet. For five hundred euros I'll want a legal-looking title as well."

"He says he will give you that."

Pascual sighs and coughs up the money. The Turk smiles, pocketing it. Afran turns to Pascual. "He says he has a good Mercedes Sprinter that will easily carry a ton and a half. If we pick it up tomorrow he will have the plates for us."

"Delivery is confirmed." Nela looks up from the phone in her hand. "Tomorrow at 13:00 hours." She tosses the phone down onto the mattress she has moved up here to her lair. "This is a burner phone. Bought for this purpose only. To receive authentication codes and confirmations. By the way, it will be evident to anyone investigating this theft that Pascual Rose's KYC data were stolen from that third-party provider. I could have covered my tracks but didn't. That gives you an excuse if they come asking questions. Anyone with the proper skills could have hacked this account and engineered the theft. The only question will be how the impostor obtained your passport, because you will need to show it tomorrow when you sign. You will need to come up with a story of how it was stolen. Either that or duplicated, which I suppose is always a possibility. Anyway, just insist you were impersonated."

"And hope to be believed."

"It's quite plausible, actually. I'm surprised it hasn't already happened. Pascual Rose is just sitting there waiting to be exploited."

"You say that without irony."

"I'm exploiting you, am I? I believe it was you who sought me out."

"It was. I just didn't expect to have my name put on one of the largest gold thefts in history."

Nela does something she rarely does: she smiles. "Isn't there a line in Shakespeare, something about having greatness thrust upon you?"

Pascual is not in the mood to return the smile. "I'll be lucky if that's the only thing that gets thrust upon me."

Afran suggests an eve-of-battle dinner, the three of them bonding over a feed; Pascual of course will pay. He has plenty of cash left, expenses having been somewhat less than anticipated so far. The restaurant is on the roof of a hotel near the port, open to the sea breeze under an awning, with harried waiters in slightly grubby white jackets. The menu features Turkish and a few French dishes, and the view of the sunset over the Sea of Marmara is spectacular. Pascual finds he is too nervous to eat and after a few bites devotes himself to the wine, a tolerable Georgian red, and watches Nela making eyes at Afran.

He has been worrying about this ever since he saw them go into a clinch at their reunion. The last thing this enterprise needs is distraction from the task at hand. Pascual is certain that Afran is the reason Nela has insisted on poaching the gold, rather than contenting herself with a grand gesture and a blistering exposé. As for Afran, Pascual is suspending judgment. In the churning wake of the Syrian disaster there is nothing implausible about a crew of Kurdish anarchists wanting to drive to India with a truckload of gold for Rojava. Pascual is just glad he is not going with them. But there is also nothing implausible about a hundred-million-dollar score attracting all the wrong kinds of attention.

Nela is most human now when it is most dangerous. The anarchist Amazon is a smitten girl tonight, hanging on Afran's words, hazel eyes locking with his soulful gaze. The content of the conversation is political, the hyperpolitical concerns of people who claim to disdain politics, but the eyes and the body language predate politics by millennia. Pascual is very much *de trop*.

After dinner Pascual professes a desire to stroll by the sea. Afran and Nela decline to join him. The squat will be locked but there is a bell and somebody will be up to let him in; thanks for the dinner and see you in the morning. Pascual gives them a cheery wave.

The wine has buoyed his spirits artificially; as it wears off, Pascual stands looking at lights twinkling on black water and wonders what he has done. He also wonders if he can find his way back to the warehouse near the Yenikapi port.

It turns out he can, with a little help from his phone and his transit card. The Metro yellow line takes him under the Bosporus to Yenikapi, and he has no trouble retracing the route he and Afran took to Mehmet's office. From there it is a short walk around the corner and under the railroad viaduct.

Pascual slows his pace. He wants to look without looking like he is looking. Jacket slung over his shoulder, free hand in his pocket, he is a man out for an idle stroll in the cool of the evening. He comes out from under the viaduct into the yard where the warehouse lies. The vehicles that were here during the day are mostly gone; lighted windows show in a one-story building that sits by the exit to the boulevard. Pascual strolls, scanning. The building directly opposite the warehouse entrance backs onto the boulevard; it would be a fine place from which to observe the warehouse if one had access to it. Pascual leaves the lot by the exit onto the boulevard, walks fifty meters back toward the viaduct and dashes across six lanes of sparse traffic to gain the foot of a flight of steps that leads up to a park on the other side of the boulevard.

Here there are trees, a promenade, a café with low tables and chairs on a strip of bare earth beneath the trees, overlooking the boulevard. From the end of the row of trees Pascual has a fine view of the warehouse, no more than a hundred meters away. As he stands watching, a car comes creeping into sight in front of the warehouse, evidently just having come through the viaduct. It is a dark-colored BMW, lights on, and its driver is either bemused by the wealth of parking spaces available or he is prowling. He rounds the corner of the warehouse, headlights falling on the fenced-off construction site behind it, then swings around slowly, rolls to the exit onto the boulevard, and turns right, accelerating rapidly away from the sea.

Pascual turns, smiles at an elderly couple taking the evening air, and begins to walk slowly back toward the Metro stop, wondering who else would be interested in an unmarked warehouse on a summer evening.

26

Nela pokes her head into the common room where Pascual is pretending to listen to a dreadlocked Scottish girl's account of a spiritual experience in Nepal and crooks a finger at him. He excuses himself abruptly, leaving the lass with an annoyed look on her face, and follows Nela into the stairwell. "What's up?"

"The exchange called."

Pascual gapes. "What do you mean? Who called who?"

"Borsa Istanbul. The custodian of the gold. They called the number I entered as your contact number, which is one of my burner phones. They want to talk to you. I told them I was your secretary."

Pascual freezes. He has had a nervous stomach since rising from an uneasy night's sleep, and now he is instantly queasy. "Good God."

Nela raises a hand. "Don't panic. It's an authentication procedure. In view of the amount of the redemption, the man said."

"I told you that much gold would draw attention."

Nela is leading him up the stairs. "They want you to confirm your identity and confirm the order, in person or via live video. We can do it from my laptop. You'll need your passport, and you should probably shave, comb your hair and put on that jacket. We can set up in the library. The books will make a better background than bare bricks."

"Are you sure we wouldn't be better off taking to our heels?"

Over her shoulder she says, "Pascual, this is a good sign. It means they aren't questioning my hack. It means I successfully made you the account owner. The delivery order came in, they verified that you are the registered owner, and now they just want to make sure you are you. Which, of course, you are. Get your passport and meet me in the library."

The library is a grand name for the room on the second floor of the squat that has one wall lined with a motley collection of books in a dozen languages on makeshift shelves and a couple of old armchairs. The rest of the space is more or less a storeroom. When Pascual arrives, properly groomed and with passport in hand, Nela has cleared away flotsam and jetsam, set up her laptop on a table and wrestled one of the armchairs around so that the books are behind it. She nods at Pascual as he enters and says to her laptop screen, "Mr. Rose is here." She vacates the chair and waves Pascual to it, saying as he passes her, "Mr. Yildirim. The compliance officer of Borsa Istanbul."

Pascual has never been prone to stage fright; role-playing and outright lying have always come naturally to him. But being thrust in front of a camera so soon after breakfast and with so little preparation almost undoes him. He manages to assume an appropriately grave expression as he sits. On the screen is a severe-looking man with a strong chin and formidable black-framed glasses. He nods at Pascual as he settles into the chair. "Mr. Pascual Rose?"

"That's right. Is there a problem with my delivery?" Pascual's reflexes kick in and he is instantly the busy international financier pestered by regulators.

"Not at all, sir. We have merely some procedures which must be performed. This is a very large delivery." The English is practiced and careful, with a pronounced accent.

Pascual nods. "I am aware of that. I have made suitable arrangements for the secure transportation of the gold."

Yildirim's black brows clamp down behind the glasses. "Yes, sir. I must ask you about that, please. The delivery address is that of a shipping company which is not known to us. There are certain companies which are accustomed to transporting large gold shipments to and from Istanbul. This is not one of them."

"I am aware of that also. I have chosen it precisely because it is not well known. Precisely because of the need for discretion with a delivery of this size. What matters is not how well known the company is, but how much I trust it. And I trust this company." Pascual's nerves have calmed as he improvises, making up utter nonsense on the fly.

Yildirim is still scowling, but he moves on. "As you wish. Now. In order for us to make delivery, you must be present in person to receive it and sign for it."

"I am aware. I'll be there."

"And we must ask you now, in order to release the gold, to confirm your identity in advance. Have you an identifying document you can show us?"

"Will a passport do?" Pascual brandishes his prized Maltese document.

Yildirim leans closer to his computer, his face ballooning. "Yes, we will accept that. Can you show me the photograph and data, please?"

Pascual opens the passport and holds it up to the laptop. "Can you see it?"

"Yes, thank you." Yildirim peers comically from the screen of Nela's laptop for a few seconds before leaning back. "Very good, sir. Thank you."

Pascual closes the passport and sets it down. "Will that be all, then?"

Yildirim looks mildly troubled, staring down at something in front of him. "Only one more thing please, sir. On your record here, there is a notation of an identifying mark. This should confirm your identity. It should be conclusive." Yildirim looks up at the camera, and now his face bears just a hint of malice. "Can you please show me your left hand?"

Pascual has to suppress a smile. This one is easy. He plays it for all it is worth, taking his time bringing the hand up into camera range, fingers spread, all three of them. "Here you are. I presume you're referring to my two missing fingers?"

Yildirim just stares for a couple of seconds, and then finally his expression softens. "Yes, sir. Thank you very much." He busies himself with papers on his desktop and casts a final glance at the computer. "You may expect delivery at one o'clock this afternoon."

"Thank you." Pascual grants the man a nod and a smile as he pushes away from the table, the busy financier anxious to get back to work.

Nela swoops in and kills the connection with a mouse click and looks at Pascual as he stands. "There. You see? I told you." The look in the arresting eyes is triumphant. "Nothing to worry about."

Pascual knees have gone weak. He leans on the table, exhales and says, "Everything. Worry about everything. We're taking delivery of a ton and a half of gold. Now is when the worrying starts."

The Mercedes Sprinter van has inscriptions from a previous owner on the side showing faintly through an inadequate coat of white paint.

Pascual tosses Afran the keys. "You're driving."

"Me?"

"I'm out of it, remember? All I do is sign the papers. You're the one taking this thing to India."

Afran looks startled, as if this is the first time this has occurred to him. Then he shrugs and opens the driver's side door. "Very well. Let's go."

Afran is not a particularly experienced driver, Pascual judges. He struggles a little with the manual transmission, applies a heavy foot to accelerator and brake, and veers between hesitancy and impetuousness in traffic. The ride is not smooth. Nonetheless he manages without hitting anybody to pilot the van out of the labyrinth and onto the main road that carries them down toward the sea.

Pascual looks over his shoulder into the back of the van. Fifteen hundred cell phones, he thinks, weighing a ton and a half. He judges they just might fit. He waits until Afran relaxes a little, cruising in the center lane, before saying, "So. What's your plan?"

"I told you. Take the gold out of the country."

"I mean in the short run. Today. What do you do after I sign for the gold? Load the van yourself, or will these friends of yours be there to help?"

Afran brakes, shifts, swerves. "Why do you want to know? You sign, you leave. Now it's my problem."

"And Nela's. Is she going to India with you?"

Afran makes him wait for an answer, concentrating on the traffic. "I don't know what Nela's going to do. That's her business. Not mine, not yours."

"True. My problem is that my name is on this. I'd just like to know what the prospects are for getting away cleanly."

Afran nods. "Nela is a very smart woman. I think she will arrange everything for you."

"Let's hope so."

A mere fifteen minutes after taking possession of the van, Afran and Pascual draw up in front of the warehouse with the blue doors. Afran hops out and unlocks the padlock on the entry door. He goes inside and a few seconds later the big double doors swing open. Afran returns and drives the van inside.

The warehouse is not large, maybe twenty-five meters square. Even with the double doors standing open, the interior is dim. Afran flicks a switch by the doors and fluorescent lights go on overhead. High storage racks bear rolls of fabric, cardboard boxes, unidentifiable bulk goods swathed in plastic. More boxes on pallets lie along the back wall. A door in the right-hand wall evidently leads to the adjacent office. Afran walks over to it and tries the handle. It is locked. "That office is empty," he says. "It belongs to Mehmet but he never uses it."

Pascual turns, looking out the double doors at the low building directly opposite. Barred windows stare back at him. "And that building?" he says.

Afran comes to his side. "Some kind of municipal office."

Pascual nods. Not my problem, he thinks. "Make room for them to pull the armored car in here," he says. "You don't want to transfer a hundred million dollars' worth of gold in full view of anyone walking across the lot."

Afran nods. Pascual wonders why he cares what Afran does with the delivery. He will be lighting out for the hills when Afran is struggling to load a ton and a half of cargo into the back of a van.

"Hello, boys," Afran and Pascual turn at the sound of Nela's voice. She is standing in the double doorway, silhouetted against the bright sunlit background. "Everything ready?"

Afran beams at her. "Now that you're here, yes. Everything is ready."

There are times when Pascual wishes he were still a smoker. The little rituals of polluting one's lungs would help to pass the time and would give him an excuse to stand in the sunshine at the entry door, watching the comings and goings out on the lot. He has taken an occasional peek but does not want to draw the attention of anyone who might happen to see him and wonder what is going on here today. Afran and Nela are having no trouble whiling away the minutes in the dimly lit rear of the warehouse, seated together on a shrink-wrapped bale on a pallet, heads close together, murmuring of Rojava or perhaps farther horizons. Pascual only hopes their mutual absorption does not lead to a lack of concentration when it counts.

His watch says it is half past noon, half an hour to go before, presuming everything works as planned, a hundred million dollars' worth of gold arrives to crush them. Pascual takes a deep breath and squares his shoulders.

He ambles back to where Nela and Afran are sitting, hands in his pockets. "I'm going to take a little stroll," he says. "Just to calm my nerves and take a look around. I'll have my phone."

"Probably a good idea," says Nela. "In case the place is surrounded with police."

"Don't even joke about that," says Afran with a nervous puff of laughter. He looks tense, unlike Nela, who gives him a brief dismissive smile.

"If the place is surrounded by police, you're on your own," says Pascual.

"Don't go far and be alert for the phone," says Nela. "They might come early."

"Just give me a shout." Pascual makes for the exit.

Outside, there is sunshine and the roar of traffic from the boulevard; here in the lot there are a good many parked cars. Pascual wanders toward the exit to the boulevard, hands in his pockets, trying to see things without looking too obviously. Near the entrance to the construction site at the rear of the warehouse a few men stand in a cluster; nobody is looking in his direction. He leaves the yard by the exit to the boulevard and turns right. A narrow sidewalk leads toward the railroad viaduct. Pascual goes under the viaduct and walks uphill. There is no pedestrian crossing in sight and what was easy in light evening traffic will be problematic in the middle of the day. Pascual watches other pedestrians take their lives in their hands dashing across in gaps in the traffic and finally imitates them, gaining the far side a couple of hundred meters beyond the viaduct. He comes back downhill on the other side and goes up the flight of steps into the park.

Pascual passed a restless night questioning every choice he has made since a Greek police inspector interrupted his breakfast at the St. George Hotel, and in the wee hours he came to a new decision.

Pascual wishes Nela had not fallen in love with Afran. He wishes he had never left his cozy squat in Marseille, never gone to Yemen, never come to Istanbul. He wishes he had not tipped his judgment and his moral sense into the dustbin forty years ago. But wishing is futile. What Pascual needs to do now is adhere to his decision that the worst thing he could do would be to sign for delivery of a hundred million dollars' worth of gold a few minutes from now. He trudges slowly up the steps toward the entrance to the park.

In addition to all the other reasons for not taking delivery of the gold, one stands out. His failure to appear will be instructive.

He reaches the top of the steps and pauses. He surveys the broad walkway running under the trees, the café tables ranged under them, about half of them occupied. He is looking for familiar faces, looking for people who look interested in what is going on across the street. If he spotted this as a convenient observation point, others may have as well.

He proceeds. Nobody is paying him any attention. The café is doing a brisk after-lunch business, serving tables clustered around its entrance as well as those under the trees. Pascual strolls down the way until he reaches the last table, which is unoccupied. He sits on a stool, looks expectantly back toward the café, a patron in search of a waiter, then casually lets his gaze drift out across the street. He can see the blue doors. They are closed, but the smaller entry door is ajar and Nela Nachtnebel is standing in the opening, phone in hand, looking anxiously this way and that.

The roar of two motorcycles comes down the boulevard. The riders wear white helmets and black jackets with a red panel on the back bearing the word *POLIS*. Behind them comes a boxy white truck with the name of a well-known international security firm stenciled in blue on its side. The convoy slows for the turn off the boulevard into the lot. Nela is jabbing at her phone.

The phone in Pascual's shirt pocket begins to buzz.

Pascual has always found it difficult to ignore a ringing phone. This one is especially taxing, he finds, watching Nela going frantic in the doorway as her hundred million dollars arrives with nobody there to receive it. The bank truck pulls up just shy of the blue double doors, the motorcycles taking up station fore and aft of it, as Nela's call to goes to voice mail and his phone finally stops buzzing. Nela is talking into her phone, practically barking; at this distance Pascual cannot hear the words, but he doesn't have to. Nela puts her phone away and walks slowly toward the passenger side of the truck, disappearing behind it. Now Afran has appeared in the doorway. He, too, has his phone to his ear, and Pascual finds this very interesting.

Pascual sits and watches for a minute or two as nothing happens. Afran has gone back inside and Nela is still hidden by the truck. Traffic tears by on the boulevard; idlers drift by him on the path. Now Nela appears again, making for the door to the warehouse, saying something over her shoulder, poking at her phone again. She goes back inside, and as Pascual expects, his phone begins to vibrate again.

"I think they are waiting for you over there."

The words freeze Pascual. They came from just behind him, they came in accented English, and they came in a voice he doesn't recognize. For a moment he sits stunned, then turns to look over his shoulder.

He has never seen this man before. He is pale, fair haired, well into his forties and showing the mileage, a hard case. He has a cell phone in his hand. Pascual is wildly searching his memory for clues to this apparition when a scrape of footsteps behind him causes him to twist in the other direction, and now the freeze is deeper, because this is a face he has seen.

Twice, in fact, and things fall into place, too late, as Pascual recognizes the bulldog look, the shaved head, the belligerent expression of the Syrian bruiser he first saw at a hedge fund office in Monaco and then again in a parked car on a street in Athens. "You again," Pascual says.

"Me," says the bulldog, and sinks onto the stool opposite Pascual. His expression says he is not here to make friends.

The blond man sits on Pascual's left, facing the street. "Call her and tell her you are coming," he says.

Russian, thinks Pascual, another piece falling into place as he pins the accent. Of course, Russians and Syrians and one stray Kurd. Imbecile, he thinks. You thought you were smart and you sat here where the whole world could see you. He says, "You know, I don't think I will."

This is met with a flat stare, a high-grade professional intimidating stare. "I think you will," says the Russian.

There is a long list of things Pascual doesn't understand, but he has a firm grasp of one principle. "No," he says. "I refuse. And don't bother threatening me. If I don't sign, you don't get the gold."

The Russian shrugs. "We don't have to kill you." He turns to the Syrian and says, "Call them and tell them if Rose is not there in five minutes, go in and kill the girl."

Pascual's head droops as he recognizes defeat. The word "them" gives the order authenticity; he knows who it must refer to. He has seen them and he has seen their handiwork, lying in the street in Monaco and in a stairwell in Athens. He heaves a great sigh as the Syrian taps at his phone. "Wait." To the Russian he says, "I'll sign."

The Russian nods at the Syrian, who shrugs and puts his phone away. The Russian thumbs his phone and puts it to his ear. "He's coming," he says. "Five minutes. Don't let the truck leave." He stands, in a hurry now. "Come."

Pascual is hustled along the walk to the seaward end of the park, where it gives access to a vast parking area built over the boulevard, which plunges into a tunnel beneath it. His escort ushers Pascual into a dark blue BMW, and with the Syrian at the wheel the car crosses the lot at speed and turns down a lane that leads to the warehouse. Two minutes after the Russian's call they are pulling up behind the bank truck.

Two guards have dismounted from the truck, and they are not happy, Pascual can see. They wear black caps and black body armor and automatics on their hips. One is arguing with Afran and Nela at the entrance to the warehouse. The other is standing by the driver's side of the truck, scowling at the new arrivals. The Russian points at Pascual. "Mr. Rose is here."

Pascual raises a hand in acknowledgment and approaches the trio by the entrance. Nela is looking bewildered and deeply suspicious. She fixes on Pascual, and he can see that if five minutes ago she thought finding him was her only problem, now she knows that the trouble runs much deeper than that. "What the fuck is going on?" she says.

"You've been betrayed."

The look Nela trains on Pascual could burn a man to ashes. "*Arschloch*," she says quietly.

Pascual raises his chin. "Not by me. Not even by the CIA."

Three or four seconds pass while Nela works on that. It is only when Afran steps out of the doorway, brushing past her, and wanders away toward the viaduct that the look on her face begins to go from searing to something else. She wheels to cast a look after him, and when she turns back to Pascual she looks as if she has taken a bullet in the heart. "No," she says.

Pascual takes her by the elbow and steers her to the door. "Come inside," he says.

Angry voices in Turkish are raised behind them as they step out of the sunlight. "Who are those people?" Nela says, beginning now to look frightened.

"The Syrians." Pascual says. "And their Russian boss."

"Russian?" The hazel eyes grow a little wider. She whispers, "Honey Bear."

Pascual says, "Tell me again how you met Afran."

He can see her working it out as he holds her gaze. "I was a fool," she says. "I knew the Wi-Fi security in Kreuzberg was weak, and I took a chance, one time."

"And Afran showed up not long after that, I bet. How did he narrow the possibilities down to you? Did you do a little boasting in a moment of weakness?"

Nela has no time to answer, as men are suddenly streaming in through the door: the Russian, the Syrian bulldog, and now two other familiar faces, Silverback and Bluto, last seen in Monaco, in casual dress today more suited to their demeanor and, no doubt, the work they will be expected to do. Trailing them is one of the guards from the truck, waving a clipboard and declaiming in Turkish.

The Russian says, "You need to show him identification, and then you need to sign this document." He does not sound like a patient man.

Pascual surveys the situation, the Syrians casually distributing themselves so as to make clear that there is nowhere to turn and the guard advancing with the clipboard. Pascual holds up a hand to stop him. He motions to the Russian to move farther away from the door, out of earshot in case the guard understands more English than he has shown. He says, "I'll sign. But there's a condition."

"You are not in a position to make conditions." For the first time the voice is raised, patience exhausted.

Pascual keeps his voice calm even though his heart has begun to pound. He knows he is walking out onto very thin ice. "As long as you need me to sign that paper, I'm in a position to make conditions. And here it is. You let her go. I'll sign as soon as I see her step into a taxi or an Uber or whatever they have around here and drive off wherever she wants to go."

The Russian gives Pascual the stare again, shifts it to Nela for a few seconds and then back. "These guards are losing patience. In a moment they are going to cancel the delivery and leave. If that happens, I will kill you both. Even if a taxi is on the way."

Pascual is desperately groping for his next move in the chess game when Nela says, "Let me make a suggestion."

All eyes are on Nela as she says to the Russian, "You could use my skills. Quite frankly, I could teach you a lot. I think you know that, don't you?"

The Russian's reptile gaze concedes nothing. "You said a suggestion."

Nela looks down her nose at him. "Here's my proposal. I'll come with you. Today, right now. I'll come over to your side. I'll work with you. I'll show you how I hacked you, I'll share what I know with your people. I'll collaborate. Are you going to say no to that? Will your superiors say no to that?"

The Russian doesn't blink. "I don't say anything. You want to come with us, you come with us."

"There's a condition."

"What?"

Nela nods toward Pascual. "He's the one who gets in the taxi, once the gold is transferred. If I see him ride away safely, I come with you."

Pascual waits for somebody to ask the question "And if not?", but nobody does. Instead the Russian makes a decision. He says, "Agreed." He turns to Pascual. "Now sign the document."

The gold is packed in wooden crates, screwed shut, each bearing a sticker with the name and logo of Borsa Istanbul. There are two different sizes, reflecting the two sizes of bars listed on the manifest Pascual scanned before signing for delivery. The one-kilogram bars that Nela anticipated are in small crates about the size of a case of wine, if considerably heavier. Those can be handled by a man with a strong back. The larger crates, containing the four-hundred-ounce bars, are roughly the size of a footlocker, with rope handles at the corners, and it takes two men to handle one. It has taken the crew of the bank truck twenty minutes to unload the two dozen or more crates from the armored truck, now backed in through the open double doors. Silverback and Bluto have rolled up their sleeves and broken a sweat transferring them to the back of the Mercedes van.

"They would have killed you as soon as the truck left," murmurs Nela at Pascual's side. "They might still kill both of us. But I don't think so. I think they will at least want to find out what I can do for them."

"Will you really work for them? Can you live with that?"

"I won't have to live with it for long." Her expression softens. "You were right about everything. I was a fool, again. I'm sorry." Her eyes flick away. "Call your taxi. I think they're finished."

The last crate is heaved into the back of the van as the bank truck starts up and rolls slowly out of the warehouse. Pascual has been playing the role of impresario, standing near the door and watching with what he hopes looks like a critical eye. The guard with the clipboard now barks something at him in Turkish and Nela translates. "He says next time don't make him wait. These operations are supposed to be run on a strict timetable."

Pascual bows his head, placing his hand over his heart. "I'm sorry." He extends his hand. After inspecting it suspiciously, the guard shakes it, turns on his heel and departs.

The motorcycles start up with a loud snarl, the armored truck rolls toward the exit to the boulevard. The spectacle has attracted a small crowd outside, Pascual sees, a dozen or so idlers in groups of two or three, just beginning to break up, go back to their jobs and spread the word about the commotion at the warehouse with blue doors. Silverback goes to swing the big double doors shut. The Russian and the bulldog have been keeping out of the way, watching Silverback and Bluto work. As the doors clang shut, they approach Pascual and Nela.

"Don't bother with the taxi," says Nela. "Just run."

Pascual sees the wisdom in this; he sees there is no time for farewells. He reaches out to give her arm a squeeze. "Good luck."

"Go," she says.

Pascual steps to the exit door and pulls it open. Behind him the Russian calls out. "Don't forget. We have her. If we have any problems, any police problems, we have her."

"I won't forget," says Pascual, and nips through the door, pulling it shut behind him. Suddenly he wants nothing more than to get as far away as he can as fast as he can. This way, up through the viaduct and into the narrow streets beyond it, where there is cover, crowds, maybe a cruising taxi.

But here is a Renault pulling up in front of the warehouse with a screech of brakes, a man jumping out from behind the wheel and dashing around to block Pascual's way as he gapes in dumb astonishment for the second time that day.

"Where do you think you're going?" says Melville, pushing Pascual back toward the door with a hand on his chest.

28

The best Pascual can come up with when he recovers his voice is the classic "What the hell are you doing here?"

"I might ask you the same," says Melville. He has forced Pascual against the wall next to the entry door; now he brings a cell phone up to his mouth and says one word: "Go."

Pascual stares into Melville's face, unchanged since he first saw the man in Marseille a scant couple of weeks but a lifetime ago, still a bland, unremarkable man except, Pascual is finally registering, for the fact that he is pressing a gun into Pascual's ribs. "A million wasn't enough for you, huh?" says Melville.

Behind the blue doors somebody is shouting. Three seconds later, somebody is shooting; the sound is unmistakable, if muffled. Pops and cracks, the tearing sound of a burst of automatic fire, and Pascual freezes in horror. He looks right and left for anything that looks like help, like witnesses, like awareness. Where did all those people go? A few loiterers remain, fifty meters away, but they have heard nothing and their view is blocked by Melville's car. "I've got Pascual," says Melville into his phone. "We're coming in."

Pascual resists as Melville herds him toward the door; he doesn't want to see the results of all that gunfire. Melville pushes the door open and shoves him inside, and he is going to have to look at it.

It takes a moment for it to register, as Melville gives him a push in the back and slams the door behind him. The first thing Pascual sees is the gunmen, two of them, brandishing nasty short-barreled submachine guns with foot-long suppressors, stepping rapidly this way and that, checking their handiwork on the floor. The question of where they came from is instantly answered by the sight of the open door to the adjacent office; Pascual remembers Afran trying the handle and realizes that just because a door is locked on one side doesn't mean it must be locked on the other. The handiwork is no longer moving, busily bleeding onto the concrete: Silverback here, head blown open, gun next to his hand; Bluto on his side, a beached whale, eyes still open but the light rapidly going out; the bulldog trying to crawl to safety with the last of his strength, coughing blood onto the concrete. And the Russian, toward the rear of the warehouse, shot in the back as he ran, a crumpled pile of clothing.

And Nela. Pascual sees her trembling and knows she is alive, curled in a fetal position, covering her head with her arms. He rushes to her and drops over her to shield her. He looks back at Melville and sees him leveling the Glock automatic at her. "Who the hell is she?" says Melville.

"She's nobody. She's nothing to do with this."

Melville takes that with a look of deep skepticism, and then after a moment his eyes light up. "Oh, my. Don't tell me this is the famous Zarlik. Hell, yes, that explains a lot. Nothing to do with this, huh?"

"You'll have to kill both of us," Pascual growls, knowing as he says it that it is not much of a deterrent.

"Why would I kill her?" says Melville. "She's the reason I'm here.

You, I'm not so sure about."

On his knees, Pascual pulls Nela into an embrace. She is trembling, hands over her face, but she is breathing, and Pascual tightens the embrace to stifle his own trembling.

One of the gunmen, a blunt-nosed, pockmarked specimen who looks and sounds Arab, reports to Melville. "Very stupid men. They try to use their guns."

Melville shrugs. "OK, sucks for them. They could have walked out of here if they'd had any sense. Let's get this show on the road. Hamid has the truck. We'll take these two in the car, you driving." He gestures at the bodies. "But get this garbage out of sight before we open the doors." Melville turns to Pascual. "Get her up, get her moving. I want to be on the road in five minutes."

The two gunmen start dragging bodies toward the rear, leaving trails of blood. Nela comes to life, disengaging from Pascual and getting to her feet under her own power. She gives him one fleeting look of horror and then she is in command again, scowling at the world. "I can walk."

Melville gives her an appraising look. "Well, well. She walks and talks. The great Zarlik. Did you really think you could get away with this? I've got computer whizzes, too. We were sitting there waiting for you."

"Murderer." Nela spits in his face.

Melville jerks back, wipes his face with his sleeve. He glares but leaves it at that, his gun hand dropping to his side. "Guilty as charged. So you don't want to provoke me. Here's what's going to happen. Nobody's going to make any trouble, and nobody's going to get hurt. We're moving the gold, and we're moving you. Then we're all going to have a nice long talk about our future. Are we all on the same page here?"

Pascual cannot speak for Nela, but the mention of a future is the best thing he has heard all day. "I'm with you," he says. "No trouble."

"You owe me a word of thanks," says Melville. "For saving your asses back there." He looks comfortable in the back seat, directly behind the driver, cradling the automatic loosely in his lap. Nela is as far away from him as she can get, canted against the door on her side, behind Pascual, who is in the passenger seat in front. The lead gunman is driving, and he is good at it, taking the Renault smoothly around the curves on this two-lane highway lined with stands of pine and thickets of brush, twenty kilometers or so up the European side of the Bosporus from Istanbul. Pascual is fairly certain the man would prefer to drive much faster, but he is going easy on the gas pedal so as not to outpace the white Mercedes Sprinter directly behind them, its springs valiantly holding up under a heavy payload. The sky has clouded over, threatening rain.

Melville has been talking in manic bursts throughout the drive, a nervous reaction in the aftermath of the carnage, Pascual assumes. Nela has not opened her mouth. Melville says, "I assume those were our Syrian friends?"

Pascual looks at him over his shoulder. "That's right."

"How the hell did they find you?"

"Social engineering," says Pascual, seeing no need to go into the matter. "What interests me is why you were ready for them."

"We weren't. We were ready for you. Don't worry, the guns were just for show. We didn't expect to have to use them."

Pascual decides this is probably true; otherwise he would not be enjoying this drive in the country. "How did you know we would be there? Faxing the delivery order was supposed to make that untraceable."

"And it would have been, if my computer whizzes hadn't been able to monitor the exchange's e-mail server. Once they got the fax, the order went right into their system, and we could read all the messages that generated. Nice try, but that's one you should have anticipated. Anyway, I was watching from the car, just beyond the viaduct, and I had my guys in the office there next to the warehouse. Imagine my surprise when you left, then came back along with a crew of gangsters, *after* the gold showed up. I didn't know what the hell was going on, but once the circus left town, I knew we didn't have much time before the gold went out the door. So I gave my guys the green light. They'd been in that office since last night, and they were getting pretty antsy. Right, Jawad?"

The driver nods. "Very boring."

Melville laughs. "I bet it was. But that's warfare for you, right? Boredom punctuated by moments of sheer terror. Anyway, I told them to go do what they had to do. If the Syrians hadn't gotten frisky, we'd have just tied them up and left them."

Pascual has been trying to make sense of the past couple of hours, and while he is not confident of getting a truthful answer, he sees no reason why he should not pose the questions. "Why did you do it this way? If you could see the hack taking place, why didn't you just contact the exchange and sound the alarm? Why did you let the delivery go through?"

"Because this way I get to meet the famous Zarlik. She's the real prize. Her and the gold, they're really a package deal."

"You're going to have to explain that."

Melville draws breath to speak but then stops; his eyes meet Pascual's and he smiles. "And you're going to have to wait. I've been sitting here running my mouth and it's time to focus on the matter at hand."

"So where are we going?" says Pascual.

"We're going to Rumelifeneri."

"And where's that?"

"Rumelifeneri is an old fishing village. Way up at the top, right on the corner there, at the intersection of the Bosporus and the Black Sea. Very picturesque, a sheltered harbor, there's a lighthouse, an old fort or something up on the heights. Lots of seafood restaurants, great day trip destination from Istanbul. And boats. Fishing boats, that go out at all hours. And the fishing business being what it is, there are captains that will take on a little cargo now and then, for a fee."

"I see. A ton and a half of cargo?"

"They can handle it. I've been assured."

"And they rendezvous with a tramp steamer offshore in the middle of the night, no doubt."

Melville smiles. "You can't ask me to give away the whole show. One of you will be going with it, by the way. I'm splitting you up. Jawad and Hamid will ride shotgun on the gold, along with one of you. Flip a coin. The other one comes with me. There will be travel involved. But short term, we need a place to park the gold for a few hours. That's where we're heading now."

The car has turned off the highway and is running along a narrower road with woods on one side and glimpses of meadows through a thin screen of trees on the other. The van is keeping pace behind them. The road bends and climbs, and they pass houses set back among the trees.

After a few kilometers of this, the woods thin out, they top a rise, and there before them, beyond scrub-covered slopes dropping away, is a steel-blue horizon under a darkening sky. "That's the Black Sea," says Melville in the tones of an impresario. "That's where Jason sailed off in search of the Golden Fleece."

Pascual is beginning to tire of the sound of Melville's voice. The road bends back into a patch of woodland, and Jawad slows and turns onto a dirt track that winds up through trees to what is left of a farm. There is a house, with the glass gone from the windows and gaps in the tile roof. There are piles of debris, a wheelbarrow on its side, a pair of empty oil drums. The house is built of fieldstone, with a roofed wooden gallery tacked onto the front of the second story, resting on rough-hewn posts. A broad opening gapes at ground level on the right-hand side, the entrance to what was once a stable; the other half of the first story shows a battered wooden door and an empty window frame. Jawad pulls up in front and everyone gets out. The van comes lumbering up the lane in their wake and Jawad waves it to the stable. They all stand and watch as Hamid turns and then backs the van up a slight slope into the stable. "Good instincts," says Melville. "Prepared for a fast getaway."

Hamid chocks the wheels with stones and comes out of the shed to join them. He is thin and dark, with a mustache beneath a beak of a nose. Melville says, "We've got a few hours to kill. Let's see if they left us anything on the stove." He waves them ahead. He has put away the gun, but his body language is making clear that he is the dog and they are the sheep.

Inside the house there is nothing but ruin and decay. The people are long gone, and the animals, dead and alive, have left their smells.

There is no furniture, only a mound of ash and a partial chair leg in the fireplace in the kitchen. Nela slumps to the floor in the main room, her back to the wall. "Make yourselves at home," says Melville. "Talk amongst yourselves, figure out who's going with the Arabs and who's coming with me. Tonight we'll run the gold down to Rumelifeneri. This rain coming in helps us. It'll keep the curious indoors."

Pascual gives him a skeptical look. "You're not worried, sending off the gold with somebody else like that?"

Melville shakes his head. "I have to trust somebody at some point. I can't dispose of a ton and a half of gold all by myself. And I'd trust Jawad with my life. I have, in fact, down there in Yemen."

Pascual stands blinking at him for a few seconds. "So what did you mean when you said Zarlik is the real prize?"

For a moment he thinks Melville is not going to answer him, discretion asserting itself again. Pascual has time to think that a refusal to answer would augur well for his future, and then Melville says, "Well, think about it. You've probably figured out that I'm not supposed to have that hundred million dollars."

"You surprise me."

"Save the sarcasm." Melville leans a little closer, confiding. "My man Jawad and I happened to come across it in the course of an operation down there in Yemen, and in the heat of the moment we just sort of appropriated it. It's not like anybody else was going to make better use of it. Better us than the warlords, we figured. They'd just spend it all on cluster bombs and qat. Anyway, we took it, and then we had to figure out what to do with it. I put most of it into that crypto account, and then the Syrians and young Zarlik here somehow became aware of it. Unfortunately, so did my bosses at Langley."

"Ouch."

"You said it. I've been officially on the run for a week now. And with Langley, you can run, but you can't hide. So my only hope is to cut a deal. And if I can give them Zarlik, who they've been wanting in the worst way for some time now, and a good chunk of the gold back, they might just agree to can me quietly and forget about prosecution. Any deal would include Jawad, of course. He was kind of dubious about the crypto move. He had to come up with the ten million for Zenobia out of what was left in one of the Dubai accounts. I told him I'd salvage what I can. If we can come away with a million or two apiece, we'll have made out pretty good in spite of everything."

"And what will they do with Zarlik?"

Melville looks at Nela, unmoving with her arms clasped around her knees. "They might prosecute, I suppose. But I think if she's willing to show the proper attitude, a little contrition, with her skills they might just make a deal with her and bring her on board. It's been known to happen."

That hangs there in the air for a minute or so, and then Pascual says, "And what about me?"

"Well, the agency seems to find you useful, God knows why. I thought I would throw you into the bargain. Either that or hold you as a hostage if they get difficult. I was thinking I'd kind of play it by ear."

Pascual trades a long look with Melville and sees that he is perfectly serious.

Melville goes back outside. Nela has still not spoken, and she sits staring into space. Pascual wanders back into the kitchen for a second look at the back door he spotted there. The rough wooden door is hanging off its hinges; it could be jerked open but the noise would alert Melville.

Back in the main room he stands looking out the window. The Arabs are conversing quietly by the open trunk of the Renault. Melville saunters toward them, nonchalant. He joins the conversation, and he and Jawad turn toward the stable where the van is parked. Jawad gestures toward it.

Pascual will think later that he should have seen it coming; what else was Jawad going to do when he heard he would have to settle for a million or two? Hamid pulls an automatic out of the trunk of the car, takes one step and shoots Melville in the back of the head, sending a gaudy red spray out the front.

29

Pascual does not wait to see Melville hit the ground. He whirls away from the window. Nela is scrambling to her feet; that shot was all she needed to hear. Pascual knows their only chance is that back door. He grabs Nela by the arm and hauls her toward the kitchen. A glance through the front door as they pass shows Hamid stalking toward it, gun hand at his side, his face an emotionless blank.

In the kitchen Pascual tears open the door and shoves Nela through it. There is shouting in Arabic behind them now, Hamid alerting Jawad. Behind the house is a gentle slope upward through the woods, over rocky ground with thick underbrush, not a fast track. Nela stumbles, recovers, picks up speed. Pascual is close behind her, panic giving him wings. He is winded after a short uphill sprint but he keeps going, following Nela.

The ground crests and Nela goes over the hump and hits the dirt, looking back. Pascual flops beside her, gasping. It takes him a second or two to spot Hamid, fifty meters away, coming inexorably up the slope, not hurrying, time on his side. Nela elbows Pascual and points: Pascual looks and gets a fresh shock; coming up fast through the trees to their left is Jawad, and instead of a handgun he has equipped himself with one of the submachine guns.

Nela is off and running again. Pascual is two seconds behind her, remembering the nasty staccato sound of the suppressed gun he heard through the warehouse doors. The brush provides some cover, and Pascual pins his hopes to that; he knows he will run out of gas before Nela does.

What they run out of first, however, is room. Abruptly they come up against a fence topped with barbed wire, running as far as they can see to right and left. Nela looks around wildly and dashes to the right. Pascual follows and sees where she is heading: a windowless stone hut in a patch of weeds. Beyond it the fence disappears into the brush. "Go," Pascual gasps. "Don't wait for me."

"They'll catch us," Nela points and Pascual sees Jawad downslope to their right, hurrying to cut them off. Nela ducks into the hut. Pascual stumbles in after her and trips over her in the dark, falling painfully on a bed of rubble. For a moment they lie still, panting, and then Nela scuttles to the back wall and says, "They will have to come in here to kill us." She struggles for breath. "We have stones." She hefts one she has taken from the ground. "If they try to come in, we throw, we strike with stones."

To Pascual it doesn't sound like much of a plan, but it is what they have. He rolls toward a side wall and sits up, then starts scrabbling for stones. Nela is on all fours, looking out the door. Suddenly she says, "*Scheisse!*" and sprawls headlong onto Pascual, knocking him over.

The stuttering cough of the machine gun sounds, all too close, along with the thwack of bullets hitting stone. Pascual is on his back with Nela on top of him, shielding him now, and as sparks, flakes of stone and ricocheting rounds fly around the inside of the hut they trade as intimate a look as man and woman have ever exchanged. It strikes him that he is going to die looking into these hazel eyes.

Not yet, though; the gun falls silent and in the next instant Nela's lips are on his, her tongue seeking his in a desperate, savage kiss. It lasts for a second and then she is scrambling off him and scooting to the other side of the doorway, crowding into the corner. She motions for him to do the same. "Next to the door," she says. "Close enough to strike."

Pascual obeys and scrambles into position opposite her, a stone in each hand.

They wait.

Pascual thinks about Sara, about Rafael. A wife and a son, more than he ever expected to have. He has, he reflects, had a life after all. A life he didn't deserve, with people to love and who loved him. And he threw it away to chase after a truckload of gold. Jason at least made it home across the sea, Pascual thinks; I am not going to.

Outside the hut a shouted command sounds, in Arabic. Pascual understands but can make no sense of it; it sounds like "Drop the guns." After a few seconds of suspense it is met with a single gunshot. Then more shots, the tearing sound of the submachine gun, sudden deafening volleys from a variety of weapons, and finally silence. Pascual and Nela stare at each other, stunned. Out in the woods somebody is running, men are calling to each other in Arabic. Where did they all come from?

The yelling dies down. Pascual and Nela sit paralyzed, afraid to move. Footsteps sound in the underbrush. A voice calls out, in English. "You may come out now. You are safe. It's all over."

Nela is not buying it, Pascual sees; her eyes have narrowed with suspicion. Pascual raises a hand to keep Nela in place. "Stay here." He peeks cautiously around the edge of the doorway.

He counts four armed men, two with handguns and two with M4 carbines, spaced at intervals in the brush, facing him. He yells, "I'm coming out." He crawls out through the doorway and stands, hands in the air. A few steps from the hut, terrifyingly close, Hamid is lying in the weeds, unmoving. A few meters further on, Jawad is a black heap, gaping exit wounds in his back oozing blood onto the rocky earth. Pascual walks slowly toward the gunmen, wondering if he dreamed that voice in English.

"Well, well," says Khalid al-Mansouri, holstering his automatic. "Mr. Pascual March. I cannot say I am entirely surprised to find you here."

Pascual halts in his tracks. "Well, I'm sure as hell surprised to see you."

Al-Mansouri's eyes go past Pascual to the hut. "Are you alone?"

Pascual almost turns to call for Nela, but something stops him. "There was a woman with me," he says. "She ran ahead and left me."

"I see. Well, you'd better come back to the house. It's going to rain on us." He turns to his men and says in Arabic, "Take the weapons. But leave this carrion here. We'll decide what to do with it later."

The rain is beating hard on the old stone house, coming in through the gaps in the roof and leaking through the rotted ceiling into the main room. "His phone," says al-Mansouri. "He was careless with his phone, as with everything else, and we were able to plant tracking software onto it. We've followed every move Jawad has made for a month. When he suddenly got on a flight to Istanbul, I suspected he was leading us to his accomplice, your Mr. Melville, and the

Mukalla money."

Outside, the accomplice is lying in the rain next to the Renault and the Land Rover that was retrieved by one of al-Mansouri's gunmen from its hiding place down the road. Even in civilian dress al-Mansouri is every inch the military man, in khaki trousers and a nylon windbreaker concealing the holster on his hip. His gunmen have come in to shelter from the rain, all of them with the same military bearing, hard faces and an easy way with weapons. Al-Mansouri wipes rain from his face with a handkerchief and fixes a grave look on Pascual. "Now you will oblige me by explaining why he also led me to you."

Pascual has been so dazed by his suddenly restored future that he has given little thought to his story. He scrambles to compose one. "If you've been watching Jawad, you saw what happened in Istanbul this afternoon."

Al-Mansouri nods. "We were monitoring from a distance. We don't have to be that close when we can track a phone. We were aware the gold was delivered to the warehouse, we were aware that Jawad and his associates were waiting for it, and we spotted you. We also spotted some rather dubious characters that arrived at the warehouse with you. I would guess they might have been the same bad lot you encountered in Monaco. Am I right?"

Pascual nods. "Along with a Russian."

"Yes. Well, the Syrians couldn't organize a successful picnic without Russian help. What happened to them?"

"Melville's men killed them all. They were waiting in the office."

Al-Mansouri's eyebrows rise. "You don't say. The Turks are going to have fun explaining that. Was it you that arranged the delivery?"

"No. I merely paid for everything. The young woman I mentioned was responsible for the theft of the gold. I chose to help her because I didn't think the CIA should wind up with all that stolen money."

"I see. And what did she want to do with it?"

"She wanted to deliver it to the Kurds in Rojava."

"To the Kurds? You surprise me."

"That was her idea. Me, I just wanted to make sure Melville didn't get to enjoy it."

Al-Mansouri grins. "Well, that seems to have been accomplished. I'm afraid the Kurds aren't going to get their hands on it, either. A court somewhere will decide the matter, I suppose. I have been in touch with the people at Langley, by the way. I imagine they will want to talk to you."

"I imagine they will. What happens now?"

"Now I think we will dispose of the bodies and drive the gold back to Istanbul. I'm afraid I am going to have to hold you for the people at Langley."

Pascual shrugs. "That's better than what I was anticipating."

"I'm sure." Al-Mansouri turns to his men. "Where are the keys to that van?"

The men trade startled looks. One of them shrugs. Al-Mansouri snaps a look at Pascual. "Who had the keys?"

Pascual blinks at him. "I think Hamid did. Jawad's partner."

Al-Mansouri barks in Arabic: "Go and strip those bodies. Find those keys." The three rush out into the rain. "Imbeciles," says al-Mansouri. "I have to spell everything out."

Pascual is exhausted. He sinks to the floor where Nela sat not an hour ago, back to the wall, and puts his face in his hands. Rain drums on the roof, splatters on the floor. Al-Mansouri stares out the window into the lowering darkness. Somewhere near at hand, tires crackle on gravel, just audible over the noise of the rain. Al-Mansouri stiffens, steps to the window, leans out. A starter grinds, an engine roars. Al-Mansouri dashes to the door. There is a tremendous jolt that shakes the house. Just outside the door, al-Mansouri looks up, reverses course, and comes diving back through the door as a cascade of rotting wood descends with a horrific rending noise and thuds onto the earth, shaking it. Pascual rises, stumbles to the window and looks out in time to see, past the wreckage of the second-floor gallery lying on top of two vehicles, the white Mercedes van careening down the track, trailing a length of rope.

"She set it rolling in neutral down the slope before she started it, very clever. Gained valuable seconds. And bringing down the balcony like that, magnificent. Complicates things immensely, of course. We'll have the devil of a time covering all this up now. God knows how we'll get back to Istanbul, to begin with." Al-Mansouri shakes his head in admiration. He turns to Pascual. "She ran away, you said."

"She did. I saw her run." Not really a lie, Pascual thinks; merely an omission.

Al-Mansouri kicks debris out of his path. The rain has stopped and his men are milling in front of the house, contemplating the wreckage. "Nobody's going to be happy about this," says al-Mansouri. "We're going to have some explaining to do."

Pascual makes no reply, looking at the sky going pink in the west. He is remembering a kiss, one he will savor for a long time.

30

"You are indestructible," says the woman in the gray pantsuit. "Like a cockroach. Or a rat."

"Thank you, that's very kind," says Pascual. He would be irked, but he is aware that the woman is the closest thing he has to an advocate and patron, and he is willing to indulge her irritation. The only name Pascual has ever known her by is Shelby, which may be her first or last name, real or assumed. Her hair is as gray as her suit and she has the pleasant, businesslike and completely sexless aspect of a nun. She turned up today without warning, and Pascual hopes that means he is about to be released from limbo. Through the window behind her he can see just a slice of the distant Bosporus between high buildings, gleaming blue and inviting beneath a cloudless sky. He has been gazing at it for a week from this seventh-floor apartment where he has been cooling his heels under the close supervision of a couple of Emirati hard cases. One of them can cook and the other can give him a decent game of chess, so relations have been cordial, but detention is beginning to wear on him. "But in this case, it's al-Mansouri you have to thank for my survival," he says.

Shelby nods. "It's a pity he couldn't preserve the gold along with your hide."

Pascual shrugs. "His guys were careless. They should have searched the bodies, should have searched the shack."

"They were careless, and the girl was damn good."

"Yes," says Pascual. "I imagine she's pretty good at whatever she does."

Shelby smiles, fleetingly. "Girl power, you better believe it. She certainly had Honey Bear in a tizzy. You met this fellow they used to get to her?"

Pascual nods. "Nothing like a good-looking bad boy to win a wild girl's heart. They chose well. They must have detected some Turkish connection to pick him to go after her."

"The name Zarlik might have done it, or some trace she left in her code. I don't know what constitutes a clue in the cyberworld. These things are beyond me."

"Once he got to Kreuzberg there couldn't have been too many other suspects. But they waited for proof, and when she told him about the gold, they had it. They sent the Syrians to Athens."

Shelby frowns for an instant. "I'm glad they didn't get her. They either would have turned her or they would have killed her, and I don't like to think about either one of those."

Nor does Pascual. He says, "I have a feeling she'll be all right."

"Maybe. Though she may have bitten off more than she can chew, with a ton and a half of gold. God knows what she thinks she's going to do with it."

"Whatever it is, I'm guessing it will be interesting. No sign of her, I assume?"

"The van was found abandoned in Rumelifeneri. Two days ago. But that means nothing. It's clearly a ruse. She could have dumped the gold just about anywhere in Turkey and had the van driven back here. I don't think she took it across a border, but who knows? She seems to be a resourceful young lady."

Pascual nods. "So, Melville. Or Pearson, or whatever his name was."

Shelby winces. "Poor Roland. He did some good work for us down in Yemen, and before that in Iraq. I suppose none of us really knows how we'll react to serious temptation until it comes along."

"He had to use agency resources to come and find me. You had to know about the Syrian hack, and the ransom demand."

"We did. Roland kept us apprised. But he said the money in question was Iranian, laundered in Dubai, part of a sting the Emiratis were running, with his assistance. He said they had a phony technology company set up to sell the Iranians some drone engines, and then they were going to swoop in and bust everyone. They just needed a credible middleman, which was you."

"All too credible. I seem to be typecast."

"Yes. It was plausible enough, and since there was none of our money at stake, well, you could say the due diligence didn't get done. The use of Pascual Rose and his bank accounts got approved. It wasn't until al-Mansouri called me with your story that we figured out that Roland was fibbing. By that time he'd gone on the run."

Pascual gropes for a fitting epitaph and comes up empty. Shelby is staring at him with a faintly amused look.

"So what happens to me?" Pascual says.

She sighs. "Well, I suppose we could turn you over to the authorities. You seem to have committed any number of felonies in the past week or so. The Turks are still trying to sort out the bodies from that shootout, and they are extremely anxious to talk to somebody named

Pascual Rose. But I don't think we're going to give them much help. You're too useful."

"I was afraid you were going to say something like that."

"You're not only indestructible, you're indispensable. We need somebody like Pascual Rose to take the blame from time to time."

"A professional scapegoat."

"If you wish. We'll get you home and then keep his passport for you, till the next time we need you. But since you mention money, I'm afraid I have bad news for you."

"Oh?"

"Roland's disbursement of a million dollars for your services has been ruled unauthorized. They're working hard back at Langley to smother all this and spin what they can't cover up, and one faction is howling about the money. And it was decided we should just quietly reach out and take it back. Otherwise, there are people at Langley who are going to insist on giving the Turkish authorities some help. I don't know if you've checked your banking app today, but you may be a little shocked."

Pascual begins to laugh, softly at first and then throwing back his head for a full-throated belly laugh. "Of course," he says when he has calmed, wiping tears from his eyes. "I never really believed in it anyway. Did you leave me enough to get home on?"

"I was able to persuade them to leave you a small honorarium which should just about accomplish that," says Shelby. "Where's home these days?"

Pascual has to think about that one, but only for a moment. "Wherever my wife is," he says.

■ ■ ■

"I'm not meeting you at the airport," says Sara in Pascual's ear. "I'll be working that night."

"I'm perfectly capable of finding my own way, thanks. Just a call to let you know I'm coming." Pascual stands with his phone to his ear, a cooling breeze off the Bosporus in his face, the towers of a modern Byzantium rising around him. "Just in case you're interested."

"And where have you been for all this time, not answering my calls?"

"I've been to the Black Sea, like Jason chasing after the Golden Fleece."

"Ah. And did you find it?"

"Sadly, no. I return to you as poor as when I left."

There is a brief silence, and when she speaks again Sara's tone has softened. "Well, that's all right, then. We'll turn out our pockets and see if we can afford a couple of *tapas* and a glass of *tinto*."

"*Vida mía*," says Pascual, meaning it. "That would be bliss."

acknowledgments

John Salter again advised the author on technical matters, flagging the implausible and steering the author back toward veracity. Any nonsense that remains is solely the fault of the author.

Dominic Martell was born in the United States and has spent most of his life there, but he has lived and traveled extensively in Latin America, Europe and the Middle East. He has worked as a teacher and a translator. The first three novels featuring repentant ex-terrorist Pascual March appeared in the 1990s, chronicling Pascual's quest for atonement in the chaotic early years of the post–Cold War period. A quarter of a century later, in the transformed landscape of the even more chaotic post-9/11 digitally connected world, Martell began to wonder what had become of Pascual and decided to bring him out of retirement.

about the type

The main text of this book is set in Hofler Text Roman, an old-style serif font designed by Jonathan Hoefler Foundary, released in 1991. A versatile font designed specifically for use on the computer that is suitable for body text, it takes cues from a range of classic fonts, such as Garamond and Janson.

Hoefler Text raised awareness of type features previously the concern only of professional printers. *New York* magazine commented in 2014 that it "helped launch a thousand font obsessives."

Lightning Source UK Ltd.
Milton Keynes UK
UKHW011000111021
392015UK00001B/51

9 781951 938109